Seduced by Voodoo

Where Darkness Reigns

Lovers Unite

Book 3

****

By: Mary Reason Theriot

Dedication

Without the love and support of my family and friends I would not have pursued this new path in life. I would especially like to thank those that have proofread copy after copy, to give me their honest opinion of the books.

To my daughter Theresa, thank you so much for your continued encouragement.

To my wonderful husband Malwen, your continued love and support mean the world to me. I don't know what I would do without you in my life. All of my books wouldn't be what they are without you pushing me forward.

To my fans, I would like to offer a special thank you for your continued support.

Copyright © 2013 by Mary Reason Theriot

ISBN-10: 1-945393-56-4
ISBN-13: 978-1-945393-56-3

Also Available by Mary Reason Theriot:

The Hideaway

The Traveler

Dr. Frankenstein

Above Suspicion

Horror in the Night

Deadly Seduction

Echoes on the Bayou

Seven Deadly Sins

A Kiss So Deadly

A Deadly Combination

CarnEvil of Souls

www.maryreasontheriot.com

Dear Reader,

There are some characters that I loved so much that they had to be brought back. *Where Darkness Reigns* contains some of my favorite characters who had to meet and join forces with other characters.

Bianca Honore's story begins in <u>A Deadly Combination</u>, but when she partners with Joshua Savoie in <u>Seduced by Voodoo</u> you learn that her heart and soul are just as black as the voodoo she practices.

Joshua Savoie's story begins in <u>CarnEvil of Souls</u>, but, as in life, true evil never dies but remains hidden until the opportune moment. Joshua comes back in <u>Seduced by Voodoo</u> to see his diabolical plan come to fruition.

Rayne Simoneaud is betrayed by her lover, Dominic St Germaine, in <u>A Deadly Combination</u>, but seeks out her revenge in <u>Seduced by Voodoo</u>.

Josie Bellows is a young vamp from <u>CarnEvil of Souls</u> who searches for the vampire who turned her so that she can find <u>Redemption</u>.

Detective Grace Hutcherson has fought vampires in <u>CarnEvil of Souls</u>, survived the battle of good versus evil in <u>Seduced by Voodoo</u> and now finds herself plagued by <u>Haunted Visions</u>.

***

CarnEvil of Souls – Joshua's Story
A Deadly Combination – Bianca's Story
Seduced by Voodoo – Lovers Unite
Redemption – Josie's Story
Haunted Visions – Detective Grace Hutcherson's Story

Prologue

They waited until the darkness of the night, when man was alone. He would be forced to face his fears. The horrors and atrocities of this world would be revealed. The frightening and unexplainable would appear.

The creatures that went bump in the night awakened. As the dark heavens peeled back, a glowing orange moon was revealed. Evil lurked under the dark skies and mortals would soon learn what walked amongst them. This was where horror and mystery made its appearance.

Of all the supernatural beings, there was one to be most feared. Vampires were a pariah even amongst demons. They were foul and barbaric creatures that walked this earth, but could there be something even more sinister?

Chapter 1

Detective Grace Hutcherson, Hutch to most, never considered falling in love. Yet, she was falling head over heels in love with Detective Mike Bailey. She couldn't get over how falling in love changed her view of the world.

She wasn't looking for love, yet, it found her. Fate stepped in and set in motion the chain of events over these last few months that led up to her meeting Mike Bailey. She was putty in cupid's hands.

Fate never asked her if she wanted to fall in love. It simply decided that she needed Mike to fill a hole in her heart. Now that she had fallen in love with Mike, she couldn't imagine her life without him.

It was funny how fate worked - fate brought the vampire and Mike into her life and now they were intertwined. She prayed that the vampire would soon be out of her life so that she and Mike could enjoy their new found love.

She feared for Mike's life, though. Joshua, the vampire who escaped from the traveling carnival, kept intruding upon her thoughts. She didn't know what she would do without Mike. He was the gravity that kept her center aligned. Without him in her life, she would be adrift in this world without a compass.

Grace woke this morning with a sense of foreboding. She was bleakly certain that something would happen today, and she prayed that it did not involve anyone she knew or loved. Joshua had attempted to infiltrate her thoughts once again last night. No matter how hard she tried to block him from her mind, he still did so. He'd sensed her ability to read his mind when she was first tracking him and had used it to his advantage. She detested how he could invade her mind and read her thoughts.

Before Joshua began to invade her thoughts, she only saw visions after they happened. She could never predict the future, but lately, she felt a calamity barreling straight for her and she had no idea what it could be.

She wished she knew more about this gift of perception and insight. How could she ward off a disaster if she didn't know what it was, when it would happen or where it was coming from?

As she locked her front door and headed to her car, she looked around the street. A sensation that someone was watching her every movement washed over her. Perhaps she was letting her imagination get away from her? She saw no immediate threat lurking in the shadows just waiting to make a move. Still, she couldn't shake the feeling that came from deep inside of her.

She leaned against her car and stared up into the sky. Maybe looking into the cloudless expanse of blue would give her some answers. Sighing, if only the answer would come to her.

She should be truthful with herself; she was nothing more than a scared animal, one that sensed an impending earthquake coming and ran around frantically looking for shelter. Whatever was coming for her, she could not outrun it. No, she would have to stay and fight.

As she settled behind the wheel of her car, she caught her reflection in the rearview mirror. She looked normal, but why didn't she feel normal? Grace never shared the knowledge about her gift of precognition with anyone other than her partners Guy Mayon and Mike Bailey. She saw the way people treated her grandmother, and she feared being treated the same way. Perhaps it was because her grandmother lived in a small town, but she couldn't be certain. The supernatural may be more tolerated in New Orleans, but she didn't want everyone at the precinct looking at her as if she had a third eye. It was bad enough that she, Guy, and Mike were treated differently since they headed up the supernatural section for the precinct. A few detectives believed the mayor was wasting the city's money. Then there were those who knew better. Between the three of them, they had seen more than anyone else who lived here and what they saw could not simply be explained away.

Pulling out of her parking spot, her mind abruptly saw a quick flash of a boy fleeing the woods with shadows chasing after him. Slamming on her brakes, she waited until the vision ended.

This vision only lasted a few seconds, but, unlike her other visions, this one lacked any clarity and was over before she could even comprehend what was happening.

She gripped the steering wheel as she calmed her racing heart. This was the first vision that came to her so suddenly and in the middle of the day. Usually, she had to walk the scene to have a vision. She had grown accustomed to the victim's emotions barraging her, but this was something more. She felt the boy's fear, but also the killer's exhilaration.

Once again, a sense of hopelessness came over her. Something evil was coming, and she prayed they could survive it.

Now that the vision had passed, she drove into work. As soon as she walked into the precinct a cacophony of sounds assaulted her. The sounds were anything but harmonious. Instead, the sounds of the precinct were varied and discordant. The most obvious of sounds was the dozens of human voices; each carrying on an independent conversation. Underneath the conversational clamor, the hum of the copy machine could be heard as it spit out papers and the continuous sound of fingers clacking on keyboards. There was also the sound of doors along with file drawers opening and closing, shoes slapping against the old linoleum floor and the incessant ringing of the phone. Topping it off was the cry of an ill tempered baby on its mother's hip.

Not wanting to be outdone by the sounds, there was a distinct smell emanating from a mixture of the older building's pungent odor, intermingled with the stench of body odors and coffee brewing; which from the smell it had been cooking for several hours. The only thing that prevented anyone from choking on the atmosphere was the ceiling fans running constantly on high speed.

As she made her way down the hall, she saw door after door leading to the various offices for sergeants, detectives, interrogation rooms, conference rooms and storage closets.

***

Hutch didn't know how she survived the day without anything bad happening, but she did. Perhaps her gut instincts were wrong. As soon as she pulled into her parking space at her apartment complex, a sense of foreboding overcame her. It hit her hard, as if someone had sucker punched her in the stomach. Instead of getting out of her car, she gripped the steering wheel and stared out into space.

It was as if someone was telling her not to go inside her apartment. She couldn't explain it, but she knew something was wrong.

She moved her eyes from side to side, taking in her surroundings. The massive oak trees flanking the complex were no different. She didn't sense anyone lurking behind them. As the sun set on the parking lot, all remained quiet.

She turned off her ignition and stepped out of the car. Opening the front door, she listened for any movement. She could sense the evil, even though she didn't see it. She could smell its dank odor as it filled the room. Was something hiding in the shadows, waiting to pounce?

As she locked her door, a voice spoke inside of her head. "Hello, Detective."

Grace went still. The voice was deep and resonated, but also seductive and alluring. He slid into her mind like honey; yet, she was bone-chillingly afraid. She tried to block him from her mind, but he was stronger, "Tsk tsk Grace. We need to talk cher. We have a lot to discuss."

She tried to ignore her racing heart and the growing sense of dread. She attempted to block him from probing her mind. Finding the strength, she told him, "I don't like you invading my mind and reading my thoughts." Before he could tell her anything else, she was able to block him from her mind. Grace hoped that he didn't learn anything important. If he discovered her weaknesses he would use it against her.

***

Joshua was furious. He had hoped to catch her with her guard down. He would learn more about this woman! They had tap danced around each other for months now and he had yet to learn anything significant about her.

Chapter 2

As Angelica Fitzgerald made her way down Bourbon Street, she wondered how she'd ended up in her current predicament. She had never even considered selling her body, but if she wanted to stay in college, this was her only way. Her friends promised that after the first time it became easier. Angelica hoped they were right, that using the escort service was easier than walking the streets. She still found it creepy selling her body. She had been too embarrassed to tell her friends that she was a virgin. She hoped she didn't panic when the time came to sleep with the man. How hard could it be? Her friends had done this for a while and made a lot of money.

***

Even under these circumstances, Joshua was glad to be back in New Orleans. He had a hard time staying in one place, but with the endless opportunities for feeding and fun, this may be the perfect place for his next playground. Maybe it was time for him to settle down and use New Orleans as the home base for his plan. He could use Bianca Honore, the voodoo priestess, to help him further his plan at a faster pace and then when she was no longer needed, discard her. For now, she served a much needed purpose. He had grown tired of waiting to put his plan into action. The discovery of his traveling carnival set his plan back. But soon, he would bring mankind to its knees.

These foolish mortals were weak, pathetic creatures. They could be easily manipulated.

A hunger grew within him, getting stronger with each second. He must eat. He could already taste the warm blood on his lips.

Joshua loved walking downtown at night and roaming amongst the people. Only in New Orleans could anyone drink freely and partake surreptitiously of drugs, which made them even more susceptible. The diverse group of people here was positively delightful. Even more pleasing was that just about everyone exposed large amounts of their delectable flesh. They absolutely glowed from the warmth of the blood that coursed through their veins. The heat and alcohol made the blood flow even faster. His eyes followed each one of them with hunger.

There were ripe, young women with rich caramel toned skin, dark hair and unambiguous eyes. There were fair skinned women with blonde hair and eyes as blue as the sky. There were young girls on the verge of womanhood with brightly colored hair and tattoos covering their body who rubbed elbows with the elite of New Orleans. They walked around laughing and trusting those around them. Anticipation rushed through him as he looked around at them. There was no other place he would rather be than here.

He blended in with this group of people. Occasionally he caught someone staring at him. He couldn't help but stare back, not letting them break eye contact. While they looked into his eyes, he probed their mind. He sometimes amused himself by placing images in their minds that gave them a rush of sexual excitement or fear. Soon, these mere mortals would cringe before him and pay him homage.

This time, he would succeed. There wouldn't be any mistakes. There would be no trouble as before. He would not be betrayed; he would be careful whom he trusted and, more importantly, he would let no one know of his plan.

As he built his following once again, he would guard his strength and powers. This time, he would do all the work and keep those he turned confined until it was time to overtake the city. He'd refuse to allow his followers to hunt, and would have blood slaves for them to feed on.

He must keep himself hidden. With the detective trying to intrude on his thoughts, he must lay low until he was ready to make his move.

A steady rain had fallen on the streets of the French Quarter, bringing a nice reprieve from the oppressive summer heat. The torrential downpour had ceased, leaving a low hanging mist that covered the cobblestoned streets. The droplets of water were almost invisible as they fell from the night sky, only becoming perceptible when he passed a streetlight or as they collected on the shingles of a nearby roof before cascading into one of the many gutters. Several fetid puddles lingered on the sidewalks. Despite the recent summer showers, the smell of booze, bile and urine hung heavy in this one particular section of the French Quarter.

Joshua noticed the young woman walking down the street. She had caramel skin and large, drowsy brown eyes. A hunger came over him as he watched her every move. It wasn't her physical beauty alone that grabbed his attention, but her very soul that drew him to her. It was rare for him to find someone with an outer beauty that matched their inner beauty. The band of silver around her wrist caught the light. He found the way she moved her body enticing. She had the appearance of someone smooth and fragile, reminiscent of an incandescent flower.

Even at forty feet away from her, he could feel her silky skin against his cheek as he bit down on her neck. He envisioned her delicate fingers entwining in his hair as he drank from her neck. He could feel her heart pound fiercely as he consumed her life force. He was dizzy from her sweet scent. Her perfume mingled with the intoxicating fragrance of her flesh. Her aura was one of sweet innocence and untouched sensuality.

She may be dressed as a streetwalker, but something about her had him believing she was a virgin. She didn't belong out here. He must save her from this life of depravity that she had set out on.

Even from here, he marveled at the beat of her heart and the pulse of her blood that ran through her veins. He could taste the goodness and purity that flowed through her. He wondered why such an ethereal beauty was out on these streets.

As he followed her, he tapped into her thoughts. He felt the deep sadness that was suffocating her. It was so profound that he could actually feel it in the surrounding air. He followed her every step, matching her pace, step by step, keeping his presence hidden from her. He was skilled at fading into the shadows to keep from being observed.

The girl was so deep in thought she never heard him come up behind her. He had special plans for this one. He stepped from the shadows and stood in front of her. His fingers slipped through her hair and cradled her head. "I desire to give you the smallest kiss, cher."

Entranced, her eyes closed as his teeth pierced the delicate skin of her neck. He pierced the artery and his tongue hungrily lapped at the blood. He felt the heat leave her body as her heart slowly stopped beating. Drawing back, his lips rested against her throat. He couldn't drain her completely; that would ruin his plans for this one.

***

The moaning of the wind through the trees was the only sound Joshua heard. He strode purposefully through the damp, dank marshlands towards the clearing.

When he reached his destination, he noticed the lit torches. A shudder moved through him at the sight of Bianca at the altar. Tonight, she had dropped her façade and revealed her true self. She was a vile creature, an extension of the demon. Her dirty, straggly hair blew in the wind and her skin was the color and consistency of wrinkled parchment paper. If he had seen this creature when she first approached him, he would have looked away. Instead, she appeared to him as a seductress who whispered raspy promises as her sweet hot breath kissed his ear.

She knew the way to win him over, promising to save him before he and his family were captured. He had already taken care of the one who betrayed the family, and if he wanted to continue with his plans, he needed the voodoo priestess's help to escape. Daylight had been close at hand, and he had nowhere to hide. She promised him he could start another family, one where they ruled this earth together. At the time, it sounded like a perfect plan. Joshua should have known she had limitations.

She believed she had him under her spell, but the fool woman didn't know the extent of his powers. She assumed they shared the same thoughts, a meeting of the minds so to speak.

He placed the woman on the altar and watched as Bianca turned her full attention to the young lady. Bianca picked up her rattle and shook it over the body in intricate patterns. The victim's body shook and lifted off the altar before paralysis set in. While Bianca performed the ritual, the young lady had a wide-eyed gaze staring up to the sky, as if she was too frightened to acknowledge that something was happening to her.

Next, Bianca took her dagger made of bone and removed locks of hair from the girls head and pubic area. Once collected and placed in the gris-gris pouch, she moved to the woman's hands. She cut away the left fingernails and toenails, adding them to the gris-gris bag.

One of Bianca's followers brought her a white rooster. It squawked unhappily as it dangled upside down in her hands. Using her bare hands, she pried open the beak and ripped out its tongue. Its wings had flapped in distress before she ripped its head off in one savage wrench. Blood poured out from the headless stump. She took and mixed the contents of the gris-gris bag with some of the blood before sealing it up. Next, she took the body of the rooster and shook it over the woman's body leaving splattered dots of blood.

Bianca turned to her followers and ordered, "Bury her."

Tonight they would find out if Bianca could raise the dead.

***

Angelica Fitzgerald stirred from her deep slumber. She never suspected that she was buried several feet underground. She shivered against the cold, damp earth that surrounded her. Her brain was slow to switch on as distorted images flashed through her mind.

Before she could fully awaken, a spasm of pain coursed through her body. As the pain worked its way through her body, she slowly opened her eyes. Darkness enveloped her. Something heavy and moist pressed down on her. Suddenly claustrophobic, she attempted to throw whatever was on her off. More dirt kept falling on her, filling her throat and nose.

Fear gripped her body. She desperately tried to push the dirt away as she shoved her hands upward or at least she prayed it was up. She had no way of knowing if she was making her way to the surface or burying herself deeper in the ground.

To her relief, her arms broke free of the ground. She somehow managed to get her feet underneath her body and shoved her body through the earth. Finding herself in the swampland, she continued to free herself from her confines. She looked around and heard tiny animals as they scurried through the underbrush. Someone had lit torches in a circle around her, and there was an altar of some kind near the center of the circle. As she peered into the darkness, she feared she may see who did this to her. Did they intend for her to die here or were they watching and waiting to see if she freed herself?

As she pulled her legs out of the grave, she lay on the ground shivering. She rolled to her knees and slowly rose. Her muddled brain took in her soiled mini skirt and heels. Dirt caked her body. Her hair fell down her back, full of dirt, twigs, and bugs. She shook her head vigorously to free some of the debris from her body.

Her first step was hesitant, unsure if her legs would support her. They were wobbly and weak, but she managed to take a small step. Her body seemed uncoordinated.

A slow, icy chill ran down the newly turned zombie's back. The sensation of being watched pricked over her skin. Fear trembled deep in the pit of her stomach as she saw the man and woman step free from the clearing.

A wail escaped her mouth as she fell to the ground, and her back arched as another wave of pain washed over her body. A ravenous hunger consumed her. Her vision swam as the hunger pains hit her once again. She was famished and must eat soon.

She watched in horror as a young man was thrust in front of her. Instinct took over, and she filled her mouth with the man's flesh. He staggered back as she delved deeper into his flesh. She took more and more of him as he writhed underneath her. His flesh and blood filled her mouth, overwhelmed her, but it did not satisfy her hunger. She needed more of him.

Before she could satisfy her hunger, she felt the shackles fall heavy on her arms. She angrily looked at the man who restrained her. She yelled at him, "You, you bit me."

Joshua laughed at the insipid young woman, "No, I killed you! I feasted on your blood and then buried you here."

Bianca stepped in front of Joshua, "And then I waited for you to rise."

None of this made sense. She had a vague memory of being bitten, but then nothing until she had freed herself from the confines of the grave.

Bianca replied to the young woman, "I am your master. You will do as I say."

"I don't understand." Her lips trembled, and tears flowed down her cheeks.

Bianca laughed at the statement, "It is not for you to understand. Soon, the need to feed will become stronger. All you will think about is satisfying that hunger. You will forget about your previous life; you will obey my orders."

Chapter 3

Water rushed over her, seeping inside her clothes, drenching her to the bones. Her mind stirred. It was as if she was in a dark slumber constructed of lost memories and brackish waters.

She opened her mouth to scream, but the water made its way in, flooding her lungs. Her arms reached outward, frantically trying to make it to the surface. Something held her back. A rope bound her arms, and she fought to free herself from the unseen forces holding her underwater. She prayed for strength to save herself and her baby.

Images flashed through her dulled mind. Bubbles spumed as she thrashed to and fro, trying to make her way to the surface as small fish nipped at her flesh. Rage and fear fueled her. Finally, she freed a wrist. She continued to pull at the other wrist. Her arm's momentum broke through the watery confines, and she thrust herself into the night air.

Fear gripped her once more. Her legs were restrained and attached to a weight. She tried to peer into the depths of the murky water, but all she saw was blackness. Enraged, she clawed at the ropes on her ankles. She was amazed that there was no pain as she ripped at the flesh of her ankles. Suddenly, the ropes gave, and she found herself free. Her long hair danced wildly around her face.

A dim silvery light danced off the water. The moon light filtered down; its rays created an eeriness to her watery grave. She made her way to shore as the fringes of rope trailed behind her like streamers. She made her way to land expelling a gush of the watery liquid trapped inside of her body.

Once she made it to land, she dragged her body out of the bayou. Surprisingly, she found that she was not exhausted from the strenuous exercise. She looked back over the bayou and waited for the ripples to calm. Sadness washed over her as she saw her reflection in the moonlit water, or rather what she had become.

The image was familiar yet somehow wrong. Her once smooth skin was withered. Her lips, once full and sensual, had retreated only to leave behind a permanent death grin. Ugly blotches now marred her skin. She shuddered at the color of her skin. As she continued to stare at her foreign reflection, she took in the sunken eyes. They were the worst, set deep within the shrunken orbits and were now two white globes that stared back at her, devoid of life and color. They were nothing more than a filmy veil of death.

If she were alive, she would scream in terror at the sight, but she felt nothing but resignation. Then in an instant it came back to her, she remembered everything that had happened to her. Vengeance filled her body, flowing through her veins.

Her ears caught the sound of a drum beating somewhere in the not so far off distance. Something compelled her to scour the land and seek out the source of that cadence. The beat of the drums enticed her further into the swampland. The rhythmic beat beckoned her, similar to an unavoidable summoning.

***

Rayne Simoneaud may be dead, but death would not stop her from exacting her revenge on those who'd done this to her. She was bound to this earth by her untimely death and could not find peace until those who wronged her had paid.

The lover who betrayed her, Dominic St. Germaine, had met his demise. The silly man thought he could keep his gris-gris bag with him in prison. As soon as it was confiscated, Bianca exacted her justice on the man. He was foolish enough to betray both Rayne and Bianca Honore.

A wicked smile formed across Rayne's face as she recalled how he died. She wished she had been given the opportunity to watch as Bianca inflicted a painful death on him using a voodoo doll she made of him.   It didn't seem fair that his death was so easy; he needed to suffer as she was suffering now.

Bianca's powers had increased, but Rayne had learned some things from Bianca. Bianca was foolish not to believe that a ghost could learn magie noire, black magic.

Rayne may not be as powerful as Bianca, but she saw what the woman was up to and she must be stopped. Rayne could not permit Bianca to complete her plans; that would be the end of humanity as they knew it. Besides, Rayne's mother had been a traiteur and so had Rayne. Her mother could heal anyone she put her hands on. Her mother dabbled with various spells during her life, but Rayne had practiced while she was alive. Now in death, she was glad she had kept an open mind about the voodoo her mother practiced. Her mother told Rayne that her powers were stronger than her own, and she must embrace her gift.

Rayne called out to the one she hoped would listen to her. Rayne's mother talked of people such as Grace Hutcherson, those who spoke with the dead, and now she hoped that Grace Hutcherson was such a person.

***

Grace leaned over, turned out the light on her nightstand and settled in for the night. Still unable to sleep in a dark room after her experience with the carnival vampires, she left the television on and turned down the volume. With the television playing in the background, she hoped it would keep her mind busy as she slept and prevent the vampire from reading her thoughts while she slept.

As she closed her eyes and fell into a deep sleep, she felt an intrusion into her thoughts. It wasn't the vampire, but someone different reaching out to her. She listened intently to what the person was saying. The voice sounded as if it belonged to a woman.

As if in a daze, Hutch got out of bed and dressed. She made her way to her car and drove to the outskirts of New Orleans. Without paying attention to her surroundings, she walked towards the bayou. The pitch black night did not frighten her; there weren't any monsters lurking about. Oak and cypress trees grew densely here; their branches frozen in a twisted, gnarled contortion, draped with thick vines and dripping with Spanish moss. Gigantic palmetto leaves fanned out along the underbrush. Towards the bank of the bayou, she noticed an ethereal glow. Unafraid, Hutch continued on. The droning hum of bullfrogs and crickets chirruping filled the air.

The air was heavy with the smell of the marshlands and the dank smell of the bayou. The apparition spoke, "You came. I was worried you would shut me out."

Grace was unsure why she was here. "I sensed that you meant me no danger. I could also sense that your soul is troubled."

The apparition laughed at that comment, "I cannot rest until my revenge is carried out."

Grace shook her head, "I don't understand how I can help you."

"I had to warn you that something is afoot. Evil lurks everywhere, even on the streets of New Orleans. The voodoo priestess' power is increasing. She has evil, malicious plans for those who walk this earth. She took on a partner, one to be feared. These two are evil incarnate, but now that they have partnered up, I am afraid they may be unstoppable."

Grace asked, "Do you know who she partnered up with?"

The apparition replied, "I have not seen him before. He just appeared one night with her. He is evil, though, possibly worse than she."

"What can you tell me about him?"

"Only that I sense there is something unnatural about him. I overheard him taunting you the other night, which is how I knew to contact you. I pray you can stop these two before they carry out their plans. Bianca, she is up to no good I tell you. I believe they are raising the dead for their army. I suspect the man is a sorcerer. He has powers similar to Bianca, but there is more to him than that."

Grace listened intently to what this apparition told her, "This man, could he be a vampire?"

Rayne laughed, "Surely you don't believe in vampires?"

Grace replied, "Well, I am talking to a ghost, am I not? Lately, a lot has gone on in New Orleans. Supernatural activity has been taking place here, as if a portal was opened somewhere. It is not something I can explain, but yes, I can affirm that vampires most definitely exist."

"And you believe this man I saw Bianca with is a vampire?"

Grace nodded her head, "If you heard him taunting me, then yes. There is only one person capable of invading my thoughts, that was until you. You are correct in your assumption that he is evil reincarnated. He has thousands of trapped souls that I have been unable to set free. We are currently trying to release these souls."

"I believe one of them is holding a creature captive. The man kept tormenting something, but I have not paid attention. I will find out more. Perhaps we can find a way to free these souls. At one time, there were several trapped souls here, but they are disappearing. Maybe it has to do with this man rather than them finding peace."

Grace closed her eyes and breathed in the night air. The energy here was highly charged. There was too much going on.

Ready to give up, a vision came to her. It was a woman who at one time would have been considered pretty, but the evil that dwelled inside her body had found its way to her outer being. Her green eyes shone in the night air, as if they belonged to a cat. Grace watched as Bianca walked up to a man and smiled at him endearingly. When he smiled at Bianca, Grace saw his fangs gleam against the blackness of the night.

As Bianca chanted, Grace watched in horror as bodies rose from the earth. She absently stepped back as more bodies surrounded the voodoo queen. As Grace continued to watch, the vampire suddenly peered into the dark and found Grace. His fathomless dark eyes seemed to peer right into her soul. His lips stretched into a sinister smile. As he moved towards her, she opened her eyes to find herself in the present.

When Grace looked around, she noticed that the apparition had disappeared. As she returned home, she wondered if she saw something that had already happened or what was to come. Either way, it was not good. The apparition was right; these two must be stopped but how?

Chapter 4

Joshua awoke to see Bianca looming over him. Her sharp fingernails scratched a pattern into his bare flesh before quickly healing. Her green eyes gleamed with interest as his eyes met hers.

He felt her trying to intrude his thoughts. The silly woman thought she could invade his mind. He sensed that she wanted to possess all of him, but he refused to allow that to happen. For now, he would play her game, but only for a short time.

She looked at him, "I will let you feed off of me."

He gave her a seductive smile. She was becoming hooked on the way his feeding made her feel. It was a euphoria like no other.

She extended an arm in front of him, "Here you go cher. Eat up."

He smiled up at her and revealed his razor sharp incisors. He sank his teeth into her flesh and drank. She had no idea that when he fed off of her, he stole some of her power. He shook his head, no if she knew that she would forbid him drinking her blood. Right now all she focused on was the feeling when he fed off of her.

After feeding on Bianca, Joshua walked over to the window and stared into the night. He smiled dreamily as he thought about how well his plans were going. Now, to speed things up. It was taking Bianca weeks to raise the dead and turn them into a zombie army. He wanted this done sooner and was ready to turn followers.

It was so easy to lure victims to feed on here; it would be even easier to turn those victims he felt he could trust. People were so gullible. Even with the crime that plagued New Orleans, it was easy to fool people. It surprised him how trusting people were of a good looking man. He bet if he knocked on a stranger's door right now they would readily invite him in for a cup of coffee. He played the part of the upstanding citizen, that way no one remembered him. He tipped the waitresses well as they would more than likely remember a poor tipper before him. Even when he tipped a victim's neck back to feed on them, realization didn't hit them until they were almost dead.

Feeling restless, Joshua slipped out of the house while Bianca slept. Tonight may be the perfect night for finding some new family members, or at least a few more feeders.

***

Debbie Hampton realized soon after leaving the bar that she had made a huge mistake. She left with him because he was so attractive. He had been extremely kind in the bar. She should have known something was wrong with him. She wasn't accustomed to men coming on to her, and when he paid attention to her, she was unsure of what to do. It was a new experience for her; one that she didn't want to end.

When he asked if she wanted to go for a walk, she was beside herself. She couldn't wait to be seen walking hand in hand with a handsome man. Besides, she had always been the good girl, and it was time for her to do something on the dangerous side. She was the one always studying or working when everyone else was out partying. Why shouldn't she have a turn?

Now, this walk along the river was turning into a hike through the woods out in the middle of nowhere. She didn't even realize how far they had walked until she noticed how quiet it was. She looked around trying to figure out where she was. There was something dark and foreboding about this place. And the smell that lingered in the air turned her stomach.

When she tried to protest, he laughed and gripped her hand tighter, pulling her along. When she looked into his eyes a chill swept through her body. His eyes were as black as coal, devoid of life.

In that instant, Debbie knew she had made a deadly mistake. When she told him to take her home, he laughed. His sinister laugh shook her to the core, "What's the matter? I thought you wanted to have some fun, let your hair down."

She looked up at him with surprise in her eyes. How did he know that? She never told him that, only thought it. As he moved closer to her, she caught a glimpse of his fangs glimmering in the moonlight.

***

Joshua caught her before she hit the ground and carried her back to the others. She was too weak to join his family. She was only good for one thing—feeding.

Chapter 5

Angela Grayson cracked open her bedroom window, swearing she could smell the pungent odor of death blow in from the cemetery across the street. She would rather be dead than here. Yes, a cold and dark death would be better than what she was about to endure. The dirty embrace of a grave plot would be better than the squalor she was forced to live in. Maybe in death she would find peace.

The sad thing was that Angela Grayson had been born to a prominent family here in Louisiana. Her dad, a renowned lawyer, and her mother, a respected doctor, had put so much pressure on Angela to make something of her life. She had not been allowed to live a normal childhood. To escape the reality of her life, Angela turned to drugs. She had tired of the tension and fighting so at the age of sixteen she ran away.

She took very little with her when she left. The clothes and shoes that filled her closet had no meaning to her. As far as the jewelry and other trinkets that her parents had bought her, she had long ago pawned those to buy her drugs.

She often wondered how long it took her parents to realize that she had run away. Her mother seldom could be bothered with her. Hell, she never made time for her husband.

Angela was desperate to feel loved, and that need led to her losing her virginity at fourteen. She reached out to any man who showed her any sign of affection; a promise of love on his part and she would spread her legs.

She discovered that she could make money on her back to pay for drugs, much more than she could from pawning her parents' valuables. Besides, once they caught on to what she was doing, they started locking everything up. They no longer kept cash in their wallets or around the house.

Sex had come naturally for her. She reveled in the power she had over men. She rejoiced in her ability to make a man desire her with just a seductive grin. They would throw money her way as soon as she gave her body to them. There have been so many men in the past.

Her life had been going good until she met Brian Donovan. Brian Donovan owned the building, and the girls who occupied it. The three story building was located in the French Quarter, and the first floor was used for the bar and the other two floors were the brothel. There were four bedrooms on both the second and third floor, but there was only one bathroom on each floor. There was a tiny makeshift kitchen on each floor as well.

This area was spared from Hurricane Katrina's destruction, but the owner did not want to continue living here, so Brian bought the building for a steal. Katrina was a massive storm that changed lives and ruined most of New Orleans within its destructive path. Katrina had hundred foot waves in the deep part of the gulf. As she moved toward land, she churned up oil wells, old boat wrecks, and even some ghosts before slamming into New Orleans. The storm surge broke through the protective levee, erasing homes, trees, roads and people. The worst came after the storm and before the waters receded. When the scent of death mixing with the hundred degree heat of late August intensified.

The city was slowly returning to its grandeur. The residents of New Orleans weren't quitters and businesses were finally starting to thrive.

Currently, sixteen girls lived here. Each one of them sold their bodies on Brian's command. He took all the money they earned, reminding them daily that he provided them with shelter, food, and more importantly, drugs. The drugs were the whole reason she did what she did. They helped her escape the grim reality of her life.

She wondered if the police knew that Brian took over after Dominic St. Germaine's arrest and subsequent death. Angela wasn't sure which man was the best boss. With Dominic, they knew what to expect, plus he never hit them. Brian, on the other hand, had a deadly temper.

Brian had taken a liking to her, and she soon discovered that he had a sadistic side when it came to sex.

When he came to her several months ago with a hit of heroin, she gladly performed the peculiar acts. She had been desperate for a hit. Now, she knew the twisted games he liked to play, but she wanted, no needed, the heroin so bad that she kept performing just to get high.

When she heard the door open and the footsteps on the stairs, she knew it was Brian. As he made his way to her room, she thought about the cold prick of the needle and the rush of heroin as it entered her vein.

Brian opened the door and held out the bag filled with the sweet, sweet relief she craved. He teased her as if it were a treat for a dog. In reality, she was the same as a pet, one begging for affection from its master.

Angela crawled on her hands and knees to him, eyes wet with tears. She no longer saw him as a man, but as a life giver. She needed that heroin he brought her as much as she needed air to breathe. She didn't care about his self-loathing. She had no sympathy for him, the girls that worked for him or even herself. Her existence depended on the drugs. Her life consisted of sleep, drugs, sex, more sex and drugs. She no longer had clarity in her life. It has become one big blur.

Brian sneered at the woman waiting for the drugs, "I want you to beg for it."

Through tear filled eyes, she pleaded for the drug. He had never asked her to beg for the heroin before. Was this some new sick torture? She begged and pleaded for something that she didn't want, but she desperately needed. As she begged for the drug, she silently asked for death as well.

She whimpered, "Please baby, give it to me."

Brian towered over her, holding the bag just above her head. It was easy for Angela to see that her begging had him excited. The bulge in his pants was clearly evident. She couldn't blame him for being turned on by the power he had over her; it was a powerful aphrodisiac.

"Will you be a bad girl for me?"

She drew out the words like warm honey on her tongue, "I will be a bad girl for you, cher."

He slapped her hard. Pain exploded through her body as she recoiled from the blow. It would leave no mark, but it still hurt.

"I don't believe you. I want you to show me." He looked down at her like the king of his domain. She looked at him like a subservient, proving to him that he was in control. He dispensed pleasure or pain at his choosing.

The need for the heroin became a tight ball in her stomach. She tried not to, but it was difficult not to glance at it now and then. He lorded it over her like he was tempting a child with candy. No matter how hard she tried, her eyes returned to the heroin over and over.

"This is what you want baby? You know what you have to do to get it."

Angela unzipped his pants to get what she really wanted. As soon as she felt the needle slip into her skin, the effect of the fix was instantaneous. First came the burst of pleasure, warm and pulsing which was better than any orgasm she'd ever had. Then her vision blurred, her muscles relaxed, and she floated away on a cloud of euphoria.

***

As Brian left, Angela's roommate walked in. Mindy ducked into her small part of the room, hoping not to draw Brian's attention.

Angela couldn't blame Mindy. She had only been with them for four months now. She still hadn't become used to the business. Mindy wasn't a bad girl and Angela wondered how such a quiet girl became involved in this business.

Mindy mentioned one night that she became involved with the wrong people and owed Brian a lot of money. Angela suspected Mindy owed Brian a large gambling debt from one of his clubs. Mindy believed that once she earned her money, Brian would let her go. Angela didn't have the heart to tell the poor girl that Brian would never let her go. Once you had worked for him, there was no out.

Currently, Mindy was one of Brian's most prized whores. He had yet to taste her goods or to show his true nature to her. The girl wasn't dumb. She could tell that Brian was a sadistic SOB. If only Mindy used her brains and ran away from here. It wouldn't be long before Brian found a new whore to replace her, and Mindy would move down in the pecking order. Soon, he would have her addicted to drugs, and she wouldn't feel the need to leave.

Angela heard that Brian brought a thirteen-year-old into the house. If that was true, they were all in trouble. Deviants would rush to the house to taste the goods of such a young girl. As sad as it was, the truth of the matter was young girls brought in prime money for men like Brian. She prayed that the rumors weren't true. The poor girl would be thrown into a nightmare, and Angela feared the type of men that would come through those doors.

Chapter 6

The drums beat louder and louder with each passing minute; it was a thumping beat followed rapidly by a tat-tat-tat. They pulse had a steady hypnotizing rhythm. The swamp came alive with each tree and shrub nearby swaying in beat to the throbbing rhythm.

The closer he got the louder the drums became, almost deafening. The noise overpowered the high-pitched womanlike scream of a minx as it scurried off into the underbrush.

The sweltering night air was thick with humidity and a dense fog covered the ground. With Joshua's superb night vision, he could clearly see the small pathway as he snaked his way through the mist. The moon and stars dared not shine on him, as if they knew to keep his face hidden as the incessant pulsing continued to beat.

The path meandered its way through the bayou with water as black as the spirits which dwelled there. The beat sounded as if it were coming from all directions; only Joshua knew their exact location. The path led him to where his voodoo queen waited for his arrival.

As with even the most primitive of voodoo rituals, the secrecy was shrouded from outsiders. Several of Bianca's followers were already chanting mantras in a heavy mixture of Creole and African dialects. The chants matched the tune of the drums as they swayed in unison to the beat.

Joshua laid the young woman down amidst a circle of candles and stone. She looked at him through glazed eyes. Joshua looked around as Bianca's followers formed a circle, all wearing long black robes with hoods pulled up to cover most of their heads and faces.

***

The young woman tried to take in what was happening, but she had a hard time staying focused. She was unsure if it was the heavy dose of drugs or if she was hallucinating. Each person in front of her wore a white skeletal mask, the torchlight and candlelight eerily reflected off them.

She watched as her abductor stood. Veronica Granger tried to remember how she got here, but it was still a blur. She attempted to sit up, but it was a feeble attempt with no results.

The man noticed her trying to sit up. While looking down at her with an emotionless expression on his face, he pushed her down to the ground once more. She saw a woman appear out of the corner of her eye. She took a small doll and placed it on her chest. Veronica watched as the man and woman walked back to the altar together.

As the drugs moved deeper into her system, she lay there immobile, limbs slack. Two of the robed figures emerged from the shadows carrying a brazier that bellowed forth sweet smelling lavender tinted smoke. They placed the brazier in front of her. She coughed as the sweet vapors wafted around her.

***

Bianca arranged two wooden bowls on the altar, one filled with water and one filled with blood. She placed a dagger made of bone and a book that appeared to be bound in human flesh on the altar.

Bianca picked up the book, leafing through for a specific page. She turned to face Veronica in the center of the circle, her followers began to chant. As each chanted, their feet rose and fell to the beat of the drums. Their chant kept to the beat of the drums, rising and falling with the staccato.

Each of her followers circled the veve, tossing the contents of the bowls they held into the fire, causing the blaze to roar to life. Walking backwards from the veve, they resumed their positions in the darkness of the night.

Bianca put the book aside and picked up the dagger. She leaned down and cut a lock of Veronica's hair. She took the hair, placed some in the bowl of blood and some in the bowl of water. The followers continued to chant. As Bianca joined in the chant, her voice rang out over the others. Their chanting grew in volume, matching hers, as they stomped their feet in perfect unison to the drums' rhythm.

Bianca picked up the book in one hand, and the bowl of water in the other. She poured the bowl of water over Veronica's head, and she hollered out in anguish. Ignoring the cries, Bianca continued to chant. She raised her arms, reached for the stars and let out a loud blood-curdling scream. In that instant, Veronica's entire body elevated off the ground. A deep guttural moan escaped her mouth as her eyes turned black as night.

As the moment arrived, several of the followers slithered around on the ground, crawling around like beasts and still chanting. The circle around Veronica drew closer to her.

One of Bianca's followers brought her a white rooster. Bianca danced around the veve with the rooster dangling from one of her hands, its monstrous wings flapping in discontent. As the dance continued, she raised the rooster up to the stars, and lowered it to the ground several times. She removed her bone dagger from her belt and severed its head. She thrust the rooster's neck into her mouth. Blood poured down her chin as she bent over Veronica and watched as the blood rivulets dropped onto her naked body.

The followers decreased the tempo of their chant as if the gods were drifting off to sleep. One follower placed a coral snake onto Veronica's belly. Bianca watched as it slithered down the girl's body, exploring the nether regions of the body. The girl squirmed in fear as the snake found a warm crevice to enter the body.

Bianca picked up the bowl of blood and stood over Veronica once more. She continued to ignore her cries of anguish. The chanting rose to a feverish pitch. The followers continued to crawl and slither on the ground as the candles magically moved in closer. Bianca raised her hands towards the sky and continued to chant. Tambourines joined in the beat of the drums as the tempo picked up even more. Veronica felt the ground vibrating beneath her. As the followers moved in closer to her, the masks they wore gave them a more haunting appearance, almost demonic.

Veronica cried out in terror as Bianca's face contorted. Over and over she continued to chant. As the music, dancing and chanting reached a crescendo, Veronica let out a piercing scream that tore through the night air. Her body began to convulse as if she was having a seizure. Twisting to and fro, she frothed at the mouth, and her eyes rolled back in her head. Now covered in blood, water and sweat, violently frothing at the mouth and thrashing about, she continued to cry out.

Soon, she would join the others and be one of the walking dead.

Chapter 7

The smell of stale beer permeated the air as Nadine Guidry made her way through the Quarter. It surprised her that people found this place enchanting with all the smells that assaulted the area. As she rounded the corner, the aroma of beignets and chicory coffee filled the humid air. The vendor who sold hot dogs near where she played was setting up. Soon the whole area would come to life with a myriad of entertainers and artists drawing out the crowds.

As she adjusted the strap to her guitar case, she continued to the center of Jackson Square. She was running behind this morning and hoped her friend saved her usual spot. Several of the other talented artists were setting up their merchandise. She took in the brightly colored paintings and other handmade goods. She waved at Madeline Dubois as she set up her stand with hand painted silk scarves. It amazed her at the amount of talent in this area.

Nadine moved to New Orleans knowing she would stand out and get discovered. That dream was quickly shot down as she soon realized just how many other people here had the same idea. However, she wasn't ready to give up and move back home. Something deep inside of her kept telling her that New Orleans was her destiny, not to give up. She should continue to pursue her dreams. This place was a world away from the small backwater town of Belle Chase where she came from.

Belle Chase was a few hours west of New Orleans and was nothing more than a small shrimping community. The population was about one thousand and most never left the little town. Belle Chase was nothing like New Orleans. There you could leave your windows and doors unlocked without ever worrying about someone breaking in. It was a simple way of life, but not the life Nadine wanted. No, she needed excitement. She wanted more than the little town had to offer. She was destined to be a professional singer and living in that small town would never get her discovered.

She strummed a few notes on her guitar, tuning it as best she could. Hopefully the tourists were in a better mood today than yesterday. Her bank account was in dire need of some serious funds. For the next couple of hours, she sang from the heart and watched as her till slowly increased. Checking the time, she picked up. During the day, she played for tips and at night she worked at one of the local bars. If someone didn't discover her soon, she would have to give up on her dreams and find a real job.

Nadine pocketed the cash and walked to the nightclub. Making her way past the other clubs, she checked to see if anyone was looking for a guitar player or singer full time. Band positions were scarce, and a vocalist position was virtually impossible to find.

As she headed home, the streets were still full of people partying. So focused on getting home, she never heard the man approach from behind.

***

In a daze, Nadine heard the vampire talk, but the words didn't register. *Blood Slave.* Just hearing the words, without even knowing the true meaning, sent a cold chill of terror down her spine. Her heart caught in her throat, and she swallowed heavily, forcing the fear back down to the pit of her stomach.

She was too afraid to ask for something to drink. Her throat was parched; her lips were chapped and cracking. She couldn't remember the last time she had anything to eat or drink.

She prayed that they killed her instead of the alternative. The thought of being used for something so vile was enough to have her contemplate ending her life. Unfortunately, she couldn't do anything about it. The restraints were so tight that she could barely move.

Nadine heard other captives talking about how they fed on them, over and over again until they were of no use any longer. Once they were done with you, you were thrown to the ones chained outside. The screams coming from the latest victim sent shudders down her spine; it must be an unpleasant experience. Perhaps being bled dry would be the better outcome. She would rather be used once, instead of repeatedly for what could be months or years.

All around her, she could smell the fear, the dirt and the body odor of those kept here. The overwhelming stench had her wishing she could cover her nose, but the restraints kept her arms close to the ground. She forced back the gag reflex each time she breathed in the air. She attempted to block out the sounds, sights and smells around her.

Chapter 8

Billy Ray Jenkins brought his trusted beagle, Bagel, rabbit hunting this morning. The morning had been going well until Bagel caught wind of something further in the woods and took off to investigate. No matter how hard Billy Ray hollered at the damn dog, he wouldn't listen.

As Billy Ray stepped toward Bagel, he blanched at the sight in front of him. Bagel was busy digging up what appeared to be a shallow grave with human remains.

Billy Ray was concerned. His dog was now acting strange. The way he tore at the remains, he would swear the dog hadn't eaten for days, if not weeks. Billy Ray knew that wasn't true. He fed the dog well this morning to keep him from devouring rabbits when fetching them.

As soon as Billy Ray moved in to put the leash on Bagel, he took off deeper into the woods. "Bagel, you get back here! Bagel, come here now!"

Instead of listening to his master, Bagel took off even deeper into the woods. No matter how much Billy Ray pled with the animal to heel, he moved further into the swampland. Bagel finally stopped in a clearing and suddenly crouched down low. Glaring at his master with eyes shining silver in the moonlight, lips in an angry snarl, and teeth bared he let out a growl that raised the hair on the neck. Bagel no longer resembled his beloved dog. Billy Ray wondered what in the hell made him act this way. It had to have something to do with the remains he found Bagel digging up. Were the remains poisoned? He must get

Bagel back in the truck so he could bring him straight over to the vet.

He would have to disturb the crime scene and bring some of the remains for the vet to test for poison. The police would not like him disturbing the crime scene, but this was his dog's life he was talking about and surely they would understand. Besides, Bagel already contaminated the area with his feverish digging.

Once Billy Ray had Bagel leashed, he looked around. He wondered how far back into the swamplands they had traveled. So focused on getting Bagel, he did not pay attention to where he was going or how far he traveled. Now he realized just how foolish he had been.

As he forced Bagel along, he became even more agitated. Bagel let out an ear splitting wail that shook Billy Ray to the core of his being and raised every hair on his body. It was as if another creature took over Bagel's body; Bagel was not Bagel any more.

Billy Ray heard a rustling from the woods. What could be out here? He let out a scream as a black shadow appeared, carrying them off into the darkness of the night.

***

Lightning flashed overhead, illuminating the dark rain clouds that released a torrential downpour at the current time. Another bolt of lightning streaked across the night sky as thunder rumbled from the heavens above.

Through streaks of lightning, there were glimpses of the dense moss covered cypress trees growing out of the black murky swamp water. This area of the swamp had remained untouched for thousands of years.

A strange chanting echoed through the ancient forest. A white painted face made its presence known with each bolt of lightning. When he smiled, you could see that each tooth was sharpened to a fine point.

As the beat of the drums pulsed through the air, heavily painted men gyrated around the flames of the fire. The heat from the fire trickled down Bianca's body as she sneered at this new captive. All around them, the rain came down in sheets, but no rain fell on them.

The captive struggled in sheer desperation against the restraints on his ankles and wrists. How had a simple hunting trip landed him in this deep of a mess? He was taken into the darkness of the woods by a dark shadow creature while trying to tend to his ailing dog.

He wished he could go back in time. He didn't want to know about the human remains any longer. All he wanted was to go home. He recalled his grandmother's warning, "Be careful, curiosity killed the cat."

He watched in trepidation as the woman walked towards him with a pouch that she pulled from her waistband. She waved it before him as she uttered another chant in a language he did not understand.

She poured a brownish substance from the pouch into the palm of her hand. Leaning over, she blew the powder into his face. The thick substance coated his throat and lungs. He couldn't swallow, and his lungs were on fire. It didn't take long before his whole body went numb. As he drifted off into darkness, unseen hands placed him on top of a wooden altar. The blade of a wicked knife glinted in the flames of the fire.

The sensation of the blade slipping into his chest woke him from his sleep. He tried to move, but his body was frozen. He couldn't even open his mouth to scream as the agonizing pain ripped through his body.

***

Sometimes when Kathleen Rochelle felt the weight of the world coming down on her, she went for a drive. As soon as Owen walked in the door, she gave him a quick kiss and headed out the door. The kids had worn on her last nerve. Then to top it off, her mother in law dropped by for a surprise visit only to complain about every little thing that Kathleen did.

Delores Rochelle felt that Kathleen didn't give the children enough attention. She believed Kathleen should give them something constructive to do instead of letting them watch television, and then perhaps they would be more entertained and productive. What Delores missed seeing was the condition of the house a few minutes before her arrival, when the kids were doing something constructive. What started out as a simple coloring activity escalated into world war three and ended with glue spilled all over the dining room table. To make matters worse, young Maddie managed to get the glue in her hair. Kathleen sent her upstairs to take a shower to wash the goop out of her hair. While cleaning up the mess downstairs, Kathleen told Owen Jr. and Betty to go into the living room and watch cartoons.

It did not take long for the bickering to start over which show they would watch. Spring break had just begun, and Kathleen was ready to pull her hair out.

After her mother in law had been there for over two hours, Kathleen was overcome with the need to get out of the house soon, or she may kill someone. More than likely the woman who was causing her headache. As soon as Kathleen heard the garage door open, she didn't say a word to her mother in law. Instead, she grabbed her keys and purse.

***

One look told her husband that if Kathleen didn't get away soon there would be hell to pay. His mother could wear on anyone's last nerve, but he knew better than to complain.

Owen trusted his wife. She needed peace and quiet, which was impossible to find in their busy household. Normally Kathleen could handle stress, but some days it wore her down, and today had been one of those days. Now with baby four on the way, her time alone would soon be at an end for at least a year.

***

As soon as she hit the interstate, Kathleen imagined herself driving all night and not going home. She would love the chance just to drive and see where the adventure took her. Of course, it was only a fantasy. She would never leave her husband and kids. They meant the world to her. It was nice to get out of the house and have nothing but silence around her. Owen at least got out of the house and went to work.

With three children under her feet most of the time, Kathleen seldom had any time to herself. However, when she was in the car cruising around, she could pretend that she had no responsibilities waiting for her at home. After driving around town for about an hour, she was ready to go home, tuck her little ones in bed and spend some quality time with her husband. She just needed her sanity to return, and then she was ready to tackle the world once again.

Tonight, a gorgeous moon hung overhead; it was an unusual color, almost reminiscent of the dying embers of the sun. She felt the pull of the moon and found herself on a road she had never taken before. The sheer beauty of the moon had her mesmerized as she drove slowly down the bumpy road. Unsure of her surroundings, she took in the beautiful scenery as she drove. It was too gorgeous to be in the car. She wanted to feel the night air on her skin and see the moon up close and personal, not through a car window. She turned off the engine but left the lights on so that she could see her way. She had no plans of walking too far, especially in her condition, but she could walk a little ways down the dirt road.

As she stepped out of the car, she was taken aback by how quiet it was. She must have driven further than she realized. She no longer heard the sounds of the city, but instead, all she heard was the wind through the trees. Occasionally a small animal moved through some underbrush, but other than that, there was a peacefulness to this place that she found serene and calming. As she moved further from the car, she heard the water as it lapped against the shore. A small bayou must be nearby, or perhaps the Mississippi River ran along this property. She wanted to see the water, but she didn't dare venture too deep in the woods this late at night.

As she continued down the dirt road, the lull of the water tempted her even more; it sounded as if it was almost right beside her. Unable to stand it anymore, she found a narrow path to her right and ventured into the woods. She would walk just a short distance, hoping to catch a glimpse of the water. Soon, she found what she was searching for. It was a short distance from the road, and it was so magical that she found herself drawn to it. The way the moonlight sparkled off of the slow moving water was mesmerizing. She didn't even mind the smell of the murky water so she moved in closer for a better look.

She breathed in the night air and the stress left her body. With each step she took, she felt more tranquil. The moonlight dancing against the soft waves soothed her soul. She stood along the shoreline and watched as the water swayed in the moonlight. Now and then a fish jumped, spraying droplets of water in the moonlight. Her breath caught at the sheer beauty of her surroundings. She wished that her husband was with her; even he would appreciate the natural beauty of this place. She needed to remember this location when she drove back into town. She couldn't wait to bring Owen out here.

As she stared out into the night, the air whispered to her, "Beware." It was a woman's voice. It felt as if the person was right next to her as the air gently grazed her ear.

A scream shattered the peaceful quiet of the night. Her heart pounded against her chest as she heard rustling around her. This area that was serene mere seconds ago was now dark and threatening. Without hesitation, she headed back to her car. As she broke out in a dead run, she heard something behind her thrashing about in the bushes. She didn't dare bother to slow down or look back, too afraid of what she may see.

She made it back to her car in record time. As soon as she got into her car, she hit the lock button and took off as fast as she could. She fishtailed on the loose gravel, but it did not slow her down. Even as she made her way down the gravel road, she refused to look in the rearview mirror, fearing what she might see.

As she made her way onto the interstate, she swore she would never go out for a drive alone at night. She definitely would not go traipsing about at night by herself in woods she didn't know. She shivered in fear at the thought of what might be out there.

The next morning as Kathleen read the paper, she noticed that a young man hunting went missing not far from where she'd stopped. Fear gripped her heart. Could he be the one who screamed? Was he possibly lost in the woods searching for someone to help him? Either way, she needed to call the police and tell them what she heard. They could at least send a search party to see if they found any clues. Her heart went out to the poor man's family. She could only imagine how her husband would react if she hadn't come home last night. She absently rubbed her hand over her swollen abdomen as she thought about what could have happened.

Chapter 9

Brian headed up the stairs for his weekly appointment with Angela. Rage ignited through him when he found Angela's bed empty. *Where was the slut? She knew she was supposed to be here.* As he walked into the small room, Angela's roommate Mindy stepped out of the bathroom, "Where is she?" he demanded.

Mindy cowered against the wall, "I don't know. She said something came up."

While Brian paced the floor, Mindy tried to make her way out the door. Brian's arms snaked around her and pulled her to him, "Where the hell do you think you're going? You are no better than she is, you know that? Sooner or later you will have a turn, and since Angela isn't here, it may as well be today."

***

A shudder wracked through Mindy's body as she imagined what Brian may do to her. She had seen the bruises he left on Angela.

Brian leered down at her, "You are a slut just like her and it's time I taught you that." He slammed her against the wall so hard, for a moment she thought she may go through the paper thin wall. Her back and shoulders felt bruised, and the hard blow took her breath away.

"I have seen you coming in after your appointments; you use your body to tease me and lead me on. It's time for you to pay what you owe me now. You should have known that you couldn't go around here with your tits and ass hanging out, flaunting them and not giving me a little action."

As he continued to shake her, his hands gripped her shoulders cruelly and painfully. Before she knew what would come next, he slapped her repeatedly in the face while screaming obscenities.

Mindy tried to block some of the blows by raising her arms, "No, please!" she cried out.

He grabbed her wrist, gave it a vicious twist and brought her to her knees. He proceeded to shove her on the bed. Dazed and semi-conscious, she barely felt what he was doing to her. He ripped at her clothes. Her heart pounded hard in her ears. Somewhere in the deep recesses of her mind, she heard his belt unbuckle, and she trembled.

As she stared up at him, it didn't even register in her mind when he slipped the belt around her neck and pulled it tight. She struggled to breathe as his face distorted. The face in front of her was that of a monster. She croaked out, "Please stop."

The belt loosened for a moment. He laughed down at her as he tightened it once again. Mindy knew this was where she would die, at the hands of this maniac in this filthy place.

She closed her eyes and thought about how she wound up here. Mindy died wishing she could go back in time and do things over.

***

It was about ten minutes before Brian even realized she'd died. As he looked down at her body, he picked up his phone and called the one person who could dispose of the body.

***

Mindy woke slowly. Darkness surrounded her. A strange shimmering glow seemed to envelop her, almost as if the moonlight had come to rest on her bed.

Somewhere in the background, she heard a strange chanting and the beating of drums. The beating of the drums vibrated through her body. A large creature hovered over her. It spread its wings as it glared down at her. She cowered on the bed as her eyes darted around the room.

As the creature looked down on her, she realized that the glowing light was coming from its eyes. A sound emitted from its throat, a high screeching noise that sent ice water down her spine to the rest of her body. She could only lay on the bed, shivering and shaking. She curled up into the fetal position, praying it left her alone.

The chanting in the background intensified and called out to her. She tried to cover her ears against the shrillness of the creature. Fear paralyzed her as the claw like arms of the creature reached out to her. She watched in horror as the creature reached into her very being and snatched her soul. Numbly, she stood up and followed the chanting that called her.

Chapter 10

Wayne Bryant couldn't wait to go hunting. His parents gave
him the 270 caliber rifle for his birthday. It took him an
hour to convince his mother to let him go out and hunt
deer.

Anxious to shoot his gun, he ran into his room and threw on
his camouflage hunting suit. He grabbed his orange
reflective vest just in case someone else was hunting.
Rushing out the door, Wayne walked briskly to the woods
behind his house. As he moved through the woods, he
thought he saw a movement up ahead. He pulled out his
gun and made sure he was ready to fire.

As he moved in to make the kill shot, the animal he was
following disappeared. Suddenly a dark black cloud loomed
overhead, and Wayne's heart stopped at the eeriness of the
sky. *Great, just what I need is rain.* He should have checked
the weather report before heading out. He was so excited
at the prospect of hunting, he didn't think of anything else.
As he went to reach in his pocket for his phone, he realized
that he'd left it on his dresser. Hopefully he made it home
before the sky opened up. Unexpectedly, he felt a drop of
rain on his forehead; he wouldn't make it home before the
rain.

A few more raindrops fell on his shoulder; as one hit his
cheek, the odor of the rain turned his stomach. He let out a
deep sigh. On top of everything else, he got caught in a
nasty smelling downpour. Of all the rotten luck! As he
went to wipe the rain off of his cheek, he felt the warmth.
He looked at his fingers and shuddered at the sight of the

blood. Yuck! Wayne looked up to see what was dripping on him. In the trees was the lifeless body of a deer strung out across the branches.

The black mass hovering overhead suddenly sensed Wayne's presence and glared down with its two penetrating eyes. The creature's stare seemed to transfix him where he stood.

It never released Wayne from its penetrating hold. His hypnotic gaze kept Wayne in a trance as the creature's magical suspension was broken, swooping down from the trees. In the next instant, the creature's darkness enfolded him as its piercing fangs sank deep into his skin. Wayne's terrifying cry soon turned into a wail that sounded almost animalistic in nature or perhaps that noise came from the creature as it feasted on human blood.

As the creature fed on him, Wayne felt euphoric. As this thing drained the blood from his body, he actually felt connected to it. Somehow, as it fed on him, he could hear everything it was thinking. Something emitting from this creature had him forget about what was happening to him. The burning pain that coursed through his body as the monster fed had subsided.

***

Rayne Simoneaud watched in disgust as the creature fed on this poor boy. She didn't know the kid's name, but he would soon be declared missing. If only she could have protected him, but she didn't get here in time to help him. She sensed the creature's hunger, and she knew its master wasn't far away. She must try to lure his soul away before the soul catcher arrived. It was the least she could do for this poor boy. She hated to see his soul trapped for eternity just as she was, as were the others.

There had been so many victims lately. These creatures were hungry and desperate for food. This particular creature fed off woodland creatures, but the boy had been in the wrong place at the wrong time. Rayne tried to warn anyone that came into the woods to leave before it was too late. She wanted to save their lives. No one should be viciously killed and forced to walk this earth for eternity.

She felt sorry for the boy's parents. She never had the chance to hold her child, but she knew how it felt to have your child ripped from you. Her child was never given the opportunity to live. Rayne was murdered while she still carried her unborn child.

She wished she could protect these parents from the nightmare they were about to be put through. Their son's body would never be found. Whatever remained would be fed to the dogs that roamed with the creatures. Rayne had only seen two dogs, but these two dogs devoured a body in no time flat.

This city she loved was enduring more than its share of hard knocks. Bianca had given the city a fair share of troubles when she worked with Dominic St. Germaine and his Mafia family. Now, she had another partner, one who was far more evil than Dominic ever was. Rayne had no idea what these two were up to, but it was not good.

***

Hutch fought against the visions playing in her mind. As if in a trance, she was forced to watch the nightmare play out before her. She didn't ask for, nor did she even want to see, this vision.

All around her, lightning crackled as the boy's screams reverberated through her mind. The murderer was shrouded in black, and his eyes glowed red in the night sky.

If only she could see the face of the murderer, or at the very least the young boy, but they were merely hazy outlines. Never once did the image come into clear detail. Onslaughts of emotions took over her body as she witnessed the boy's murder.

She had never seen images like this before, and it scared her. She often wondered if she saw a car accident before it happened, if she could prevent it. Now she saw a murder as it took place, and there was nothing she could do to help the victim.

If only the vision were clearer. She could almost make out the area where the murder was taking place. She believed it was in the woods nearby, but she couldn't be sure of the exact location. The other images were too distorted. However, the fear the boy felt came through strong. She could also feel hate and loathing, but she didn't know if it was coming from the monster or the boy.

Over the years, her gift had served her well. She had solved accidents and a few crime scenes as if she were standing right there when they happened, but she'd never had a vision like this one. She felt the emotions that went through both the victim and the murderer. Why was this happening to her now? What brought about this sudden change in her precognition skills? Did it have something to do with the psychic link she had with the vampire? She tried to get a better image of the killer, but all she could do was sense a presence.

Suddenly, an image flashed through her mind; it was as clear as day. On the ground was a hunting gun. Whoever this boy was he had been out hunting. She needed to alert the dispatcher to let her know of any children, especially teenage boys reported missing. There was no need to wait the normal forty-eight hours before searching for him; he was dead. However, if they knew where he went missing, Hutch may get a better feel of the crime scene. Maybe if she walked the crime scene, she could get a clear image of the killer.

Unsettled by her latest vision, Hutch picked up the phone and called Mike. Of all the people she could trust, it was Mike. He listened to what she had to say and didn't judge her. He would not look at her with disbelief or want to have her committed to the loony bin right away.

***

Mike Bailey was on his way home from a long stake out when his phone rang. As soon as he answered, Hutch confided in him without giving him a chance to speak, "I had another vision Mike. It was hard to make out, the images were hazy, almost distorted, but I do know a young boy was killed by a vampire."

A shudder went through Mike at the idea of Hutch having to witness a vicious attack, "Did you make out anything?"

Hutch let out a deep sigh, "I tried to make out something that would help us save this boy, but it was just too distorted. The only clear image I made out was the shotgun."

Mike muttered, "Damn! It's not your fault. I just hate that this vampire is stalking you the way he is."

"Mike, I don't believe that this is the same vampire. This was another vampire."

"I'm coming over. Guy and I watched the club all night and never once saw Brian enter. If he does own the club, he doesn't make an appearance there every night."

Mike had heard rumors that Brian Donovan had taken over where Dominic St. Germaine left off. If so, then Mike wanted to put Brian away as well. If he took St. Germaine's place in the Mafia family, then there was a chance that he would continue the human trafficking ring. That was something no one wanted to see happen.

He'd also heard that the upstairs of the building was where Brian kept his girls. They didn't have enough evidence to bust Brian. Unfortunately, he learned a few tricks from his former boss to keep from being detected.

***

By the time Mike made it to Hutch's house, she felt drained and defeated. No matter how hard she tried, she could not get the images to reappear. She no longer saw the boy being viciously attacked, sensed his fear or smelled the odors that surrounded the area. No, she was once again in her bedroom.

She heard Mike knock on the door, and it took all her strength to get out of bed and to the door. On her way there, she knocked over a glass of wine she had on the nightstand. By the time she made it to the door, it became a struggle to take each step.

After she had let Mike in, Hutch called the dispatcher and asked to be called as soon as any missing reports came in for a teenager. The dispatcher informed her that half an hour ago the Bryant family called to report their son missing. "His name is Wayne Bryant. He went out hunting and never returned. With it being close to nightfall, the boy's father became worried and tried calling him on his cell phone, but he left his cell phone at the house. The dad searched for him, but didn't find any sign of him. The sheriff is rounding up a search party right now."

As soon as Hutch hung up with the dispatcher, she told Mike about the missing teenage boy. It didn't take long for Hutch to get dressed, and they joined the search.

Chapter 11

All the search turned up in the woods where Wayne Bryant went hunting was a skull - regrettably, a human skull. Remnants of hair were all that remained on the skull. Whoever it belonged to died a while back; no flesh remained on the bones. The cadaver dogs were brought in to search for the rest of the remains. Hutch feared there wouldn't be much left to find.

The skull appeared to be from a teenager, but it was impossible to tell the sex of the victim out here. It would be sent to a forensic anthropologist to find out more details.

Almost one hundred searchers scoured the woods searching for the missing hunter. The New Orleans Police Department, members of the church the Bryants belonged to, and the Department of Wildlife and Fisheries scoured the woods hoping to find the young man. Those who worked for the Department of Wildlife and Fisheries knew this area like the back of their hands and moved through the area with complete ease. Several of the local hunters also donated their time to help locate the young boy. They suspected he wandered further than he realized and managed to get turned around in the dense marshland.

With the discovery of the skull, a feeling of dread came over the search party. If someone was out here killing teenagers, then maybe the boy came across the wrong person instead of getting lost.

As Hutch and Mike headed back to meet the other search party members, a sense of déjà vu came over Hutch. There was something familiar about this area. As she walked around the familiarity became even more convincing. She was positive this was the crime scene. She kicked over leaves near a tree. If her vision was correct, this was where the gun fell. As she moved leaves about, her foot came across something solid. She called for Mike, "I found something."

Mike put on a pair of latex gloves and brushed the leaves away. "It's a gun." The knowledge that they more than likely found Wayne's gun settled like a rotten apple deep in the pit of her stomach.

Hutch walked over to where the crime scene techs were to inform them of what she and Mike found. She looked back over at Tony Burge; he was still white as a ghost from finding the skull. She must admit that was probably the last thing he ever expected to find in the woods. He kicked at leaves the same as her except he found a skull. When he picked it up and saw the blank eye sockets looking back at him, she thought he would pass out. Instead of passing out though, he started hyperventilating. Hutch thought they would have to call in the ambulance.

Officer John Arceneaux attempted to calm the man, "Don't worry, it's not Wayne."

He shook his head, "Yeah, but it is someone who was killed isn't it?"

"It is difficult to say right now. The skull has been out here for a while. It could have washed up from a grave."

The crime scene techs were scouring the woods for more bones. If there was a skull, then the rest of the bones should be close.

***

By the time Hutch got back to her apartment, she was worn out. She hated when cases turned out like this one. They all knew they wouldn't find the young man alive.

She wearily crawled under the covers and fell into an exhausted sleep that had more to do with the emotional roller coaster than actual physical weariness. At around two o'clock in the morning, she woke up with a feeling that something was wrong. She forced herself to lay still in bed, and strained to hear any noises that didn't belong. She heard nothing but the normal sounds of the night; however, she sensed that something was not right. She got out of bed and slipped on her robe.

She moved through the house without turning on the lights. It was strange how foreign familiar objects could look in the dark. The furniture seemed to leap forward when she turned her head. She stopped and looked at the front door. She swore that a figure was walking through the closed door, as if it was reaching out to grab her.

As she made her way through the apartment, she began to feel uneasy. It was as if someone was watching her and there was a horrible smell, as if there was something dead in her apartment. She jumped when she heard a noise coming from somewhere behind her. She rushed back to her bedroom and slammed her bedroom door behind her. After locking the door and securing a chair under the doorknob, she unlocked her gun from the lockbox. She stood facing the door, gun drawn, breathing heavily and heart racing. Hutch was unable to get back to bed and desperately needed fresh air, so she quickly dressed and headed to the precinct.

As she drove downtown, she couldn't shake the sense of impending doom. Did the vampire strike again last night? Was his being on the prowl what awakened her? As she walked into the precinct, her nerves were stretched tight.

When she saw Mike today, she would ask if she could spend the night at his place. Her beloved apartment was no longer a haven of peace, but a prison. Some days she swore that someone had been in there while she was gone. It was happening more often. The other day she swore that someone had moved some of her things around. She considered telling Mike, but it sounded foolish even to her. She couldn't prove it, and the apartment was always locked up tight.

Chapter 12

Revenge consumed Bianca. It twisted inside of her, deep in her very core. Venom dripped from her as she thought of those who'd wronged her. If it hadn't been for Dominic St. Germaine, her plan would be in motion by now. Instead, that selfish son of a bitch had to ruin everything for her with his betrayal, and he would pay.

Tonight was the perfect night for magie noire, black magic. Tonight magie noire would prevail as it consumed this place. This was a night of strange beginnings, or endings.

The temperature bellowed steam off the roads as the humid air hit the scorching blacktop. Even at this hour, there was no relief from the oppressive heat. Tonight, she planned to raise the spirits of the dead once more. She had attained the darkest realms of voodoo.

Her black soul tainted everything in its path. She had a heart as cold as ice, and there was no light that shone in her eyes. She was all death. Pure evil ran through her veins, erasing any goodness that may have ever existed in her. She was wicked through and through. The devil himself feared her.

Tonight, she planned on raising the man who betrayed her. A rush of anticipation flowed through her at the very idea of being able to control him and his every move. This would teach him the consequences of betraying the likes of her. He would be more resistant to being raised, but she was stronger.

Standing here in the cemetery, the humidity in the air hung thick and oppressive. She couldn't recall a hotter night here in Louisiana. The only illumination came from the moon and stars up above.

A six foot boa constrictor gracefully draped around her neck. Normally docile, the reptile seemed on edge tonight. She tried to calm the beast before she started. Instead of obeying her commands, the snake moved its head back and forth in front of her face, flicking its forked tongue in and out of its scaly mouth. The creature had never been this restless. She stroked the boa once more, not only drawing from its power, but calming it as well.

As she began her ceremony, the ghosts rose from their graves, furling and unfurling as if performing a dance. As Bianca continued her chant, they were dragged forward by unseen forces.

The spirits Bianca raised appeared at her calling, ready to draw in the newest spirit. The boa sensed their arrival and constricted around her neck. She closed her eyes and continued her chant.

As Dominic St. Germaine's soul was drawn from his grave, she removed the voodoo doll from her pocket. At first she planned to have Dominic join the other zombies, but trapping him in the voodoo doll would allow her the pleasure of torturing him whenever and however she wanted. That very thought exhilarated her.

It took almost a week to finish this doll; she had to make sure the doll was powerful enough to contain this particular spirit. As soon as his spirit entered the voodoo doll, it twitched and tried to get out of her grip. She tightened her hold on it and grabbed a razor blade. She made a small incision on one area of the doll, nothing detrimental just enough to cause him pain. A sinister smile crept across her face as she made another slice into the voodoo doll. This would be a wonderful addition to her collection. When she captured a soul in the voodoo doll she could torture it at will.

As the drummers and dancers waited for her word, the boa began to relax, finally able to rest. At the shake of her head, the pounding of the drums filled the night air. It was loud and frantic. There was nothing as intense as this ritual. She let the pounding of the drums move her body and cleanse her soul. She could feel her power strengthen with each beat of the drum. She had officially transcended to another level, one that no one before her had ever accomplished.

***

Dominic St. Germaine opened his eyes. He looked around to see where he was. Darkness surrounded him. The smell of decay filled his nostrils. He felt around his tight confines and knew the answer. She got to him and now he would be her radio controlled corpse that walked and moved at her will.

Reaching out, he touched the top of the coffin. It took all of his strength to break free of his confines. Damp, soft earth fell around him as he pulled himself up. Once he was free, the moonlight bathed the cemetery in an eerie light.

Dominic's eyes flared with hate at the sight of Bianca. He lurched forward, hands extending, craving to squeeze the life out of her body. No matter how hard he tried, his body wouldn't cooperate. His arms returned to his sides, under the control of Bianca. He was merely a puppet whose strings were being pulled by her.

Bianca let out a maniacal laugh, "Yes Dominic, I summoned you." He noticed that she held one of her voodoo dolls in her right hand and fear washed over his body.

Bianca informed him, "Your soul belongs to me now." Bianca's green eyes turned as red as the flames of hell. All around him the night air whispered, murmuring stories of ghosts long gone, terrible tragedies of life and death. Shadows danced around the cemetery grounds.

***

The chanting woke her from her deep slumber. She had no idea she was buried six feet under the moist, dark earth. She shivered as her brain slowly switched on. Flashes of random memories danced through her mind. Each memory became a distorted image.

Someone whispered in her ear, *"Time to wake up."* Her eyelids fluttered open. A tight spasm of pain seized her body. Her body trembled as the pain made its way through her body.

Darkness greeted her. She strained to see through the blackness that enshrouded her. She placed her hand in front of her and could not even make out the shape in front of her.

Suddenly claustrophobic, she thrust her arms upward in a desperate attempt to get out of her confines. As she broke through the barrier above her, dirt rained over the tiny space, filling her mouth and nose. Terrified, she plunged her other arm into the earth, trying to free herself. She shoved herself upward. Warm, wet earth fell around her body. She had no way of knowing if she was making her way up or down. She frantically tunneled deeper into the ground, shoving her fear aside.

As she clawed at the dirt, she broke free from the soil. With one final shove, she broke through the cemetery floor and stood blinking in the moonlight. She looked back at the hole that had been her prison. Her black as night eyes blinked hard against the night sky. She took a deep breath and spit out the remaining dirt trapped in her throat.

She fell to the ground as she continued to cough up streams of muddy liquid. Whimpering, she wiped her mouth with her dirty hands.

Around her the night whispered. The chanting that awakened her from her slumber continued to call her. Up above an owl hooted in a tree nearby. The moon shined down brightly.

Something inside of her told her she must follow the chanting. As she made her way to the chanting, it stopped. Unsure of where to go next, she moved back to where she came from. As she looked down at the mound of dirt, tears filled her eyes. Someone awakened her from her eternal rest, but why and how?

Knowing that she couldn't go back home, she sought out the darkness of the night to find shelter. As she caught her reflection in a vacant store window, fear gripped her. She stopped and stared at her reflection in the window. Was this what she had become? She was nothing more than a vile creature that walked this earth. Her skin was pale and ghostly white. Her once blue eyes were now black as night. There was no sparkle left in her eyes, no shimmer left in her hair. Her once luxurious hair fell flat against her back, straggly and unkempt. At least she was buried in something nice. This dress was her favorite to go out and party in; it had been a sexy little number when she was alive. Now, the black of the dress showed how lifeless her skin was.

As she attempted to find a place to hide, depression settled deep in her soul, that was if she even had one. There were a few houses left in one section of town that were vacant since the hurricane hit several years ago. There she may be able to find a place to hide from the world as she decided what she should do.

She stuck to the shadows as her body moved extremely slow. It took her what seemed to be hours just to move a few feet. It would take her an eternity to get to her destination. She may have to look for an abandoned house nearby. As she walked through the streets, she noticed a manhole open, and she could hear voices fast approaching. Without thinking twice, she ducked into the open sewer.

As she looked around, she confirmed this would be a good place to hide. Here she could walk with ease under the city above. Here, she did not have to worry about running into another human being. This place was fitting for a creature such as her. She would find out who did this to her and exact her revenge.

Chapter 13

There was no moon out tonight; darkness enveloped everything. As she walked down Bourbon Street, she noticed the dark shadows that lurked in the doorways and recesses along the street. Even the streetlights that usually helped illuminate her way barely cast off any light. She had walked these streets more times than she cared to admit, knew where trouble lurked and avoided being near those areas.

As she made her way further down the street, she tripped and tried to catch herself. She was still high from the last joint she smoked and found herself distracted. Almost instinctively, her body swayed to the jazz music that drifted through the streets.

New Orleans was a town that never slept. There was so much energy in this city, nothing could keep it down. The southern nights were seductive and warm, just like a lover. But, she learned the hard way that New Orleans could also be as dark and cold as death.

Karen Renault ran away from home several years ago, swearing that any place would be better to live than with her overprotective parents. They never allowed her to do anything she wanted to do and had overly strict rules. Now, she wished she could go back in time and live her life differently, but that wasn't possible. So many nights she wanted to pick up the phone and ask her mom and dad if she could please come back home. Pride got in the way and prevented her from making that phone call. She could never tell her parents what she had done to survive on the streets. Karen couldn't bear seeing the hurt and shame in her mother's eyes. Karen learned the hard way that there were things much worse than rules your parents implemented.

It didn't take long for the alcohol, the all night parties and drugs to control her life. She forgot about her dreams and any plans of making it big. All she cared about was making enough money for her next hit.

As she stumbled along the French Quarter, she found an alley that looked to be devoid of any life. This would be a good place to sleep off her current high. She settled in behind a dumpster to hide from any of the gutter bums that had a tendency to lurk about.

As she fell asleep, a feeling of apprehension crept up her spine. She bolted upright and looked around. A shadow fell across her feet. Before she could let out a scream, her young life was cut short.

***

As the creature made its way through the alley, it could hear a woman breathing. The silvery light of the moon painted the alley in dancing shadows. The street was silent as the creature made its way down the alley.

Sticking to the shadows, it skulked through the dark. The creature paused before making its move and listened to make sure no one was near. All that echoed through the night was the soft rasp of the woman breathing.

As the creature looked at the sleeping woman, its pulse quickened. The aroma of living flesh and blood was sharp and clear now. The sweet meaty scent of the woman filled the creature with an insatiable hunger.

Its sensitive eyes were capable of perfect vision in the darkness of the night; the creature looked around once more before making its move. No one was near; no one would hear her scream.

As the creature made its move, the woman turned ever so slightly, allowing it to catch a glimpse of her milky white skin. Her hair glimmered in the moonlight. Rage and anger filled the creature at the woman's beauty. At one time, it had been beautiful as well. The sound of the woman's heart beating and the smell of her blood taunted the creature. A ravishing hunger overwhelmed its senses.

The creature must move the body; it couldn't devour it here. There was a chance that someone may walk by. The woman stirred as the creature lifted her up. Knocking the woman out, it moved quickly to the riverside where it could devour as it saw fit.

As soon as it dropped the body to the riverbank, its claws dug into the soft flesh of the unconscious woman. Blood splashed across the bank as the flesh of the woman's chest was ripped open. The need for the woman's flesh was greater than the creature expected. As the creature's head darted down, its razor sharp fangs bit into the woman's neck. A warm spray of blood flowed down the creature's throat as it greedily drank the fresh blood.

The victim's breathing had ceased. Her body was in ruin as white bone gleamed in the moonlight. The creature tore away flesh and bone to get to the most succulent parts of the body. As ribs were broken, the sound echoed through the night while the creature reveled in the sweet taste of the organs.

The creature looked at the gore it left behind. Her sightless eyes stared up at the creature. The creature hated what it had become. At one time it had been beautiful, but no more. Those were distant memories. Now, it looked for weak things to consume. It preyed on the beautiful as it filled with rage at what it had become. Once its fury was spent, it headed back towards its home.

***

One Eyed Jack was looking for a place to sleep where no one would bother him. Earlier, he had found a bottle of whiskey that someone threw in a dumpster and wanted to partake in a drink or two before falling fast asleep. He didn't understand why anyone would want to waste good alcohol, but their loss was his gain. After a few minutes of searching, he found a secluded spot by the river where he could drink his cares away and not worry about someone bothering him. Few people came this way at night.

As he made his way to the riverbank, he saw someone sleeping there and realized that he would have to go some place else. As a wave hit the riverbank, the person didn't bother to move. Old One Eyed Jack wondered if maybe this person was passed out and wouldn't notice him.

He pulled out the little flashlight he found the other day and shined it over to the sleeping person to see if they moved. He let out a snort; this person must be three sheets to the wind if they weren't waking up with a flashlight in their eyes. As he made his way to the other side of the sleeping person, he almost passed out from the sight in front of him. He ran back up the levee screaming like a little girl. He would have nightmares for years to come. When he reached the street, he took a gulp of his whiskey and went in search of a cop. There were usually several out patrolling in this area. He soon found one and explained, "Dude, der is a dead woman over at de river. Mon Dieu, someone put a curse on dat one. Mais, I have never seen anything like it."

The cop looked at the man with indignation, "How much of that hooch have you had to drink tonight sir? I can smell it on your breath."

One Eyed Jack held the bottle closer to him, "Mais non, I only had a sip of dis stuff. I took a drink when I got back up here to calm my nerves. I'm telling ya dere is a dead body down dere. Someone cut out her heart."

Officer Boudreaux was in no mood for some drunk's antics tonight, but he had to check this out, no matter how ridiculous the charge was. "Come on; show me where the body is."

He shook his head, "I ain't going near dat body. I will point to it with my flashlight, but I won't go anywhere near dat body again, mon ami. Dat one has a curse on it, I tell you."

***

Officer Boudreaux radioed in that he was going to check out a possible crime scene and asked the dispatcher to stand by. The old man standing next to him was probably too drunk to even realize that what he saw was someone who had passed out. Since patrolling the French Quarter, he had seen a lot of belligerent drunks and people so strung out on drugs they could not stand. He had had to call more than one van to pick up stone cold drunks to let them sleep off their stupor in the jail house.

As they neared the river bank, One Eyed Jack put his feet firmly on the ground and shook his head, "Mais, I ain't going any closer." He took his flashlight and shined it in the vicinity of the body, "Dat is where da body is located. I will wait right here for ya. Ya don't have to worry about me running off, non. I just don't want to see dat again."

Letting out an exasperated sigh, he exclaimed, "Okay, sir. You can stay right here until I get back. Now, I don't want you running off, you hear?"

"Mais oui. I told ya I will wait right here for ya."

Officer Jack Boudreaux had been with the New Orleans Police Department for almost two years. In those two years, he had lost his rose colored glasses and knew that you could expect the unexpected in this business. As he neared the body, he gently kicked the shoes of the victim to see if they even budged. Since the person didn't respond, he moved closer and shined his light on her face. His entire supper threatened to come right back up. Forcing the vomit down, he called the dispatcher, "You need to send crime scene techs and a detective down here. We have a dead stiff that was butchered." Officer Boudreaux looked at the body one more time before forcing himself to turn away and draw in a deep breath.

Without looking at the body, he said a novena for the poor soul and walked back up to talk to the drunk. Maybe he saw something without even realizing it.

Chapter 14

When Detective Mike Bailey first came to New Orleans, he was in the Navy and stationed here.   After serving ten years in the Navy, Detective Bailey decided to leave that part of his life behind him and joined the police force. His first street patrol was the French Quarter, also known to the locals as "The Vieux Carre" which meant "The Old Square." This historic district was one of the city's oldest neighborhoods. The French Quarter, founded in 1718, consisted of approximately 85 square blocks with the mighty Mississippi River bordering the Southeastern part.

After working for the police force for a number of years, he became jaded and took a sabbatical. During that time, he worked with his best friend, Guy Mayon, as a private investigator. That was when they stumbled upon a carnival of vampires killing victims across the United States. The police commissioner at that time asked Mike and Guy to return to the force and work in a special department that strictly dealt with the supernatural that the present mayor was establishing. New Orleans was having problems with walking zombies and vampires around that time period. They had no idea if any of the vampires escaped, and Detective Grace Hutcherson expressed her concerns that the ring leader of the vampire carnival had indeed escaped. Guy and Mike feared that the voodoo queen, Bianca Honore, who worked with the Mafia, was also still practicing her magie noire. There had been a slew of unexplainable robberies, and one witness reported that the intruder seemed to be in a trance. If this was true, then there was a possibility that the voodoo queen was using her magie noire in New Orleans.

As Mike pulled up to the crime scene, he noticed Hutch's car was already there. They kept their relationship low key since they worked together, but he was ready to move it to the next level. Besides, they practically saw each other every night. Most nights he didn't even go home anymore. Guy suspected that the two of them were dating.

As he got closer to the crime scene, he felt the tension in the air. They were called to the crime scene since the supernatural was suspected, but from the way everyone was acting, this was something more. Everyone talked quietly amongst themselves and just looked over at the body, but no one went near the scene. That was never a good sign.

Hutch walked his way as soon as she noticed him. Before she left the scene, she took a moment to genuflect, making the sign of the cross, before proceeding to meet him.

Mike asked, "How bad is it?"

She shook her head, "Someone wanted to make sure this woman was good and dead. Her internal organs are missing, cut out. The coroner believes that the organs were ripped out of her. Whoever did this had enough strength to reach right into her body and remove the heart, liver, lungs and kidneys. They also drained the body of blood. Whoever did this wanted EVERY last drop of blood."

As Mike listened to Hutch describe the body, one word went through his mind, vampire. Now he knew why they were there, "Was this done by the one who has been invading your thoughts?"

She shook her head, "I am not picking up a trace of him at the scene. That doesn't mean that he didn't do it. He only allows me in when he chooses. I can sometimes catch him off guard, but as soon as he feels me picking up on his presence, the link is broken."

Mike didn't like the fact that this vampire could intrude on her thoughts so easily. He feared the creature was stalking her, which was another reason he wanted them to move in together. He was afraid to let her out of his sight. Now that he had someone he cared about, he didn't want to lose her.

***

Guy Mayon was a New Orleans native. He was proud of his Cajun heritage and loved his hometown dearly. Even with its flaws, he couldn't see himself living anywhere else. Guy was not bothered by the constant humidity that made everyone sweat or even the coldest of winter days that seemed to cut you straight to the bone. There were others here that shared the same pride, which was why even after the disastrous hurricane Katrina, this city was being rebuilt. You could see the pride and love in the way the residents here preserved their French and Spanish heritage. What some people saw as run down and dilapidated buildings, he saw as the city's history.

Guy even loved the various people who made up this city. A diverse variety of people walked these streets, which made up the decadence of New Orleans. They were what made this city flourish.

Guy walked over to Mike and Hutch and stated, "You guys need to admit that you are a couple and be done with it."

Hutch looked up at him, "I don't know what you are talking about."

Guy just snickered, "Mmhmm, so that is going to be the way, huh? Okay then, let's get back to work."

Before moving in for a closer inspection of the body, they waited for the crime scene photographer to finish taking pictures. The coroner looked over at Mike and asked, "So, do we need to invest in garlic to wear around our necks?"

Mike replied, "From the look of this body, it may not be a bad idea."

The coroner shook his head, "I was afraid you were going to say that. Man, we have seen zombies and vampires together. What's next, werewolves?"

Mike let out a chortle, "I wouldn't doubt it at this moment in time. I never know what kind of low life we may be dealing with next."

* * *

As they walked into the police station, the receptionist caught Hutch, "The coroner wants y'all over there ASAP."

Hutch asked, "Did he say why?"

"No, just that during the autopsy he found something important."

Mike interrupted, "He didn't say anything about what he found?"

"No, sir. He said for y'all to head right over instead of settling in here."

Guy opened the door, "I guess we better go see what is up."

On the way over to the coroner's office, they speculated why the coroner wanted to see them ASAP.

***

Dr. Calvin Ortego had been with the New Orleans coroner's department for over fifteen years now, and lately the number of unexplained cases was staggering. The mystery that seemed to thrive in this area was what lured him to New Orleans. He could honestly attest to the fact that he had worked stranger cases than his fellow coroners. Once the news of the vampire deaths became public knowledge, his coroner peers began to contact him about unexplained deaths they were working on or had worked on. It seemed they also had bodies drained of blood, but unlike his case, there were no puncture wounds on their bodies. However, some of the bodies had decomposed to the point where it was impossible to distinguish if any puncture wounds were present.

When he first started in this business, he never once suspected he would be investigating deaths caused by vampires or that zombies walked this earth. He would be the first to scoff at the very idea of such things. Now, the first thing he did when a body came into his morgue was to recheck all the vitals and make sure the doors were locked before leaving. He didn't want any bodies walking out of his morgue like the funeral home had happen to them. Mais non, that was not the kind of publicity they needed here.

Dr. Ortego was in his office when the detectives arrived. He met them out in the corridor before escorting them into the morgue.

Mike extended his hand out to Dr. Ortego, "We understand that you wanted to see us right away."

As they walked to the autopsy room, Dr. Ortego went over the toxicology reports he received. "I want you to understand that this is just a preliminary report, but my associate felt that it was important enough to tell me right away. Once I saw the toxicology report for myself, I had to agree."

Mike, Guy and Hutch waited in utter anticipation for what the good doctor had to tell them. They saw the puncture wounds and the removal of the organs so cause of death was pretty obvious.

Dr. Ortego continued, "I know when we looked at the body we thought we knew the cause of death, but I like to make sure all the i's are dotted and t's crossed before signing off on any death certificate. I had a toxicology report run just to see if the young woman was possibly high or drunk, which would explain why there were no defensive wounds on the body. You would think if someone was sucking all the blood out of a person, they would put up a fight. This young girl not only had enough heroin to kill a horse, but she also had another toxin in her blood stream."

"So, this killer didn't think the heroin would be enough to subdue her?"

Dr. Ortego shook his head, "The killer may not have known she was already high as a kite."

Hutch replied, "The suspense is getting to us Doc. What did the toxicology report show?"

Not wanting to spoil the surprise, Dr. Ortego replied, "Let's just say that for once I am glad my associate decided to think outside of the box and check for exotic poisons as well."

Guy asked, "Okay, so what made her think of the exotic poisons?"

"Well, we know for a fact that the voodoo queen used a poison from Haiti to make her zombies. Now, when we have a dead body we run toxicology reports to check for that drug, but she went one step further and included snake and spider venom as well. She remembered reading something about voodoo priestesses and queens having familiars and snakes."

Hutch replied, "I am impressed."

Dr. Ortego agreed, "I am too. Especially since her gut instincts were correct. It turns out the victim did indeed have snake venom in her blood stream."

Mike pondered this for a moment, "But why would a vampire need to use snake venom? He has killed before and needed nothing but his mind and strength to do the job."

Dr. Ortego replied, "I wondered the same thing. It is as if the snake venom was used as a neurotoxin to help subdue the victim."

Guy responded, "So the killer needed additional help? A vampire wouldn't need extra help."

Dr. Ortego nodded his head and escorted them to the body waiting for autopsy, "Exactly. I am running DNA on the saliva from the wound to determine if we are dealing with a male or female and to see if we can come up with any more clues as to who did this. I guess that if this were an actual vampire that killed this girl, then there would be some variations in the normal DNA sequence. After all, they are supposed to be the walking dead."

As Mike looked down at the body, he told the good doctor, "As soon as you get some results let us know."

"Always Detective."

Mike went over in his head everything the doc said. He brought up some very valid points. An experienced vampire would not need to use a neurotoxin. "Hey doc, wouldn't whoever used the snake venom have to worry about transferring it to them if they were going to drink the blood."

"Typically yes, but not if they had an antidote or built up a resistance to this particular neurotoxin."

Guy asked, "So, how do you build up a resistance to this neurotoxin."

"They start off by giving themselves small doses, but it takes years to do this. I don't see a vampire needing to build up a resistance to this particular neurotoxin."

Hutch replied, "No, but a voodoo queen that keeps a snake draped around her neck may want to keep an anti-venom handy. She may also make sure she built up a resistance to the venom."

Dr. Ortego nodded his head in agreement, "Yes, you are correct. You honestly think this is the work of the voodoo queen?"

Hutch inspected the body once more, "This may involve more than just the voodoo queen. Something tells me that our voodoo queen and vampire have joined forces."

Mike was starting to believe that Hutch was correct in her premonition. If so, they were in for a lot of trouble. Nothing good would come from those two joining forces.

Guy asked, "Is there any way to find out which kind of snake venom was used."

"I am having the lab test the venom, but it is a monumental task. There is no telling how long it will take. When I know something, I will let you know."

***

Guy was more curious than anything. It wasn't like they would be able to locate the killer just by determining the snake used to poison their victim.

As they walked out to the car, Guy exclaimed, "Why can't this just be a nice and easy first degree murder? I swear, something about this city seems to bring out the motier foux, crazies."

Mike reminded him, "If it weren't for cases like this, you and I wouldn't have this particular job."

***

He couldn't deny the truth behind that statement. Guy didn't like that they had no idea what they were dealing with this time around. Was it a vampire or a wanna be vampire? Both could be extremely dangerous and very unpredictable. Then there was the possibility they were dealing with a cult intrigued with vampires. He needed to check and see if there had been any satanic cult rituals lately. It should be easy to find out. He would see if any sheep or livestock were reported as gutted or beheaded. Sometimes they were known to siphon the blood from the animal. It could be that they grew tired of mutilating animals and moved on to something much worse. They must keep an open mind on the different scenarios and not become focused on proving that this death was vampire related.

Chapter 15

Adam Ledet woke to a loud clanking noise. Still not fully awake, he went to propel himself off the side of the bed, but his moves were cut short; something wasn't right. Something had a hold of his ankles.

As the sleep left his eyes, he noticed he was enveloped in total darkness. He tried to focus, but he soon realized he wasn't in his room. Fear moved through him when he discovered that his arms and legs were restrained. It had taken a moment or two before he realized that the loud clanking noise he heard was from the chains restraining him.

Fully alert now, adrenaline rushed through his veins like a runaway train barreling down a track. Who could have done this to him? What happened to him? He tried to go over the details of last night, but he drew a blank. The last thing he remembered was walking home from his job at the bar on Bourbon Street.

Fear, anger and confusion barraged his mind. Questions flooded his thoughts. Where was he? Was this a cruel joke?

Adam heard a movement coming from somewhere in the room. He hollered out, "This isn't funny. You need to let me go!" He tried to stay calm, but his voice betrayed him.

He waited for an answer, but only heard the rattle of the chains. He swallowed down the fear caught in his throat. Were there others in here with him? He remembered a while back reading a newspaper article on human trafficking. He prayed that wasn't what happened to him. He couldn't imagine being kidnapped and used as a sex slave. The very thought sent chills down his spine.

Adam tried desperately to at least free his arms from the restraints. He contorted his hands in various directions hoping to slip his hands free from the cuffs. As he struggled to free himself, he wondered what kind of person would do this to him. Was his abductor a man, woman, stranger or acquaintance? Once in a while he swore that someone was in the room with him.

Adam was unsure of how long he had been here, but as he watched the shadows dance around the room, he realized that this was no joke. Someone was holding him prisoner.

Fear crept into his body as he thought back to the recent loan from Brian Donovan. His friends warned him that he would be sorry if he made a deal with Brian. He wasn't worried about Brian's threats. Adam assumed the man would pressure him to pay the loan as soon as possible, but never this.

As time crept by, the noises in the room played on his nerves. He began to fear the unknown. He imagined everything that could happen to him, the amount of pain and suffering he would be forced to endure before he died. He was fairly certain that he would die.

He tried once more to peer through the shadows to see where he was. Even after his eyes grew accustomed to the darkness, he could not make out any shapes in the room. The one thing he was certain of was the smell. The stench was all consuming. Every time he breathed in the air, he cringed. It smelled of blood, urine, feces, body odor and death.

Unable to take being in the restraints anymore, he tried to free himself once more. Once again, he squeezed his fingers tightly together. His skin burned as the metal cut into it, catching on his knuckles. Ignoring the pain and the warm blood trickling from his hand, he continued to work on freeing his hand. He oscillated his hand, and his breath caught when he felt his hand begin to slip free. He gave his hand a fierce tug and to his surprise his knuckles slipped free. His hand was free! He smiled to himself over the fact that he freed one of his hands. Using his free hand, he began to work on the other hand.

Once his hands were free, he moved to his ankles. They would be the most difficult to free. He tugged at the restraints furiously, twisting one ankle and then the other in an unnatural position as he tried to free himself from his restraints.

The oppressive heat in the room didn't help matters. Sweat poured down his body at the exertion of attempting to free himself. He imagined the sweat was tiny snakes slithering down his body, snakes wanting to find a place to hide from the evil of this place. He shook his head, trying to clear his head. He must think of a way out of this.

Chapter 16

Brianna Easterly made herself comfortable in her small courtyard in the French Quarter as she tried to ignore the noises that filled the night air. She despised living above the restaurant, but until business picked up, this was all they could afford. At least they had this one little luxury. If it wasn't for this small piece of heaven, she doubted she could stand living here.

Her husband, Walt, was already sleeping, but Brianna was too restless. She plugged in her earphones and listened to the soft sounds of music. The noise helped drown out the surrounding noises while she read one of the eBooks she'd downloaded earlier that week. As she sipped on a glass of wine and read, the stress of the day left her body.

As she took another sip of wine, she watched the moonlight dance across the yard and the various patterns it made on the ground. If only they could move to the country, away from this crazy city. Nighttime was her favorite time of the day. Night was when magic became possible.

She laughed when she thought about telling Walt why she so loved the nighttime. It took him a while to get used to her eccentricities. For a while after they married, he tried to stay up with her and enjoy the night, but the night air wasn't for him. He preferred to sleep rather than enjoy the night.

A wispy cloud moved across the moon and darkened the area for a moment. Once the cloud floated away, her beloved moonlight returned. Just as quickly another shadow moved across the small yard. In the corner near her rose bushes was the shape of a man. Her heart lodged in her throat when she caught him staring at her. Instead of being scared though, she found herself hypnotized by his stare.

She stood up, finding herself drawn towards the mysterious figure. She reached out to caress his cheek and discovered his skin cool to the touch. His eyes changed only for a moment. There was something so profound and dark hidden behind his lifeless stare. The depths of his eyes sucked her into the dark abyss. This was the magic of the night that she held so close to her heart. This was the magic she was waiting for.

Without uttering a word, he bent down and kissed her fiercely. He leaned her body back while pinning her wrists behind her back. She was utterly helpless to resist him. She was caught in his web of intrigue and dark sorcery and didn't care about the things he was doing to her body. When he eased her to the ground, she didn't think of her husband fast asleep in the bed upstairs. She only thought of this man taking over her very thoughts.

She reveled in the way his cool skin felt against her warm skin. This man had her mesmerized. The heavy scent of the roses filled the air around them, making her head swim. She never even felt when his fangs pierced the delicate skin of her neck. When he sucked on her neck, exhilaration washed over her body. Her body reacted to his touch as if she desperately longed for him. She ran her hands through his hair and clutched onto him as he continued to drink from her. His lips were so cold against her heated skin.

A moment of clarity came over her. She shouldn't be here with another man when her husband was upstairs waiting for her. She loved her husband more than anything and would never sleep with another man.

***

Joshua sensed her clarity and invaded her thoughts once again, creating a euphoria that caused her to lose all thought of her husband. He continued to drink from her, relishing in her very taste.

He felt her let her mind and body waft away as her life slipped away quietly. He left her lying by the roses in the peace of the night.

***

Walt rolled over and reached out to bring his wife closer to him. Not feeling her warm body in bed next to him, he looked over at the clock to see that it was almost four o'clock in the morning. As he got out of bed in search of his wife, he knew exactly where to look for her. Brianna more than likely wasn't paying attention to the time and drifted off to sleep while reading a book. He'd never met a woman so mesmerized by the night.

As he walked out into the courtyard, he sensed something was wrong. Brianna wasn't in her normal spot, but instead, she was lying face up on the ground near the rose bushes. Walt's anguished cry pierced through the night.

Stumbling blindly back into the house, he somehow found the phone and called nine one one. The rest was a blur.

Walt didn't remember talking to the dispatcher or letting the police officers in.

Detective Mike Bailey answered his ringing phone without even bothering to glance at the caller ID screen. A phone call this early meant there was a murder somewhere that needed his team's attention, "Bailey."

The dispatcher informed him, "Sir, we have a body that the coroner believes you should come see."

After Mike had written down the information he needed, he called Guy and woke up Hutch. Guy told him he would meet them at the crime scene since it wasn't far from his house.

It took no time for Mike to get to the crime scene. The streets were almost devoid of life. As Mike and Hutch got out of the car, Mike looked around. Everyone in the French Quarter was either asleep or drunk, and those drunk were staying contained to Bourbon Street.

The only cars on the street were about half a dozen police cars with their flashing red and blue lights glimmering against the windows. The crime scene techs had just arrived in their van and were busy unloading their supplies. Unfortunately, this was just another night in New Orleans.

Mike was thankful that the local news had yet to hear about the most recent murder. Hopefully, they could process the scene and remove the body before they arrived.

Officer Boudreaux greeted the detectives as they walked into the courtyard. "If it hadn't have been for the puncture wounds on her neck, I doubt you would have been called.

She looks as if she died peacefully in her sleep until you see the neck wounds."

Detective Bailey watched as a number of uniformed officers and crime scene techs scurried around the crime scene. They were silent as they examined the scene in front of them. Guy looked at his two partners and asked, "Any ideas?"

Hutch took in the scene and tried to read the energy around her, "He came from the rear and surprised her. She was sitting over there on the settee reading. He had her in a trance as soon as she noticed him."

As Hutch continued to read the scene, the vampire sensed her presence, and he intruded on her thoughts. He whispered, "She was weak."

Hutch stopped, frozen in fear for a moment. She took a few seconds to calm her nerves and made sure that she had him blocked from reading her thoughts once more. It was so hard to read a crime scene when the vampire was always using that time to invade her mind. Mike could sense the change in her and asked, "Are you all right?"

"I'm fine now. She was weak; that was why he didn't turn her. He is being careful with whom he chooses to join his following this time. He has a certain type that he wants."

Mike mulled over what she said. He had no doubts she was correct in how she read the scene. Mike watched as Dr. Ortego headed their way, "Dr. Ortego."

"I'm sure you know why you were called out?"

Guy nodded his head, "It looks like a vampire bite."

"Yes, she died from exsanguination. I think we need to head over to the chapel and pray. This killing was a lot less gruesome than the other murders, but nonetheless, a lady's life was taken too soon." As they continued to talk, Mike watched as the body was moved to a gurney.

Guy looked over at his partners and could tell by the exasperated look on Hutch's face that she was already tired of this case, and they were just starting.

***

Hutch picked up the paper the next morning and saw that their murder was in the news. The poor woman's death didn't even make the front page. It was as if death in New Orleans only warranted a small article on the back page.

A husband found his wife's body early yesterday morning. The victim died from excessive blood loss and was marred by two puncture wounds on her neck. The victim has been identified as Brianna Easterly, wife to Walt Easterly. As of yet, no funeral arrangements are available. When the New Orleans Police Department was questioned, the public relations department said that a statement would be forthcoming.

Hutch noticed that a small picture of the victim was included under the caption. Hutch wondered how many articles would be written on the back page of the paper before this vampire was caught. She guessed they should be grateful that the reporter didn't mention the word vampire. It wouldn't be long before that word was on everyone's lips, though.

Chapter 17

The insatiable hunger hit the creature once again. The thirst for blood was more than it could stand, it could hold out no longer. The poison from the snakes it snacked on dripped from its fangs.

Several months ago, a cottonmouth snake had ventured into the creature's home. Seeing a way out of its misery, the creature decided to feed on the snake while it attacked out of fear. Instead of killing the creature, the snake's venom moved through the creature's body and now when it fed the venom dripped from its fangs. Soon after the creature made that discovery, the creature found snakes to snack on. The blood satisfied the cravings while the venom helped to immobilize its prey.

The alleys of The French Quarter had become a favorite hunting ground for the creature. Late at night the drunks, druggies and homeless roamed these streets. These people were easy prey.

From the shadows, it saw the prostitute walk to the alley. She was no challenge for the creature.

The creature smelled the air and hungered for the blood pumping through the woman's young body. The creature's eyes followed each step the woman made. Following her every step, the creature prepared to attack. It was too hungry to move the body to a place more secluded for feeding. Its muscles tensed and its fangs were exposed as it prepared to attack.

The woman did not have time to react before the creature sank its fangs into her throat. Hot blood instantly filled its mouth. The taste was so much sweeter than anticipated as it flowed down the creature's throat.

***

The pitch black darkness of the night sky reminded Mike of the chicory coffee that was so popular here in New Orleans. The night air was thick and filled with mystery. As he walked down the streets of the French Quarter, a jazz tune filled the night air with its forlorn melody. A dense fog rolled in from the mighty Mississippi River masking the walkway and dampening the air. Even though it was October, it was still warm. Of course, the weather at this time of the year was fickle. It could be freezing in the morning and sweltering by mid-afternoon.

Tonight's humidity cut him right to the bone. It was also the perfect night for a murder. The moon was full, and the fog snaked through the city. There weren't too many people out on Bourbon Street tonight. Generally, at this hour the alcohol was flowing like the river nearby, quickly and freely. Maybe they knew that evil lurked about the town and hurried to their destinations.

As soon as he reached the alley where the body was located, he stopped to survey the scene. The fog that snaked eerily through the alley seemed to hover over the body.

One of the chief technicians, Daniel Crawford, was busy taking pictures of the crime scene and collecting evidence.

Unfortunately, when he was called out, there wasn't much evidence to process.

The medical examiner was kneeling down in front of the female corpse. He let out a deep sigh and took a deep breath before heading into the alley. Now he wished he hadn't taken a deep breath of the stale air. It was filled with the dank smell of the river mud, stale cigarettes, urine and old beer - not a pleasant smell at all.

Mike ducked under the crime scene tape and approached the crime scene. "Dr. Ortego, I take it you're the reason I was called in?"

Dr. Ortego looked down at the body crumpled in the alley and nodded his head, "Exsanguination was the cause of death. However, I am positive that it was your vampire. Her neck was broken as she was being drained of blood. This was just like the body discovered while the carnival was in town. I will run a DNA sequence to see if the DNA from the previous murder matches this one."

Mike observed the body, "From the look of her clothes and shoes, he found a hooker to feed off of tonight."

Dr. Ortego pointed out, "She also has track marks. I have a feeling we will find a high level of heroin in her system."

Mike called over to Officer Crawford, "Make sure you take several photos of the victim's neck."

Crawford rolled his eyes, "It's covered; don't worry."

Mike bit his tongue at the officer rolling his eyes, trying to control the anger boiling up inside of him. It showed a sign of disrespect, but then Mike should know better than to tell him how to do his job.

Mike asked Crawford, "Who found the body?"

He tilted his head to one of the cruisers, "A bum looking for a place to pee stumbled upon the body. He probably searched the body for drugs and money before calling it in. The clothes looked a little too neat for someone dumped at the site."

As Mike headed over to talk to the witness, his cell phone rang. It was Hutch, "We have another body. Guy and I are headed that way now."

He let out a sigh, "You have to be kidding me. I assumed this guy would be full after feeding off of this one."

Hutch agreed, "We may be dealing with more than one vampire. This one is clear across town. Mike, this one isn't as clear cut as the one you are working on. The body looks like the victim found by the river. Her internal organs were removed."

A sick feeling washed over Mike as he listened to what Hutch had to say. "I had planned on talking to the man who found the body, but something tells me he didn't see anything. Give me the address, and I will meet y'all over there."

It took Mike almost twenty minutes to make it across town. The body was found by a housekeeping maid wanting to take a nap in a vacant room.

As he made his way to the hotel room, the smell of death permeated the air. Mike had a feeling the maid wouldn't be sneaking into rooms for a while. Taking a deep breath, he prepared himself for what he was about to witness. If this scene were like the last, it would be a hard one to stomach. As he headed into the room, the coppery smell of fresh blood greeted him. He expected to find blood all over the room, but instead, there was very little.

Dr. Ortego walked into the room right after him, "Looks as if we are going to be busy tonight. I ended up leaving my associate with the other body."

As Mike looked down at the body, he thought about the rash of murders escalating. Now they may be dealing with two separate killers, but they were both on the same mission - to drain the body of blood. The mutilation of this body was much worse than the previous body.

They needed to do something to stop these killers, but what? He felt helpless and that was not a feeling he liked. He was supposed to protect and serve and right now he wasn't even in control of this case. They were dealing with a murderer who they couldn't identify and until they identified that killer, it was the one in control. This was no mere man that they were dealing with. It had to be a spawn of Satan, a demon.

***

That night Hutch's dreams were more of distorted images than anything else. She found herself walking the streets of the French Quarter. A noise coming from the sewer drain drew her attention. An unknown force pulled her into the bowels of the city. As she walked through the sludge, a movement in the back caught her attention. She found herself face to face with a creature like none she had ever seen before. Her heart caught in her throat as the creature just stared her down.

This must be a hallucination; dealing with vampires and such had her imagination working overtime. She tried to force herself to wake up. Instead, she watched as the creature advanced on her. As the creature closed in on her, Grace could read her thoughts and see all the way to her heart. This creature was an abomination.

Grace could see beneath the creature's skin and watched as blood moved through its veins that snaked through its body straight to its heart. As Grace peered deeper into the creature's body, she could see the beating of the heart and could clearly make out the thump-thump pattern of its beats. Grace recoiled at what she saw living inside of the heart. Deep inside the recesses of its heart was a black void that was slowly taking over the creature's very being. Could Bianca and the vampire have created this creature? Had it somehow escaped? More importantly, could this be what was murdering people so viciously around New Orleans? As the creature went to pounce on Grace, she bolted upright in bed. She looked to her side to see Mike sleeping peacefully in bed. Moving into the crook of his arms for comfort, she prayed she could go back to sleep without any more visions.

As Hutch listened to Mike sleep, she thought about the things she had witnessed lately. There had been so many deaths and mutilations. This time last year, she would have never admitted that vampires walked this earth, but now, she wondered what other fairy tales were actually true.

Tomorrow they would need to search the sewers to see if this creature lived there. Even if this dream were a mere delusion, she would feel better knowing this creature didn't exist; they had to make sure.

Chapter 18

Joshua could smell her as she made her way near him. There was something intoxicating about her scent; it was a clean, womanly scent. As with all vampires or predators, he knew the scent of his prey. As he smelled the air one more time, he noticed something different about this woman. Just from her scent, he knew he must possess her soul. She had a precious, beautiful soul. Maybe, her soul would help calm the tortured souls that he had claimed over the years.

The taste of her fear was strong, pungent and almost overwhelming. It tasted salty and bitter on his tongue. Instantly, he was at her jugular. As his fangs gleamed in the moonlight, he grabbed a fistful of hair and pulled her head to one side. As his fangs sank deep into her sensitive neck, he inhaled and saturated his pallet with her sweet scent.

Once he was done feasting off of her body, he looked down into her eyes. They stared back at him lifelessly, vastly different than before he fed on her; they were hollow, cold and empty.

He picked up the dead body and brought it outside. Pulling off the lid of a steel fifty-five gallon drum he had here on the property, he shoved the limp body into it. This would be the perfect delivery for the beautiful Detective Grace Hutcherson. He had felt her trying to intrude on his thoughts. Perhaps by finding this body on her doorstep, she would get the message to leave him alone.

As he dropped her into the drum, her legs splayed out in a "V" pattern. While pushing her legs down, the sound of bones splintering echoed in the night air. Before sealing the drum, he threw in her purse. Joshua figured he might as well make the detective's life easier and let her know who the victim was.

As he sealed the drum, he noticed Bianca walking his way. He let out a silent groan. The woman couldn't let him have any time to himself lately. Sunrise wasn't too far away, and he wanted to get the body to the detective's house before morning. If Bianca stopped to talk, it would be tonight before he could make his delivery. While this latest girl may have a pure soul, his hunger was not sated and he needed a snack on the way back home.

As Bianca made her way over to him, he paid attention to the way she almost glided over the ground instead of actually walking. If he didn't know better, he would swear she was turned. She moved like an immortal, one that had lived for centuries. He wondered how strong her powers had become for her to move with such ease.

Between the two of them, they were growing a substantial sized army; yet, Bianca wasn't ready to move onto the next step. Joshua suspected she was taking money from Brian Donovan as his hired killer to grow her fortune. It seemed as if she never had enough money. He hadn't shared with Bianca the knowledge of his billions he'd accumulated over the century.

He wondered if the detectives knew that Brian Donovan had taken over as the new Mafia boss. At least Bianca was smart enough to change her method of killing to make it appear to be a vampire wannabe killing. This helped to keep the detective's eyes off of them.

Joshua thought of what his life had become. This wasn't the life his master expected him to live. His master could never find out that he was being watched over by a mere mortal, a voodoo priestess nonetheless. Right now Joshua was biding his time, waiting for the opportune moment to eliminate Bianca from his life. Currently, she served a purpose. Unknowingly, she was helping him to achieve his dreams. When it was time, he had no qualms ridding this earth of her.

Bianca looked down at the body, "Who is this?"

"Just supper. I plan on delivering her to the detective to shake her up."

Bianca shook her head, "That isn't wise. We don't want to draw any more attention from her."

He tried to keep his irritation of her remark from simmering to the surface, "This will scare her off so she won't keep trying to read my mind."

"Why don't you just get rid of her? Then you don't have to worry about her."

Joshua had often wondered the same thing. Could it be that he found this mortal intriguing? "No, if we kill her now, then we are sure to cause an investigation."

"You don't have to kill her; you can turn her, or we can have her join the zombies."

Joshua shook his head, "No! She serves a purpose for now. I can read her mind and find out if they are close to finding us."

Bianca looked at him with skepticism. "Fine, you can let her be for now, but I don't want this body left on her doorstep."

Without arguing further, Joshua easily carried the drum to a clearing, doused it with gasoline and set it ablaze. Bianca joined him, and they watched the girl's body burn.

Before the sun rose, they headed into the house. He detested the sunrise. Dawn was the hour when the sky changed, and darkness was no longer bathed in blood. At night, the world belonged to his kind, but unfortunately, the daylight belonged to the humans.

Even before being turned, he enjoyed the night and its mystery. At night, the imperfections of the world were hidden. The trees resembled large, malevolent giants. Their branches reached out with gnarly fingers, ready to scratch and grab at anyone who dared to wander into their path. As the sun rose in the sky, the vampires were forced into hiding; the blood that permeated the night disappeared. The darkness of the night was transformed into cornflower blue skies with white billowy clouds. In the daylight, even the trees lost their malevolent appearance and became gentle swaying beauties that reached up to Heaven.

The screams of those they tortured were replaced with the songs of birds as the first rays of the sun broke through the darkness. As the sun rose higher in the sky, the world was transformed into a place of peace and harmony. The daylight hours were a safe haven for the mortals; soon though, it would not be that way. Their beautiful world would soon be disrupted, and a nightmare would take over.

Joshua watched from the shadows and dreamed of the future. No one could stop him from completing his goal and with each passing day his family grew in size and power. The zombies were becoming quite ravenous, and it wouldn't be long before they could control them. Once unleashed on the public, they would devour whatever crossed their path. Currently, they were fed in small increments. Once the vampires drained the bodies of blood, they were thrown to the zombies so that they could eat the brains and whatever else they wanted. Once a vampire bit the zombies, they were turned and craved human flesh. Joshua would never consider these creatures his kind. They were simply the walking undead. They did not show the same strength or characteristics as those turned when mortal. They were abominations, but he allowed Bianca to have her way for now. Soon it would be his turn.

Bianca did not understand who she'd partnered with. He was more than a predator, a hunter and mind reader. He collected the souls of those he killed. Even now his powers grew stronger. He was the most powerful vampire there was on this planet, and yet no one knew his true power.

As he overlooked the grounds, he wondered just how many blood slaves they had right now. It may be time to gather a few more. Mardi Gras was a productive season for them. Although they had acquired quite a few blood slaves, they could always use more. They must keep them far from the zombies. They were only given to them once their purpose was served.

Chapter 19

Greg Arnold made his way through the streets of New Orleans with ease. Even as drunk as he was, he doubted anyone could tell. Heck, just about everyone here was drunker than him.

Suddenly a sense of unease washed over him. He swore someone was watching him through the crowd. He turned around and saw two eyes almost glowing at the end of the street. Not wanting to find out what this person wanted, he took off in a run He hoped to make it to his hotel before whatever belonged to those glowing eyes was on top of him.

Whatever alcohol had been in his system quickly dissipated as fear consumed him. After deciding to take a short cut through an alley, he was enveloped in the darkness of the area. His harsh breathing seemed to echo in the night air as he made his way to the end. A noise behind him caught his attention and he tried to disappear into the wall, praying that he could blend into the background.

As his eyes adjusted to the darkness, he saw the eyes again. The eyes reflected strangely in the moonlight. They were making their way to him and sniffing the air as it advanced. When the creature appeared before him, he cried out harshly in fear. His cries turned into a blood curdling scream when the creature standing in front of him revealed the fangs it had for teeth. Greg's cries resembled the haunted shrieking of the damned. With nothing more than a sneer, the creature sank its fangs into his neck as it ripped away at his chest. As the creature drained Greg of his blood, the neurotoxins paralyzed his body, rendering him helpless.

Once done feeding on the man, the creature looked down at the mutilated body. This attack was so savage that it had ripped off the victim's head and massacred most of the body. Even more disturbing was the lack of blood anywhere near the body.

A noise at the end of the alley caught the creature's attention. It feared being discovered, so it left the body where it was and fled into the darkness of the night.

***

As soon as Guy, Mike and Hutch dropped into the manhole, the smell of death overtook them. Hutch was satisfied that it was more than just a dream she had. She informed her two companions, "This is where the creature lives."

As they moved deeper into the sludge, Mike could feel its presence in the air. Mike asked, "Did you get a good look at whatever lives down here?"

Hutch shook her head, "It was mainly distorted images. Whatever it is, I am fairly certain that at one time it was human."

The deeper they moved into the sewer, the heavier the smell of death became. All around them, they smelled urine, feces, blood and more importantly decay. They knew they were in the creature's lair when they saw the discarded bones.

They drew their guns and searched high and low for the creature. Mike replied, "It must be out hunting." A noise in the back of the sewage drain confirmed that they were no longer alone. A chill snaked across Hutch's spine as she turned back to see glowing eyes peering at them through the darkness.

What was looking back at them may have been human at one time, but no longer. Its skin was a ghastly gray and showed signs of decay. When it let out a vicious growl that resonated to their very core, fear almost paralyzed Hutch. At the moment the creature advanced, they fired with each taking aim for a different part of the creature's body.

As Hutch looked around at the pile of bones, she stated aloud, "It appears that this creature was living down here for quite some time."

Guy agreed, "I have a feeling that in the beginning, it brought the victims down here to feed on. There is no telling what caused it to start leaving the bodies for anyone to find."

Hutch thought back to her vision, "I think as the disease progressed it lost all concept of what it was doing."

As Dr. Ortego arrived, he heard the end of the conversation and replied, "I agree with Detective Hutcherson. We have been doing research on the DNA samples that we were able to pull. If our findings are correct, this could be a disease attacking the body. As it spreads, whatever was once human becomes completely lost, and all that remains is what the victim has turned into. We have the DNA samples from who we know were killed by vampires and then the samples of what we suspect is a wannabe vampire. I am wondering if this creature here is your wannabe vampire. At one time, this was a female human. We need to be careful in case there is venom that runs throughout its body.”

Hutch asked, “So, what do you think we are looking at Dr. Ortego? A mutation of the vampire?”

As Dr. Ortego studied the body, he replied, “I am not certain yet. It will be hard to ascertain for sure since we do not have an actual vampire to compare it to, but some type of mutation.”

***

Back in his office, Dr. Ortego flipped on a switch that turned on the overhead projector, “Here is what we have found so far.” Hutch watched as a strange looking double helix swirled on the screen. “The vampire DNA isn’t all that different from human DNA except that it is altered by the virus. Out of curiosity, I collected some samples from various bodies here in the morgue to see which ones may indeed contain this virus. Some that had no puncture wounds did contain the virus. The more we study some of the recent murders we noticed that the gene is mutating.”

A shiver went through Mike as he studied the body and listened to everything that Dr. Ortego said. “Perhaps the ghost that visited Hutch was correct in her comments, and Bianca is up to something. I have a feeling if we ran the prints through our database it would come back to someone who has recently departed this world. I also bet that we would learn she was buried in a cemetery that has many complaints of strange activity at night."

Guy looked over at Mike, "So do you believe that this woman could be someone Bianca raised from the dead?"

Mike nodded his head in agreement, "And if so, then we are all in trouble. We have no way of knowing how many more Bianca raised from the dead without digging up each and every grave. What if she raises those that deserve to be in hell? What if she is raising serial killers, criminals and basically the dregs of society to join her army? These men had no conscience in life, and there is no way they have a conscience in death."

That very thought chilled Hutch to her soul. That was just what they needed, an army of the criminal walking dead. "If she is raising the dead for some diabolical plan, why was this creature the only one we found down there?"

Guy wondered the same thing, "What if she didn't realize that she raised this person? Maybe she was so focused on another that she wasn't paying attention to the surrounding graves."

As Mike listened to what Guy was saying, an idea struck him, "What if she was focused on raising Dominic St. Germaine?"

Hutch looked at him in disbelief, "You think she raised the man who betrayed her?"

"Think about it for a moment. She raises the man who betrayed her, only to continue her torture on him. We can't prove that she killed Dominic in prison, but what if killing him wasn't enough for her? What if she experimented at first, and when she could successfully raise the dead, she would bring Dominic back from the dead. She would want to keep him under her constant control this time. Perhaps she and Joshua found a way to trap his soul just like Joshua trapped the souls of those in the carnival."

Guy thought about it, "We don't need to dig up the grave to find out if Dominic St. Germaine's body is in the grave. We can use the ground penetrating radar to see if a body is actually in the grave."

"But we don't even know if she just raises the soul or has the actual body risen from the ground."

Guy looked down at the creature in front of him, "Something tells me that she has to have the whole body rise from the dead."

Mike asked, "How long do you think it will take to find someone with ground penetrating radar?"

Guy smiled at him, "Not long at all, mon ami. While you were playing private investigator with me, the agency had one. I had a need for it in several cases, but none of the cases we worked on together called for it."

"Damn, how many other toys do you have?"

"Oh, I have quite a few toys we can use when the need arises."

***

Mike rubbed his hands together as he thought about using the ground penetrating radar. He often wondered if there were more than one body buried in some of the graves. It would be easy for a killer to slip in an extra body or two when the need arose. When he learned that the Mafia had a strong presence in New Orleans, he began to wonder about the possibility of more than one body in the newer graves. It was easier to hide a body in plain sight; the graves were already dug, and it would be easy enough to drop a body in a pre-dug grave. Once done, one only had to cover it with dirt. The grave worker wasn't going back in the morning to see if the grave was still the correct depth. No, they would get that body in the ground as quick as possible and move on.

Mike told Guy, "I want to use the radar."

Guy shook his head, "Mais non, mon ami. That little piece of equipment is too expensive for a novice to use. I'll let you walk with me so that you can see what is underneath the ground." Guy looked over at Hutch, "What about you? Do you want to watch as we study the graves?"

Hutch shook her head, "Y'all go ahead and have your fun. After I am done here, I need a hot shower."

Mike gave Hutch a quick kiss on the lips, "I will see you at the house later on. Make sure you keep the doors locked while you take your shower."

***

Hutch could see the worry in Mike's eyes and gave his hands a quick squeeze. She appreciated the concern, but at the same time she was not accustomed to someone worrying about her safety.

As soon as Hutch walked into their master bathroom and caught a reflection of her face, she let out a grimace. The sleepless nights and stress of the case were catching up with her. Her face looked as gray as that creature's face they killed earlier today. Her clothes looked as if she had slept in them all week, and she smelled worse than the sewer she had been in. As she looked at her clothes and saw the stains on them, she made a hasty decision to drop them in the trash. She didn't want to think about what was on her clothes.

Instead of a shower, she fixed herself a hot bubble bath. While the water was running, she walked into the kitchen to pour her a nice glass of sangria. After the day she'd had, she needed something stronger than wine, but something in the back of her head kept telling her to keep her wits about her.

Entering the bathroom once again, the steam enveloped her from the hot water and the heady scent of the gardenia bubble bath was a welcome relief. As she set the glass of wine on the edge of the tub and stepped into the tub, the weariness of the day set it. She was so tired; her eyes felt as if they were full of sand. She had to blink several times just to clear them. She let out a sigh as she leaned back in the tub and let the warmth of the water relax her muscles.

Chapter 20

Paul Gilbert parked his maroon BMW under a security light near the church's entrance. The street light cast grotesque shadows on the pavement. His family had gone to this church for as long as he could remember. Even though, the neighborhood wasn't as safe as it once was, he couldn't bring himself to find another church. Besides, he liked Father Trahan and would hate to switch churches only to find that priest was stale and stagnant.

The thunderstorm that hit the city earlier this afternoon was dying down. All that remained was a light drizzle. Dawn was a few mere hours away.

As he walked into the church, he looked up at the crucifix, dipped his fingers in the holy water and made the sign of the cross. Paul nodded to the other occupant in the chapel. As he genuflected, he made the sign of the cross and settled down for his hour of the night vigil. As he began to say his prayers, he never noticed the other man leave.

After saying a few prayers, he walked over to the votive candles. He lit one, kneeled down on the prie-dieu and raised his eyes to the statue of the Virgin Mary.

He had hoped that this hour of reflection would help him find peace, but his feelings of regret, guilt and unworthiness permeated his very being. As Paul reflected on the past few days, he wondered how things went wrong so fast. Why did he let greed take over his rational thinking? He knew that there was no such thing as easy money. When Brian Donovan came to him with this business opportunity, he should have said no. He'd heard the rumors around town about the possibility of Brian taking over where Dominic St. Germaine left off. Instead, Paul saw dollar signs and lots of them. Now, Paul's reputation was tarnished but also his life and soul. How could he look his wife and daughter in the eye knowing what he was helping Brian do? He suspected that Brian would use the warehouse to sort drugs, but he never thought Brian would be involved in something so much worse. How could anyone want to associate themselves with the dregs of society as those participating in human trafficking?

Paul hadn't planned to go there, but after receiving several complaints from neighboring businesses about the lights being out near the warehouse he had to go check it out. Several of the other warehouses had been robbed recently, and the owners were worried that the robbers were hiding near Paul's warehouse, using the darkness to slip into their businesses. Paul had replaced the halogen bulbs right before Brian rented the warehouse, so curiosity got the best of him. He assumed that perhaps Brian didn't want the neighboring businesses to see his men coming and going from the business. But that didn't mean they had to disable the lights to accommodate their plans. After Paul had confirmed the lights were indeed out, he decided to confront Brian. What Paul walked into was much worse than a few lights being dislodged. He witnessed men bringing in young girls, women, and even boys, all varying in ages, into the warehouse. Paul was revolted at the sight. Instead of confronting anyone with what he saw, he slipped back out into the darkness of the night.

When Paul went home that night to his daughter and wife, the guilt of what those poor souls were going through in the warehouse weighed heavy on his mind. He had to call the police, but shame and fear kept him from making that phone call. He prayed while attending adoration the answers would come to him.

As he genuflected, he realized that he had to make things right and accept the punishment for his greed. He feared that his family would be forced to suffer the consequences of his atonement, which they didn't deserve. He had betrayed God, and his family.

Paul rested his elbows on the prie-dieu and put his face in his hands as the tears built. As he sat there silently crying and praying, he inhaled the scent of the burning votive candles. He prayed for so long that the candles had died out. All that remained was a whiff of smoke as the fire reached the end of the wick.

As the quiet of the chapel settled into his very being, time seemed to stop. As his replacement for adoration walked in, the calmness that Paul desperately sought finally enveloped him.

When Paul turned to greet his replacement, his face paled upon seeing who was there instead. The tranquility he'd just found disappeared. He struggled to calm the desperate thoughts floating through his mind. Why was he here? He could know about what Paul saw.

Paul froze in fear when he felt the gun muzzle push into his back. "Let's go."

Once he was out the door, an intense pain wracked through his body. His body was propelled down the stairs from the force of the gunshot. Landing face down on the sidewalk below, his brain never registered when his attacker kicked him in the face for good measure. His life's blood flowed freely from his broken, mangled body as his eternal soul slipped away.

***

Brian wanted to personally watch as "the cleaner" took care of this little problem. He should have known this man would be curious and eventually learn about his warehouse. He had to silence the man before the police were warned about what he saw.

Brian instructed his men, "Go take care of the man's family."

***

Paul's soul hovered over the scene and began to quake with fear when he heard that they were going after his family next. He knew what Brian had in store for his wife and daughter, and it was not death; Brian intended to put them up for auction also. He must warn his wife before the men got to his house.

Being new to the spirit world, it took him a while to get used to floating through buildings and such. He made good time getting back to his house. When he arrived at the house, he didn't see the men. He had to convince his wife to leave in a hurry, without scaring her half to death. Once upstairs, he peeked in on his daughter before going to see his wife. As he leaned over his wife's sleeping body, he was instantly filled with regret. He would miss seeing her like this. If only he'd had one more night with her. He whispered into her ear, "Hannah. Hannah! I need you to listen."

***

Hannah felt a chill in the air and reached for the blanket. For a moment, she thought she heard Paul come into the room. She could have sworn she smelled his cologne and felt him bend down and kiss her. She called out, thinking he must be in the bathroom, "Paul, is that you honey? Where are you?"

Paul called out, harsher to get her attention, "Hannah, I need you to listen! You and Colette must leave. It is imperative that you leave the house now honey."

Hannah sat upright in bed. This time she was certain she heard Paul's voice, but she didn't see him. In the darkness of the room, she made out his shadow. Paul watched as his wife started to pale, "Oh my love, there is not enough time to explain. Please, do me this one favor. I need you and Colette to leave. Leave town now! You mustn't dawdle. Some dangerous men are on their way here cher."

Hannah had tears in her eyes. She reached out to the apparition in front of her, but she felt the coldness of the air, "Oh Paul. Please tell me I am dreaming."

"My love, please, there is no time to explain. You must go and go now."

A shiver came across Paul. He feared that the men were near the house. "Hannah, go NOW!"

Hannah didn't wait for further explanation. Even if this were a dream, she would rather go with her gut instinct - to run. It didn't take her long to wake up, throw on some clothes, grab her purse and load her sleeping daughter into the car.

Paul got into the passenger seat of the car with her, "Go, Hannah. You must go now!"

Hannah didn't wait for further explanation. She went to turn on the lights of the car and pull out when Paul told her, "No, my love. Don't turn your lights on just yet."

As Hannah drove away from the house, she caught a glimpse of a car pulling into their driveway. Terror filled her as she realized that her gut instinct had been right.

She turned to look at Paul and asked him what was going on. As she listened to what he said, she shivered in fear. How could Paul bring this into their lives?

When she looked over at the passenger seat once again, no one was there. Colette stirred in her seat, "Mommy, where did Daddy go?"

Hannah looked back at her, "I don't know honey. I wish I knew."

Hannah wasn't sure what happened, but she feared that something bad happened to Paul. That somehow he prevented something bad from happening to her and Colette. She picked up her phone and called the New

Orleans Police Department, requesting to speak to a Detective Mike Bailey. She recounted word for word what Paul told her, but she refused to let him know where she was or where she was going. She feared that Brian Donovan would not stop looking for them until she was dead. No, it was best for her and her daughter to disappear.

Now, to figure out where to go with no clothes and someone hunting them down. For now, she planned to drive as far as she could.

Chapter 21

Father Trahan tossed and turned in his room. Every time he closed his eyes, he saw the Virgin Mary statue and some of the other religious relics in the church crying blood. He was unsure if this was a warning or a nightmare. Lately, when he visited the sick in the hospital or walked around downtown, he swore he saw dark shadows peering at him, watching his every move. The only place he truly felt safe was in the church, and now the dreams had him fearing evil had made its presence there as well. He kept his crucifix, St. Benedict medal, rosary, and various miraculous medals on him at all times.

What if his fears were correct and the devil was trying to take over this city. He and some of his fellow priests feared that the devil had infiltrated politics in some of the larger cities in America and was slowly taking over those cities. Had the devil decided it was time to take over New Orleans? The signs were staring them in the face for a while, especially after Hurricane Katrina hit. Church attendance had dropped, and some of the parishioners left the city in search of a new life away from New Orleans. Another important factor to consider was the exponential rate that crime was increasing. What worried him the most was people didn't seem to care about, or even want to help, their fellow man. Gone were the days of the good Samaritan. Now, it seemed that people only cared about themselves, and it broke his heart.

With the economy in a depressed state, the soup kitchen here always had a steady line of people needing food.

Father Trahan talked to some of those who partook in the church's kindness, and he could see the sloth in them. They would rather depend on handouts than find a job. Several times he found a job for one or two of the unemployed, and they did not even bother to accept the job offer. It may not be the most soul satisfying job, but it was an honest day's work for an honest day's pay.

As Father Trahan drifted off to sleep once more, a noise in the front of the church woke him. He couldn't place the sound, but something deep in his being told him he must go see what was wrong.

As he walked into the church, he happened to look over at the Virgin Mary statue. What he saw made him stop in his tracks. He swore the statue was crying. Not wanting to take the time to confirm this sight, he rushed out the front chapel doors. His fears were confirmed when he saw a body lying on the pavement and what looked to be the shape of an SUV leaving the scene. As he rushed to aid the person lying on the pavement, he called nine one one and explained to the operator what had happened. As Father Trahan waited for the police to arrive, he said the last rites over the dead body.

Sadness and disbelief made its way into Father Trahan's heart. He knew this man; he and his family had always been such devout Catholics. Once the police arrived, he planned on telling them he wanted to tell Hannah and Colette about Paul's death. This should be done by someone who they knew, not a stranger.

It was not long before the early morning sky was lit up with the flashing lights of the multitude of emergency vehicles.

As the body was being taken care of, Father Trahan walked back inside to pray to St. Gertrude for this man's soul and all of the other souls in purgatory. As he kneeled down at the prie-dieu, he raised his eyes to the statue of the Virgin Mary. His heart caught as he stared at her in amazement. He stood up and walked over to the statue. He slowly raised his arm and wiped at one of her tears. Putting his thumb up to his mouth, he could taste the salt on his tongue. The statue was crying real tears instead of blood. He looked around the chapel and watched in disbelief as the other relics released tears from their eyes. He needed no other confirmation than what he saw to confirm he had not been dreaming earlier, but he had seen a vision of what would be.

He walked back to the prie-dieu and continued to say the St. Gertrude prayer. Each time this powerful prayer was recited, a thousand souls were released from purgatory.

****

As Detective Mike Bailey stepped out of his car, he made the sign of the cross. He never expected to work a case on the steps of a Catholic Church, or any church for that matter. While not raised Catholic, living here in New Orleans he had found that this faith brought him some comfort. It helped him find some peace from the death and violence that he saw day in and day out. In his line of work, one needed some kind of faith to help them get through the day.

The morning fog created an eerie sight in front of the church. As the damp air hit his face, he wondered if these were tears from heaven as evil had touched so close to the church.

Mike approached Officer Boudreaux to find out why he was called instead of his whole team. "This is not the place I would expect a murder to take place."

Office Boudreaux shook Detective Bailey's hand firmly, "Mon ami, I believe this has something to do with your old case. This murder has all the indications of a mob hit. As soon as I arrived on scene, I could tell from the bullet wound that this man was executed. Father Trahan walked out just as a vehicle pulled away. He said even without the vehicle having turned on its lights he was certain by the shape it was an SUV."

As Mike listened to what the young officer had to say, he stroked his goatee, absorbing the information. As Mike walked over to the body, the smell of fresh blood assaulted his senses.

Dr. Ortego was leaning over the body to examine the wounds, "What can you tell me Doc?"

Dr. Ortego stood up to acknowledge Mike's arrival on the scene. "Well, this victim was not drained of all its blood and he has all his parts so I am wondering why they called you out here."

"The powers that be have their suspicions on who killed this man. They requested that I come out and investigate."

"Well, if they believe that this is a mob hit, then they may be correct. I won't know until the autopsy, but it looks as if this man was shot point blank, execution style. The bullet entered right at the base of the skull and exited right above the collarbone. It appears they were both walking down the stairs, but from the angle of the exit wound, the killer was behind the victim. It was a clean shot. Someone wanted this man dead."

Officer Boudreaux informed Mike, "Father Trahan went inside to pray, but he made it clear that he wants to be the one to tell the wife and child."

Mike replied, "Well, if this is a mob hit, there may not be a wife and child to tell. If this man was executed, the killer more than likely went for the family also. Unfortunately, they were probably the first to die to torture the man with the knowledge that his faults killed his family."

Chapter 22

Hailey Sinclair woke to find herself in a musty closed off room. The ground beneath her was a dirt floor. A thin ray of light made its way through a crack in a boarded up window.

Her memory was merely distorted images that were moving too fast for her to understand at the moment. She remembered walking back to her hotel from a bar on Bourbon Street and bumping into a handsome man.

She vaguely remembered the man attacking her - wait, no that wasn't right. He didn't attack her; he kissed her or at least she thought he did. She must have drunk more than she realized. If only she could remember what happened to her. The only thing she remembered was the mesmerizing man. She couldn't imagine not being in his arms, even though she didn't know him. He held her attention the moment their eyes met. His eyes kept her in a trance. Something about his persona was intriguing yet dangerous.

She should have known better than to go into the alley with him; yet, she couldn't stop herself. Something about him had her wanting more, and she forgot about common sense. She knew better than to go somewhere with a complete stranger, but she did go, and now she must suffer the consequences.

Even now, she pictured his dark eyes and his glistening hair in the moonlight. She remembered his skin as white as snow and cold to the touch. The very smell of him was intoxicating. When he spoke to her, she was completely his.

She tried to shake off the remaining fog that lingered in her mind. She attempted to stand up and found herself too weak to stand. Suddenly, she remembered the man biting her neck, not kissing her. When he tipped his head down to hers, she waited in anticipation for the kiss that was to come; instead, he tilted her head back and bit her on the neck instead. What kind of freak did that? The sting of his teeth penetrating her tender flesh still lingered in her mind as did the smell of her blood. It overpowered her senses at the time.

She remembered the most erotic sensations overcoming her. Instead of fearing what he may be doing, she found herself wanting more of him. She shivered at the thought of his mouth on her once again.

Biting her neck still didn't explain why she was here on this dirt floor, though. It also didn't explain why she could barely stand up. She felt as if she was coming down with the flu. She was cold and achy all over. It felt as if a heavy weight was on top of her, pinning her to the ground.

Extreme exhaustion consumed her. Unable to fight the fatigue any longer, she gave in to sweet slumber.

She was awakened by the noise of footsteps in the distance. She soon realized that she could hear all sorts of creatures scurrying around in the dark. A cacophony of sounds assaulted her finely tuned ears. Groggily, she woke up to find herself in the same place where she fell asleep. When the door opened, she noticed that the sun had set. She'd managed to sleep the whole day away. Now, it was time to find out what her captor had in store for her. A shiver of trepidation moved through her body as she thought of the unknown. She despised surprises and preferred knowing what was going to happen.

Joshua looked at his newest addition, "I am glad to see that you are awake."

She recognized the voice right away. It was the man she'd bumped into on the street. Fear filled her, and she tried to back away from him.

"Are you feeling any better?"

She looked up at him. How did he know that she felt bad? Did he give her something? What did he plan to do to her? Would he torture her before killing her? She didn't want to be unmercifully tortured; she would rather he kill her and get it over with.

Joshua explained, "You may not understand what is happening to you right now, but I will teach you all that you need to know."

Unsure of how to answer him, she just looked up at him. "Teach me what? And where am I?"

He replied, "This is your new home, and I am your master. I turned you so that you can join my family."

She looked up at him with rage in her eyes. She had no idea what he was talking about, but this man must have one or two screws loose. He must be a twisted individual to do this to another human being.

Joshua replied, "Come. I mean you no harm."

She still didn't respond. She found that she couldn't speak
to him at this moment. She was both afraid of him and yet
intrigued at the same time. Hearing the words spoken
helped put her at ease some.

She found that it was much easier to sit up now and slowly
made her way from sitting to standing. As soon as she
stood on her two feet, her stomach turned hard. It took her
a moment to find her balance. The stranger grabbed a hold
of her shoulders to help steady her. Her stomach turned
again. This was in brutal response to hunger, a hunger like
she had never experienced before.

The man looked down at her and smiled, "You must be
hungry by now. Let's go and get you something to eat."

She took his hand as he pulled her along. After leaving the
small shed she was held in, she found herself somewhere in
the swampland. A noise in the distance caught her
attention. She noticed a deer stepping from the woods into
a clearing and her legs moved towards the animal with
more speed than she had ever known. Her mouth watered
at the thought of eating. Her instincts took over, and she
charged at the animal. Even though an inner voice was
telling her to stop, she bit down on the deer's neck and
drank the blood that spilled out. Right now nothing else
mattered; the warm, delicious blood soothed the ravenous
hunger which controlled her very being.

As she looked down at the dead deer, she felt sick to her
stomach. Depression and disbelief soon took over. What
had she done? What had she become? This had to be a
nightmare. There was no way she just drank blood from a
deer, was there?

As Joshua moved up to her, she wanted to run from him, but couldn't. She needed him to tell her what was happening to her.

"I had supper laid out for you. You didn't need to feed off this animal. Are you still hungry?"

She looked up at him in disbelief. How could he not be bothered with the fact that she just killed an animal in front of him and drank all of its blood? "Yes, I am still hungry."

"Good, then let's go eat. I am famished."

As Hailey followed him into the small cypress house, she saw a man and woman restrained to chairs. "Being that it is your first night as a vampire, I thought it would be easier to supply you with your meal. However, from what I just witnessed, you have a natural instinct within you to feed."

Looking at the man sitting in the chair, she should be repulsed, but instead she found herself staring at the vein bulging in his neck. Once again, her mouth watered in anticipation. Something deep in her gut told her that this was wrong, that she knew better, but she couldn't stop herself. She moved in closer to the man who desperately tried to free himself.

Could she do this? Could she take the life of another human being? She'd already taken the life of an animal, but this was different. Something felt evil about this.

She watched as the man who did this to her bent the woman's head back and fed. She should hate him, but she could not find it in herself to hate him. Something told her that she would never be normal again. Yet she couldn't bring herself to hate him.

As she watched him feast off the young woman, she found the whole thing erotic. The smell of the blood teased her senses, making her hungrier than before. She walked with determination to the young man. After feeding off of the man, she looked down at the body suddenly realizing what she had become. She did not believe in the supernatural, and here she was feeding off of a human.

The reality was almost too much for her to handle. There was no way she could explain this to her parents, family or friends. They wouldn't believe what happened to her. They would think she was a lunatic. What would her parents think when she never returned home? Would they even notice she was gone? They barely noticed anything other than their own lives.

As the blood she consumed made its way through her system, she felt the weakness that she'd experienced earlier ebbing from her body. Her arms were no longer tingling, and she felt stronger than ever before. Her senses became more acute.

Walking outside, she took in her surroundings once more. Joshua came up behind her, "You must learn to use your new senses. Learn the different sounds and smells that surround you. This will help keep you alive and from being discovered. Now that people are becoming more aware of our existence, we must be careful. I will teach you how to find your food."

She just nodded her head as she surveyed the area. Her eyes could see in the darkness of the night better than she'd ever seen during the day. She could hear as an animal scurried in the forest. She could smell its blood. She could even hear its beating heart. Even with everything that was going on with her, she felt calmer than before.

There was something thrilling about being the predator. She felt powerful as she sensed the heartbeat of her victim ebb from his body while she drank his blood. The feeling of the kill was so intense, but she found it difficult to feel sorrow for the victim. It should be disheartening to kill an actual human, but she was surprised that she found it easy to do so. There was no reason to be regretful. After all, she must eat to survive.

Joshua looked deeply into Hailey's eyes, "I guess you figured out that you are a vampire."

She nodded her head in agreement. There were so many questions that she wanted to ask him, but she was not sure where to start.

"My name is Joshua and we are in the swamplands near New Orleans, Louisiana."

Hailey asked, "Why did you turn me into what I am instead of just killing me?"

Joshua laughed at her question, "There was a fire in your eyes, and I knew you would make a perfect addition to my family."

"So there are more of us here?"

"Mais oui. There aren't as many as I would like. I must make sure that those I bring into this family are worthy of this gift."

Hailey looked for the others who lived here. He chuckled, "They are out feeding and doing my bidding. Bianca is out as well. This gives me time to teach you what you need to know before she returns."

Hailey could hear the contempt in his voice for whomever this Bianca was, "Who is Bianca?"

Joshua sneered, "Bianca is the voodoo queen who saved me a while back. For now, I live here with her."

From his posture, Hailey could tell that Joshua was unhappy about his present situation. She decided that asking more questions about Bianca would only anger him, which was something she didn't want to do.

Hailey and Joshua talked for such a great length of time that she didn't notice how much time had passed. She turned just in time to see glowing green eyes heading their way. She had to be the woman Joshua was unhappy with. This woman did not look happy to see Hailey with Joshua.

Bianca asked Joshua, "You just had to turn another one didn't you?"

Joshua sneered up at Bianca, "I told you that those zombie vampires you make are a poor substitute for those that I make."

"Be that as it may, mine are more controllable than those you make."

Joshua knew from experience that there was no reasoning with Bianca; he turned back to Hailey, "Come, I will show you where you will live from now on."

As they passed by the zombies, she jumped back in disgust. They looked like the face of death with sallow and withered skin pulled tight around decaying bones. They were merely a pile of grotesque, cracking skin and brittle bones which no longer flowed with blood. Their eyes stared upward, nothing more than white, colorless orbs and what once were cheeks were now crags, sunken and hollow. Their lips were pulled back in perpetual grimaces that showed off their newly acquired fangs.

As Hailey followed Joshua, she could feel the other woman's eyes burning a hole in her back. She would have to watch her back. Hailey suspected that Bianca would make sure she was not around much longer. Jealousy could be a bitch at times, and this was one of those times.

Chapter 23

Brian Donovan's hangover was one for the record books. It was worse than any hurricane that hit this town. He picked up the bottle of whiskey and threw it down in disgust. It was bone dry. He stumbled outside where thousands of people lined the streets waiting for the Mardi Gras parade to head their way. There were scores of floats, each equipped with a blaring sound system. This was probably the craziest time of the year in New Orleans.

As he headed to the bar, the music coming from one of the floats was playing so loud that it vibrated through his body and aggravated his headache. He walked up to the bartender and ordered a Bloody Mary, hoping that the tomato juice would help settle his stomach. He should find some food, but all he wanted to do lately was drink so he could forget and not think.

He was having nightmares of the young woman Dominic St. Germaine had had him dispose of. She invaded his dreams more frequently lately. It couldn't be guilt doing this. He had killed more than his share of people, but she was the only one that he killed who was pregnant.

A drunk tourist walked in, informing the bartender that he needed another drink. The bartender handed the guy a plastic cup of beer and ushered him back out the door. As the man staggered away, Brian glanced at the parade floats passing by. Most of the floats were elaborately decorated flatbeds being pulled by large pickup trucks. Each float carried fifteen to twenty members of a Krewe, who were more than likely just as drunk as him. Krewe members threw colorful beaded necklaces, candy, flying disks, panties, garters, koozies, and stuffed animals to the anxious crowd. Normally if the crowd was thrown something they didn't like, they threw it right back. Mardi Gras was a time for massive partying here.

Brian leaned back in his chair and watched as the floats passed. The weather was warm for this time of the year. It was late February and just about everyone was wearing shorts and t-shirts. Most everyone standing on the sidewalks were already heavily adorned with beads.

Up in the sky, thunder rumbled as dark gray clouds moved in. He hoped that the rain held off until he made it back to his apartment. He doubted any of the partygoers cared about getting wet; however, he had no desire to get drenched while partying in the streets. He had grown tired of the Mardi Gras scene. All he cared about was making sure his men grabbed some girls for the upcoming auction. It took a while to get everything started up again, but he was ready to begin auctioning off girls. He planned on starting small and slowly growing this area of his business. He had done well pushing drugs on the streets, but the police were becoming stricter on drug pushers because of some new plan the current governor had.

Brian had considered seeking out Bianca for her help with the current governor. If he kept hindering Brian's business, he might have to do that.

A loud noise from the parade route interrupted his thoughts. An obviously inebriated Krewe member had fallen off a float and stumbled into the crowd. He doubted anyone on the float even noticed he was missing.

Brian caught a glimpse of someone in between the floats, and he froze in fear. He shook his head, knowing what he was seeing wasn't real. She was dead; they had made sure of it. Yet, there in between the floats was Dominic St. Germaine's lover that he killed. Rayne Simoneaud was looking right at him. He patted his waist band, making sure that his gris-gris bag was still safely tucked away. He hadn't taken the gris-gris bag off of his body since Rayne's death. He had never seen anything like her death before, or since.

***

Brian stared all around him, taking in his surroundings. He was unsure how he came to be here, but this was where he had dumped Rayne's body that strange night.

Everything looked the same today as it did back then. This place was a different world than the one he lived in. He was probably a half hour or so away from the city, but it seemed to be a million miles from civilization. The humidity here was ten times worse than in the city. The marsh grass grew in profusion and herons stood in the shallow water as their beaks searched the bottom for food.

Shaking himself out of his reverie, he went to start the small boat engine only to find it bogged down momentarily in the silt of the swamp. It took a moment for the small engine to start. As soon as the water was agitated, millions of mosquitoes buzzed all around him. Despite the repellant he had on him, the blasted pests ate him alive.

A movement at the back of the boat caught his attention. As he looked around to see what caused the sudden noise,

he turned white as a ghost. Sitting in the back of the small
bateau was the ghost of Rayne Simoneaud.

When she saw the fear in his eyes, she let out a cackle that
rang through the air. Brian rubbed his eyes to see if the
apparition may be a figment of his imagination. He took so
many drugs and drank so much alcohol that it could be
possible he no longer could tell what was real and what
wasn't. His head was spinning from the heady mixture.

A noise in the bayou caught his attention as the apparition
stared venomously at him. A bull alligator made a low,
snorting sound as it slid sinuously down into the water from
a bank nearby. All that remained of the alligator was his
glittering eyes and nostrils as it slowly floated towards the
bateau.

A shiver of fear snaked through him as the boat began to
rock gently. He despised alligators; they were too much like
him as they killed without regret or feelings. He always
feared that one of these days an alligator would tip the
bateau and send him into the murky water where the
gators would start a feeding frenzy on his body. He could
imagine them tearing off chunks of his flesh before dragging
him down to the bottom of the bayou to drown. But they
would not devour him then; they would wedge him
underwater, possibly between a pair of sunken logs for days
to ripen and rot. Alligators liked to make sure that their
meals were nice and aged before enjoying them. They
allowed the swamp water to bloat the corpse, softening it
up before mealtime. This was nature's tenderizing action.

As the bateau rocked more, he looked back to see if the
apparition was still there. He forgot about the alligator

heading his way. Before he could react, the ghost pushed him overboard, and he landed in the water with a loud splash. His body would join the millions of bodies that were hidden in these waters, many were bodies he had put here himself. He doubted anyone would notice he was missing or even care.

Rayne smiled as the alligator started to turn and drag down the body of Brian Donovan. Revenge could be so sweet.

***

Andrew Wallace was livid. How did he let himself get suckered into this fishing trip? He didn't even like fish.

He swore to his wife Joy that he was going to be more assertive and tell people "No." He wasn't going to allow people to push him around, yet here he was doing something he despised. How did he let his idiot best friend talk him into this fishing trip? Jim Rollins knew he didn't like the outdoors, but he begged him to go with him so he wouldn't have to go by himself on the bayou.

For the life of him, Andrew couldn't figure out why he agreed to this trip. In his mind, he was screaming "No." Andrew let out a string of curse words as his fishing line got caught up for like the billionth time today. Why did he even bother acting like he was enjoying this? Heck, why did he even bother with casting a line? He would be better off letting the line float in the water. Then he wouldn't have to fight with the blasted thing and try to untangle it from the debris in the bayou. Once again, it had become tangled on another cypress stump or some trash littering the bottom of the bayou.

Jim hollered out, "Mon Dieu, look at all dem gators over dere."

Andrew rolled his eyes, and watched the vicious attack, "They must have found something good to eat. Whatever you do, don't take de boat anywhere near them." Andrew had no desire to be a dessert to whatever dinner the gators found.

However, he was curious about what had the alligators in such a state, so he took out his binoculars. He peered at the rolling mass of alligators and paled at what he saw, "Mon ami, you better blow that air horn of yours."

It had taken several blasts of the air horn before the alligators dispersed. Andrew and Jim both had to swallow back bile as they saw what the gators were fighting over. As they made their way to the remains, the smell of death and decay hung heavy in the air.

Floating in the water was a headless torso. Andrew leaned over the side of the bateau and puked while Jim hauled the remains in the boat. Andrew was still retching when Jim called nine one one to inform them what he was bringing in. This experience had given him the power to say "No." He especially would be saying "No" to fishing.

***

Detective Mike Bailey looked down at the text on his phone. It read, "Brian Donovan's body has been found. Someone fed him to the alligators." In Mike's opinion, Donovan's death had been too quick. There was no telling how many unfortunate victims were already auctioned off by his hands.

Chapter 24

His trip to New Orleans was better than Brent Cole ever
planned. During the day, the city was a tribute to its
culture, but at night, the city came alive with an energy he
had never known; it was an unrecognizable labyrinth.

As he ran down Bourbon Street, he picked up his pace. His
shirt and pants were drenched in sweat, and he swore that
they were at least two sizes too small for him. Even though
he was picking up his pace, it felt as if he was running in
place.

When he turned around to look behind him, he tripped over
something on the sidewalk. As soon as he made contact
with the concrete, he bit his tongue and cut the palms of his
hands. Yet he never felt the sting of biting his tongue and
scraping his hands.

Even now as he picked himself up from the sidewalk, he
looked around. He was positive that he could hear
someone breathing behind him. Whoever was chasing him
was merely toying with him, wanting him to suffer a slow
death.

He pushed himself up off the sidewalk and headed for an
alleyway in search of a place to hide. Since arriving here in
New Orleans, he found the streets packed with people, but
the one night he needed someone, the streets were devoid
of life. As he ducked behind a dumpster, some resemblance
of self-control began to return to him. He took a moment
to catch his breath and listened for his pursuers.

What he witnessed back there couldn't be real. Someone must have laced his drink with something.

A chill came over him when he saw a shadow fall where he was hiding. He looked up to see a woman in front of him dressed in a robe. The stench that exuded from her churned his stomach. She smelled of death. This woman was stunning, but when he looked into her eyes, all he saw was emptiness.

He shuddered as the woman transformed right in front of him. Her black as coal eyes turned a mesmerizing green, and her face shifted to that of a demon. This creature in front of him transformed into a skull covered with skin. Her once full head of hair was now nothing more than wispy strands. When she reached out to him, her hands became a claw-like limb. The very sight of her brought fear to his heart, and he knew that the fate before him was damnation.

When she spoke, her voice seemed to pierce his soul, "You, you have a fighting spirit. I think I will keep you for my army."

***

As the cobwebs of sleep dissipated from his mind, Brent Cole rolled from his side to his back and let out a loud moan. A throbbing pain deep inside of his body dragged him unwillingly from sleep. His head felt as if someone was playing a conga drum inside of it, and the tempo was rapidly escalating. With each surge of pain, his brain threatened to explode. When he moved, it felt as if battery acid was coursing through his veins. As he tried to sit up, he found that he could barely move. It felt as if someone had put weights on top of him. The only noise he could hear was the sound of his pulse roaring through his ears.

Lying still, Brent tried to recap the events of last night. There had to be a reason why he felt as if he had been run over by a tractor trailer. No matter how hard he tried, his memories just wouldn't cooperate with him. His thoughts were muddled.

He recalled the fruity concoctions he'd had at the last bar and decided they must have been more potent than he realized. This was a mother of all hangovers. That would explain the memory loss and the other symptoms he was experiencing right now. His stomach was queasy, and every muscle in his body hurt. Small currents of electricity coursed through his body. He knew better than to go out drinking last night. He never could hold down his alcohol, and this only proved it.

Now he was paying handsomely for last night's experience. He rolled over to see the time. He sure hoped he didn't miss his plane back home. As he rolled over in the bed, panic took over his body. He wasn't in his hotel room. The surroundings didn't look familiar. He seemed to be in a small, dark room with only a small bed as furnishings. As he sat up in bed, he winced in pain. He cradled his head, holding onto it as if any minute it would split in two. With every little movement he made, the muscles in his body burned as pain ricocheted through his body.

Maybe, he should lay back down. If he remained perfectly still, perhaps he would eventually feel better. As soon as he lay back down, he slipped back into unconsciousness. The sweet embrace of sleep was the only thing that brought him any comfort, he readily surrendered to it.

When Brent opened his eyes once more, he wondered how long he had been out. His surroundings were still hazy as he clawed his way back to the world of consciousness. As he took in his surroundings, he noticed that his headache was gone. The headache may have left his body, but the queasiness that he experienced earlier was now an unrelenting stomachache. It felt as if a sea of molten lava was churning deep in his abdomen.

He cautiously swallowed down the bile in his throat. His mouth was sour from the acrid taste of sleep. He was parched, but too afraid to drink anything. He worked his tongue around in his mouth in an attempt to generate some saliva, but it was useless. His tongue only managed to stick to his lips and teeth like drying glue.

He contemplated sitting up, but he was afraid any movement may start the cacophonous symphony in his head once again. Worse than the pounding headache would be upsetting the lava churning in his stomach and having it erupt. No, he was better off huddled up in this spot instead of on the floor praying to the porcelain god.

Brent found himself drifting back to unconsciousness and welcomed it once again. When he woke up once again, he found that he was bathed in darkness. He began to panic; why was everything enveloped in black? He prayed he wasn't going blind. Losing his vision was one thing, but he didn't want to add to his rapidly growing list of complaints. A lump of fear formed in his throat as he pushed it back down.

When he opened his eyes, he noticed a small amount of light filtering through the door. Shadows danced across the walls of the room. There were no windows in this room, and he wondered what time of the day it was. He still had no idea where he was or how he got here.

This time he forced himself to sit up. The small movement left him breathless, and the pain immediately assaulted his body once more.

Brent let out a moan. The pain was the last thing he wanted to return. His head once again felt as if it would burst at any moment. Unable to take the light headed feeling, he laid back down.

Suddenly, a young girl was shoved into his room. Brent smelled the most enticing aroma as she looked around fearfully. The hunger pains hit him almost at once, contorting his face. Instincts took over, and he began feeding on her immediately. He did not stop until she was drained of her blood. As her body fell to the ground, he sat heavily on the bed. He grasped his head between his two hands and he realized what he was. He was horrified at what he had become and what he'd just done.

He had heard the rumors about vampires walking this earth, but he laughed at such old wives' tales. He thought they were just superstitious nonsense, but he must now face the reality that those stories were true; he was living proof.

He had become what nightmares were made of, the walking dead. He was cursed for the remainder of his existence.

After feeding, he stepped outside and realized for the first time how his senses were now heightened. Even though it was dark out, he could still see for miles. He could hear a small rabbit or other creatures scurrying through the underbrush nearby. The air here had a foul odor to it, as if something was decaying nearby. He'd heard the rumblings of stomachs nearby and could smell blood in the air.

Chapter 25

Joshua felt Bianca once again trying to read his mind, and he forbid that to happen. As if sensing his reluctance, she pleaded with him to come to her. He knew that she wanted him to feed off of her, but he also knew that she wanted to steal his power.

He had to be careful; he had watched her seek out the stronger slaves to control them and make them bend to her will. Once she had them under her control, she killed them in order to steal their power. He refused to allow her to control him.

As he headed to her bedroom, the heavy rains pummeled the roof. When he opened the door, he looked over her naked body.

She looked up at him and smiled. She was a sight to see. Her green eyes almost glowed in the night. Her hair was black as a raven's wing and cascaded down her body, trailing over her breasts. She may look like a beautiful seductress to others, but Joshua saw her true self. She was a hideous creature with scraggly hair and gnarly limbs. She was a true priestess of the devil; some would consider her a dark mambo. Black voodoo had long claimed Bianca's soul.

She may not be able to read his mind, but she could control his body. His lust for her was becoming overwhelming. As he closed the door, she crooked a finger beckoning him to come to her bed.

To get what he desired, he must give in to her cravings as well. A wicked thought crossed his mind. She had no idea that every time he fed off of her he stole some of her powers. He did it gradually to keep this knowledge from her.

After making sure Bianca's needs were well satisfied, Joshua felt a restlessness building up inside of him. He decided to walk the streets of the French Quarter while Bianca slept.

***

As Stacie Allen walked into the elegant hotel, she wondered about the man who turned her. She hadn't thought about him since that night she slipped out of the carnival. The world her maker chose for her may be what he wanted, but it was not the world she wanted.

It took her a while to get used to her new life, but now she was happy with her life. Other than feeding on human blood, her life was no different than before. She found that her clients enjoyed the sensuality of being fed on and afterwards the only recollection they had was it being the most pleasurable experience they ever had. It kept them coming back for more. She was grateful Joshua taught her how to embrace this new life and how to make the best of things.

She doubted anyone even noticed she left the carnival that night, what with everything going on there. A few days later, a quick blurb in the paper mentioned the rides were impounded. She left just in time. The only one she wondered about was Joshua. The other members of the carnival she had no actual connection with and did not care about their outcome.

As she knocked on the hotel room door, a seductive smile formed across her face as the rotund man opened the door. She smelled the air and her fangs protruded in anticipation of her next meal. This man ate well, and she could already taste the rich blood on her tongue.

As she straddled him, she wondered if she could even find his neck. It didn't take long for the man to get overwrought and pant in anticipation. As she rubbed him down with her special massage oil, he moaned in delight.

She had learned that massaging and getting her clients worked up got the blood moving. As her fangs sank into the fatty flesh, the blood coated her tongue. The blood was just as good as she imagined; it was thick, creamy and salty. She drank heavily, savoring the taste.

After her client left, she checked out of her room. As she headed out of the hotel, she noticed the time. Daylight would soon be here. She must hurry and get back home well before the sun rose. She hated the pain when even the early morning rays hit her skin. As she rounded the corner, the tattoo on her wrist began to tingle. She sensed the presence of another vampire. She smelled the air and was thankful that the fog was moving in. She could smell the residual decaying blood on the vampire, but there was something more. She was sure that it was her master. It had been a while since she sensed his presence, but he was nearby. That had to be why her tattoo tingled. She smelled the air once more hoping to find his location.

As she turned around, she heard him call out to her, "Hello, cher. I see that you made it out before the police moved in."

Stacie bowed down to her master, "Sir, I did. I take it you have been well."

He nodded his head as he studied his child, "Well enough. How long have you been in the city?"

"Since that night you told us to disband. I stayed behind, sir. It is the only home that I know, and I couldn't leave this town."

Joshua replied, "I am beginning to understand the lure of New Orleans. A century ago this was my home, but I am only now finding a love for this place."

"Yes, sir. There is something magical about this place."

He asked, "You are doing well, then."

"I started my old business again, as if I never left. Only a short time had passed since I was turned, and no one even noticed I dropped off the face of the earth for awhile. At first, it depressed me until I found out that these men loved for me to feed off of them. More importantly, they didn't even remember me feeding off of them. They believe they had the best sex ever and keep coming back for more."

It pleased Joshua that one of his protégés was doing so well. "Have you turned anyone yet?"

She shook her head, "No. I don't want to bother with a following of my own. I am doing well with things the way they are. Followers could hinder my plans."

***

As Joshua listened to her talk, pride filled him She had made use of her new found life, but he wasn't sure if he should tell her of his plans. As he probed her mind, he could feel her putting up a block, and it caused him some uneasiness. He wasn't sure that he could trust her yet. He would have to keep an eye on her.

He took her hand in his, "If you ever need me, I am not far from here and will hear your call."

She squeezed his hand and looked into his eyes. For a moment, she thought she saw a flicker of sadness in there, "I don't live far from here if you want to stop over."

He shook his head, "I have been gone far too long as it is and must return before daybreak. If you ever need me, just call."

She smiled up at him, "I will Joshua. If you find yourself in a situation where you need help, please don't hesitate to ask. I owe this new life of mine all to you."

As Joshua watched her walk away, he wondered if he could use her to accomplish his plans. Only time would tell.

Chapter 26

Mariam Honore watched her granddaughter with genuine shame. Could it be that Bianca's mother had been right in her predictions about this child during her pregnancy? She swore to Mariam that Bianca would be evil; she wanted to end the pregnancy, and she asked Mariam to help her do so. Mariam Honore could not bring herself to end her grandchild's life though. She told her daughter that her hormones were talking and that her child would not be born evil.

On the night Bianca was born, her daughter pleaded with her to kill the baby. Mariam could not bring herself to do it. After the baby was born, she took one look at that precious child and fell in love with her. Mariam could not fathom how something so angelic looking could be evil. No, they would raise her right, and there would be nothing to fear.

Mariam now knew that Bianca was born with powers beyond those of a normal human. She possessed supernatural powers. Her granddaughter was an abomination upon this earth. How could Mariam miss this while Bianca was growing up? Where did she go wrong? Now she must stop her granddaughter from destroying this world.

Mariam Honore looked over the land Bianca called home, and a fear of trepidation moved through her. She watched in horror as the chained zombies snapped at one another and desperately tried to free themselves to find food. Mariam was unsure of exactly what her granddaughter was preparing to do, but she knew it wasn't good. She must find some way to prevent this. Mariam reached out to the spirit world to find someone who could help her.

***

Rayne watched the chaos and mayhem that Bianca Honore created. She shook her head in disgust at what this woman had done to the dead. Rayne was foolish in her beliefs that she alone could stop Bianca. Her powers were too strong, and there was only so much that a dead person could do without being caught in one of Bianca's incantations.

These poor souls in front of her were not at rest. Bianca turned them into flesh eating zombies that were trapped in shackles and awaited her command. Rayne watched in horror as one of the zombies devoured a poor rabbit that wandered too close to the abominations. When Bianca released these creatures, it would be the end of the world as people knew it. No, she couldn't let that happen. She must stop this. She must warn Hutch of what was about to happen; she had to show her somehow what Bianca planned. Rayne wished she knew Bianca's exact location. She had a feeling they were near the St. Germaine property, but she did not know an exact location to give the detective.

A movement in the trees caught Rayne's attention. There was another watching over the zombies. Rayne was certain that the stranger was another apparition like her, but still she must proceed with care. As Rayne moved in, the apparition sensed Rayne's presence, "Come, my child, you need not be afraid of me."

Rayne observed the apparition closely. There was something familiar about her. There was a striking resemblance to Bianca. This put Rayne on guard. Could this by why Bianca was so powerful? She had summoned help from beyond the grave?

Mariam Honore reached out to the spirit standing in front of her one more time, "My child you have nothing to fear. I am not like her."

Rayne took the woman's hand and grasped it, hoping to sense if there was any evil in her. Mariam gasped at the contact, "You are a traiteur are you not?"

Rayne nodded her head, "It is a family trait. I was practicing to be a healer. Since my demise, I have continued to learn, hoping to stop Bianca. I was foolish, though, in thinking I alone could stop her."

Mariam shook her head, "Cher, I believe it will take more than you to stop my granddaughter. I refused to listen to the premonitions of how truly evil she was. I am a foolish, old woman who thought she could change her. I thought if I taught her the white magic she would do good things. I tried to raise her right, but she was drawn to the magie noire."

"We must stop her. If you can't then I understand, but I won't allow this to happen."

Mariam said vehemently, "No, my granddaughter must be stopped. We cannot allow her to go through with this plan."

Rayne informed her, "I am talking to someone who may be able to help us. I had warned her once before that Bianca was up to no good. It took all my power to enter her mind for a short time. When I called her, she came. I must call her once again. She must be given the exact location and what is about to happen."

Mariam replied, "I fear that a mere mortal will be unable to stop these abominations. This is the devil at work, and we need divine help. We must find a Catholic priest who will listen to us."

"Mais, I don't think we will find such a person."

"We have to try! This is a battle of good against evil. Your friend that talks to ghosts will not be enough. We need a man of God; someone who can banish the evil from this place and free the trapped souls."

Rayne contemplated what all this woman was telling her. "Where will we find such a priest?"

"You will need your friend's help. Only she can talk to the living and convince them to help us in this plight."

Chapter 27

Tammy Winston believed that she'd found paradise after moving to New Orleans. She bought a one way ticket three years ago from Minneapolis and never looked back. Most nights it was so warm here that she could sleep in the park. What these southerners considered cold was nothing like she was used to. She wondered just how many of those who lived here could handle the cold up north. Although she must admit that when it did get cold here, it was a cold that penetrated all the way to the center of your bones. It was a cold that you actually felt, but it didn't last long. Best of all, there was no snow here.

Most nights she could sleep in the park, weather permitting. On the rainy nights when she needed to seek shelter indoors, there were plenty of places to hang out in. Most bars here were open all night and since she was drop dead gorgeous, no one had ever told her she must leave. Her favorite bartender at Masquerade gave her free drinks as long as she hung out at the bar. Men flocked naturally to her which drummed up business for the bar. He was always telling her that when she spent time at the bar his sales for the night doubled.

There were plenty of truck stops where she could take a shower. She knew which gas stations and area restaurants she could go into to potty. She befriended one of the street vendors, and he offered her free food if she hung around and helped draw attention away from his competition. Most of those she befriended gave her food and drink without asking for anything in return. Some of the street vendors and night clerks at the gas stations were very friendly and treated her with respect, not like some local bum. Down here they watched out for one another.

Several of the strip club managers had offered her jobs, but she was not desperate enough for money to work there. One of the local bar managers, Brian Donovan, was overly persistent about her coming to work for him. He offered her drugs hoping to lure her to work for him. Each time she rolled her eyes and walked away. Several of the girls who worked for him had warned Tammy to watch her back whenever he or his goons were near. She heard whispers that he was into some appalling stuff, including human trafficking. After hearing the rumors, she could never work for someone like him. Besides, she did good panhandling and working odd jobs.

During tourist seasons, she preferred to work at jobs where she could wear something revealing and attract a sugar daddy or two. She found a few willing to keep her in a hotel for a couple of days. If they broke her number one rule of no hitting, then she left without a second thought. Other than that she was happy to let them wine and dine her.

Her favorite places were the fancy hotels that some of the men visited during their stay. They had the softest beds, plenty of hot water and more importantly, she didn't have to pick up after herself. She could seriously get addicted to room service. Whenever she wanted something, she only had to pick up the phone, and they brought it to her.

These hotels were so much nicer than the flea infested hotels she was accustomed to growing up. She had no desire to stay in another one of those. Sleeping in the park was better than staying in those rooms. There wasn't enough antibacterial spray to kill the germs there.

She loved to daydream of the day when she made it big, lived in a penthouse suite of a hotel and never had to lift a finger for anything. Her meals would be brought up to her, and someone would come in to clean up whatever mess she made. This was just a dream though. No one would discover her on the streets of New Orleans or anywhere else. She just didn't have that type of luck.

She came from a poor family in Minneapolis, and her childhood was miserable. Growing up, she couldn't wait to move away. Her mom and dad were either drunk or high, which was why to this day she didn't touch the stuff. When she sat at the bar, the bartender offered her free alcoholic drinks, but she preferred soda. When someone bought her a drink, the bartender pocketed the money and gave her a drink that looked similar to whatever had been purchased without the alcohol.

She cringed whenever she thought of her childhood. Her dad's favorite sport was beating up on her mom which was likely the reason for her staying high on drugs or alcohol to forget about her miserable life. Tammy had no idea if her parents were still alive and she didn't care.

Tammy fell asleep that night thinking of her miserable childhood. She had crawled into one of the slides in the park to sleep when something awakened her. Even though she woke still groggy from sleep, she noticed that there was a chill in the air. Unsure of what awakened her; she stayed still and listened to the surrounding sounds. She trusted her instincts, and if something disturbed her sleep, there was a chance that something was out there. Her instincts saved her butt on more than one occasion.

She knew it was midnight since she could hear the church bells tolling. As the sounds echoed through the night air, uneasiness took over her body. Outside of the slide, she could hear the wind picking up as it blew through the trees. There was another noise out there though. It sounded like a moaning and sent chills down her spine.

She made her way out of the slide to get a better look. A thick blanket of clouds covered the moon, encasing the area in complete darkness. She noticed that even the street lights were out which was unusual. With the wind blowing, the area seemed spooky. As the wind died down, the stillness of the night was worse.

It was never this quiet here. There was no noise tonight. It was indeed creepy. Now she wished she'd accepted the earlier offer to join the man for dinner. At the time she wasn't ready to call it a day, so she turned him down. Now she wished she was any place but here.

A noise came from the edge of the park, and she looked around fearfully. Now she was afraid. Her imagination started working overtime, trees became gnarled creatures reaching out to grab her and signs became ghosts rising from the ground. She was near complete hysterics and shivering violently.

She laughed at herself. "Girl, what is the matter with you? There is nothing out there." After shaking off the last of her hysterics, she decided to see what was going on around the French Quarter. As she bundled up her belongings, she heard a noise even closer to her this time. The hairs on her neck rose. Every nerve in her body told her that someone or something was out there watching her.

She peered into the dark trying to locate what made the noise. Could it be that whatever was out there knew she was listening to see where it was hiding and remained quiet for the moment? Then she heard it, the sound of twigs breaking. Someone was walking in the park. It sounded as if they were heading this way.

Calling out into the night, "Who's there?"

Suddenly, she was in a nightmare; a nightmare she couldn't wake up from. As she saw the figure appear in front of her, she became frozen with fear. She couldn't get her feet to cooperate and run. It was as if she was rooted to this one spot. No matter how hard she tried to get her body to move, she was unable to do anything to save herself. She opened her mouth to scream in terror, but it was too late. The creature moved in on her quickly. Before she could comprehend what was happening, the creature sank its fangs into her neck.

***

Stacie Allen had observed this young woman for a while now. After her talk with Joshua the other day, she was ready to build her own following. This would be a unique following; she would have an elite escort service of vampires. Before adding someone to the group, she had to make sure they were worthy. She had no doubts that this young woman was perfect. From what Stacie observed, she had no family and slept most nights here in the park, which was how she knew where to find her. She didn't mean to scare her, but Stacie feared if she explained her plan to the girl, she would think she was crazy. The last thing Stacie needed was someone telling her friends that a vampire approached her, asking her to join her escort service. That would kill her business.

The girl was still woozy from being bitten, so Stacie helped escort her to the house. The girl was lighter than she expected, so they made quick time in getting to where they needed to go. To bystanders, it looked as if Stacie was helping a drunk friend home.

Once they arrived at Stacie's house, she placed the girl on one of the guest beds to let her sleep while the transformation happened. Stacie knew from experience that it was easier if you were allowed to sleep it off. It could be painful as the poison moved through your body.

A couple of hours later, Stacie heard the young woman moving around and headed back upstairs to check on her. "I'm glad to see that you are awake."

Tammy looked around, hoping to recognize her surroundings. "Where am I?

"I thought you might like to sleep in a warm bed for a change and brought you to my house."

Tammy tried to remember what happened last night, but it just came to her in bits and pieces. She remembered something waking her up from a dead sleep, but that was the last thing she remembered. "That's nice of you, but it isn't necessary." Tammy went to get up, but her head wouldn't stop spinning when she sat up. Instead of leaving, she laid back down. Tammy mumbled, "Maybe I will lay back down."

Stacie sat down on the bed and stroked the young woman's hair, "You need to rest as much as possible. The change is easier when you sleep it off, cher."

Tammy heard the woman talking, but the lure of sleep was too great. It wasn't long before she was out once again. By the time Tammy woke up the second time, it was nighttime. The moonlight danced across the room.

Stacie walked into the room with a warm smile, "It is good to see you awake. I hope you are feeling better now."

Tammy stretched languidly, "I feel better now than I did when I woke up earlier."

Stacie let out a soft laugh, "You slept for two days."

Tammy looked up at her surprised. It felt as if she had only been asleep a few hours. Stacie held out her hand, "Come, I am sure you are hungry."

Tammy hadn't thought about food, but now that she mentioned it she was hungry. Still unsure of what was happening to her, Tammy asked, "What did you do to me?"

"I turned you. You are a vampire now, cher."

Tammy looked at her with uncertainty, unsure of what to think. Vampires didn't exist. Why would this woman say such a thing?

When Tammy looked down at her skin, Stacie laughed softly, "Cher, the physical changes are hard to notice. You are paler, your eyes are now black and you are cool to the touch. Other than that, you are the same."

As they left the room, Stacie turned back to her newly turned follower, "Oh, there is one small change that I should mention; you will now feed on blood. Mortal food will no longer appeal to you. Only blood will quench your hunger."

As Tammy listened to what this woman told her, she shuddered at the thought of drinking blood. She was extremely squeamish at even the sight of blood, and now she was supposed to drink it.

Stacie could tell that she was uneasy about the thought of having to drink blood, "Oh, cher you will get used to it. I plan on teaching you ways that are enjoyable for not only you, but the one you are feeding on as well. While some vampires do drain the victims of all their life blood, when you do that, then you have to worry about disposing of the body which can be messy and cumbersome. If you take my advice, you never have to kill those you feed on."

"What about sunlight?"

"Ah yes, sunlight. That is something that may kill you. We must be heavily clothed and use a lot of sunscreen. If you find that you must go out in the sunlight, make sure that you are only out for a short period of time. The sunlight will burn your skin even with the clothing and sunscreen. It can be an excruciating pain."

Tammy absorbed everything that she was telling her, "Are we damned?"

"Only if you see it that way, cher. Me, I see it as an extended life. We have an eternity to do everything we want to do. I found a way for us to become richer than you could ever imagine. That is what you wanted, oui?"

Tammy looked up at her in surprise. "You can read minds?"

"Oh cher, I can do that and much more. You will find out that your powers are almost limitless."

Chapter 28

As Father Mark Trahan showed the group of detectives into his office, he was unaware that he was about to open a door that he would be unable to close. Father Trahan did not look like your typical Catholic priest. He was a big man, standing six feet two inches and two hundred twenty pounds. Most people did a double take when they saw him in his vestibules. Before joining the military, he was the high school quarterback and never imagined he would become a priest after his tour was over. He found his calling while stationed overseas. Instead of re-enlisting after his four years were up, he chose the seminary and answered God's call. His parents were stunned.

He asked the detectives, "Can I get y'all anything?"

Guy Mayon replied, "No, Father Trahan; we are fine. Thank you for agreeing to see us."

"You didn't fully explain what you needed from me over the phone."

As he listened to what they had to say, disbelief was evident on his face. Guy Mayon tried to explain the situation, "Father Trahan, I know this is hard to believe, but we have concrete evidence that vampires exist. I need you to put aside your beliefs and teachings and listen to what we are saying, really listen. We believe that a vampire and a voodoo priestess are raising the dead and are getting ready to use them for their own demonic plans."

Hutch chimed in, "I believe most of these souls are ones bound to this earth, unable to move on. There is a chance she found a way to trap the souls in purgatory."

As Father Trahan listened to what these detectives had to say, a chill of apprehension moved through him. He had long believed a battle existed here on earth between good and evil. If what they were saying was true, then it sounded as if the devil wasn't preparing for a battle but a worldwide takeover. If he stopped and took a look at the world nowadays, it seemed that evil had spiraled out of control. It was everywhere you looked. There was no escaping it. If it weren't happening in real life, you could find it in movies, television, video games and so on. If they did not do something soon, he feared that the devil would have the upper hand.

As the young female detective continued to talk, he stared out the window and looked over his beloved city. When Father Trahan first joined the priesthood, he never expected to be in charge of a church right here in New Orleans. His calling was to do mission work. While stationed overseas, he felt the need to spread the word about God; some of those people needed to hear God's message of love, hope, and salvation. Mission work may have been his plan; however, it wasn't God's calling for him. He was kept stateside and ended up in New Orleans, closer to where he grew up.

As he listened to what these detectives told him, dread built in the pit of his stomach. He would need to rely on his military background and his faith if he hoped to save this town, or possibly the world, from this evil. Was this God's plan from the very beginning? Did God foresee this and know he was the one who could conquer this evil?

He thought back to his teachings in the seminary. One bishop told them that following God would prove to be a constant test of one's faith. If you went back through history, those who believed in God were tormented, tortured and persecuted for their beliefs. This would be a true test of one's faith. He would need to rely heavily on God and his faith to defeat this evil he was about to fight.

He had never backed down from or declined a challenge. No, he would do this wholeheartedly. Good must triumph over evil.

Father Trahan knew of a few people he could call to inquire about releasing the trapped souls that Detective Hutcherson had spoken of. He would make some inquiries into the vampires and zombies. He had heard of others trying to raise the dead; he needed to see if anyone had ever been successful and how they dealt with them.

The Catholic Church was filled with more secrets than the general public could ever fathom. He wondered if anyone even knew just how powerful the church was.

He turned back and looked at the three detectives sitting in his office. He would need more people assigned to their team. They were about to wage a war against the devil himself, and there was no way just the four of them could defeat Satan alone. They needed as much help as they could gather.

Father Trahan informed them, "I must do some research and make some calls. I need y'all to put together an army that we can use to help battle these demons. We can do an exorcism of sorts to help free the trapped souls, but before I perform any rites, I must talk with several people."

Detective Bailey stood up and shook Father Trahan's hand, "Thank you Father. We will let you start working on your end, and we will arrange a SWAT team to help stop these creatures."

Father Trahan swallowed hard, "These people must understand that there is a chance they will not survive this fight."

Detective Mayon exclaimed, "Father Trahan, we are cops. We know every day when we walk out our front door and head to work there is a chance that we can be killed in the line of duty. Everyone fully understands the chances we take and will want to help out, but we will make sure they know the circumstances."

Father Trahan nodded his head in agreement. This was an assignment that must be completed, but he could not send a man into a battle without them knowing the chances of survival. These people would be putting their lives in danger, but also their very souls on the line if the devil got a hold of them.

That night before bed, Father Trahan said his prayers as usual. "Our Father who art in Heaven, hallowed be thy name. Father, please give me the strength to make the right choices in the days to come and to do Your will as You see fit." After he finished saying the rest of his prayers and the rosary, he fell fast asleep.

As soon as he closed his eyes, horrific images flooded his mind, images of those he was about to fight. It was two o'clock in the morning when he woke up frightened and drenched in a cold sweat. He'd seen such evil images and could only assume that God Himself wanted him to know what was ahead of him. Before falling asleep once again, he prayed that they would defeat the evil that lurked about, waiting to strike.

The next morning Father Trahan woke up feeling the weight of the world on his shoulders. As he prepared for the seven o'clock Sunday morning Mass, he wondered if the sparsely attended Mass would perhaps be filled to capacity. Lately, Mass attendance had drastically declined. He hoped that people would find their way back to the Church. He wondered if maybe the Catholic Church needed to look into changing some of the strict ways they had kept to tradition for over two thousand years. More and more people left the Catholic Church to attend religions that were more modern and trendy. Other religions seemed to focus on the children, as well as the adults. He had seriously considered adding a Children's Mass to keep the children intrigued with the Catholic religion and their teachings. The Church needed to look at the family unit and not just the adults to help build their attendance.

Before heading to the cathedral, he read over his sermon once more. He wanted to make sure that it sounded as good as it did the night before. He liked to keep his sermons short and to the point. His analogies were drawn from the current events, which sadly there was no shortage of lately. With the shootings in schools and bodies being found in the alleyways of this city, evil had made its presence known, and it was time to fight back. People should love their neighbors and not covet what they had. You should care for one another and not try to harm your neighbor. Sin was everywhere he looked, and unfortunately, there was no avoiding it. Everyone had to confront sin on a daily basis and try to overcome its temptation. Sin must be stopped before it seeped into their hearts. When he looked at his parishioners of late, he felt as if they were merely sheep on their way to slaughter. The modern world made it so hard for a mere human being to avoid the temptation of sin. Father Trahan felt as if his pleas were going unheard. He prayed that they would continue to stay strong in this modern world as it continued to test their faith.

Chapter 29

Isabel Acosta feared that the devil had finally come for her soul. He had come to whisk her away to hell; death was breathing down her neck at this very moment.

When the handsome man with the mesmerizing eyes walked up to her, she thought that for once she would enjoy this trick. This man was more handsome than any of her previous tricks. She could deal with the smell emitting from him since he agreed to pay her price. She was having severe withdrawals and desperately needed a hit. Right now, anything would do as long as it got her high.

If he were like most of her tricks, he would be done in less than twenty minutes. Then she could go see Antoine on the corner and get her something to make her forget her worries.

When they rounded the alley, the look on his face told her that she was in serious trouble. She didn't see the blank expression on his face until it was too late. The look he had made her insides tingle with a warning vibe. If she had noticed that look earlier, she would have told him to buzz off. Never ignoring the warning signs was what kept her alive this long on the mean streets of New Orleans.

When he pushed back her hair and bent her head back, she assumed he was into the kinky stuff. When she felt the pain from his teeth biting into her neck, she suddenly felt like she was floating. It was like no high she'd ever experienced. The next thing she felt was a coldness wash over her. She could feel herself falling into a black abyss. The devil was bringing her to the bowels of hell as she fell deeper and deeper into the dark abyss.

Isabel didn't bother to scream. It would do no good. No one out here cared enough to save her. Her mom told her that the life she chose for herself would send her to hell. For once, her mother was right.

* * *

As the young woman Joshua just fed on slumped to the ground, he picked her up with ease. Even in death, she was light as a feather. She would be a good snack for the zombies tonight if Bianca didn't want her.

Chapter 30

By the time Father Trahan made it back to the rectory that night, he felt overwhelmed. He'd spent all day researching everything he could find on vampirism, zombies and spells that were performed to raise the dead. He found quite a bit of research on exorcism, but he wasn't sure if that research would help free the trapped souls in the carnival. Everything he found on exorcism was for possession and not trapped souls. He came across a few obscure articles regarding demons that were known to steal souls for the devil, but that was about it.

As he prepared for bed, he pondered everything he'd learned. There was still so much research to do if they hoped to defeat this evil. He found a few ways to protect them from a voodoo priestess and her charms. Voodoo went against everything he was taught regarding the Catholic religion, but he did know it went hand in hand down here in New Orleans with the locals. Those that practiced voodoo here tended to mix voodoo with the Catholic religion. He made an appointment with a voodoo expert for tomorrow morning. Hopefully, he could shed some more light on this fascinating subject. If it meant that he had to wear a gris-gris bag, carry his rosary and a canister of salt, he would.

If Jesus could walk this earth and confront evil on a daily basis, he could too. They may be humanity's only hope. There would be times where he had to step outside the boundaries of Church guidelines in order to defeat this evil. There may be no other way.

Last week if anyone had asked him what he thought of vampires and zombies, he would have scoffed at the idea and replied that they were mythical creatures. After what he had learned, he knew that they were very much real. His life would never be merely preaching and presiding over ceremonies again. The worry of donation collections each week being enough to cover the operating costs seemed insignificant now. No, now he must save these souls and stop evil from winning. It was satisfying knowing he would be the one to help save tortured souls.   It was a near impossible task, but he refused to give up. If he failed, it would not be because he did not try.

When the newspaper published the article regarding the St. Germaine family being Mafia, he finally understood why Father O'Connell was the only priest that the St. Germaine family saw. Since Dominic's death, the family had not shown their faces in the Church and the donation box was lighter without their contributions. As Father Trahan looked around at the various items that the St. Germaine's "blood" money bought, he wondered when the Church became so materialistic. Jesus did not care if the place he stopped to preach in had stained glass windows or ornate altars. In his heart of hearts, Father Trahan knew he would have to ignore the politics of the Church and concentrate on his task at hand. If he failed, the whole world would suffer. This was his last thought as he fell fast asleep.

Instead of dreaming of horrific creatures, his dream was confusing and disjointed. He dreamed of souls lost and wandering the earth. Suddenly, an old woman appeared in the midst of the souls and started warning him of something using manic hand gestures. As he neared to hear what she had to say, the image in front of him broke up.

When Father Trahan woke up, he immediately planned on doing some more research. He was unsure of which direction he would take to find out the information he needed. As he said his morning prayers, he asked for God's help.

He kept going over the dreams he'd had lately. Some nights the dreams were more disturbing than others. He wondered how Hutch hadn't gone insane from what she saw. Even the saints throughout history who saw demons must have felt it weighing down on them, but they still did not go mad. It took a strong person of resolve and faith to see what they witnessed every day and keep their sanity.

He believed there were some who walked this world that saw man for what they truly were. Mankind shouldn't be equipped to grasp what resided past the veil of this world; yet he was certain there were some out there who could. He must find those who possessed this gift; he hoped they could help win the fight of good versus evil.

He remembered hearing a story in the seminary of a person in an asylum who swore he could hear voices warning him that one of the doctors at the asylum was a snake like creature. He wondered if the man was still alive and how he would go about finding out his name. There may be something to his story after all.

As he entered the kitchen of the rectory, he discovered Father O'Connell was awake. Four priests shared this particular rectory in an attempt to save the Catholic Church some money during these trying times. Father Trahan didn't mind; it reminded him of military or seminary life. They all got along and the extra company was nice, but they still found time for themselves. The rectory was large enough to house all four priests and a live in housekeeper. Mabile Jackson had lived with them since Hurricane Katrina demolished her house. It was an easy decision for the parish since Mabile had worked for the Church for over a decade now. Mabile was going on seventy, but she didn't act a day over fifty. She did light cleaning and cooked for them. They were a close knit family here and could be honest and candid in their talks. Mabile acted more like a mother hen than employee and never hesitated to scold them for their bad habits.

"Good morning, Father Trahan."

Smiling, "Good morning, Father O'Connell. I hope you slept well last night."

Father Chris O'Connell laughed, "At my age, any sleep is a blessing. You look troubled this morning."

"Not troubled as much as seeking guidance." Unsure just how much he should tell Father O'Connell, he weighed his next words carefully. Father O'Connell may have looked the other way when it came to the St. Germaine family, but he also didn't believe in making waves regarding the Church's policy. Father Trahan wasn't sure how many waves he may make with this newest information. "I have been asked by someone to help save some troubled souls."

Father O'Connell suggested, "Come, let's pour us a cup of coffee and go sit in the study."

The study here was one of Father Trahan's favorite rooms. There was no TV, and it opened out to the small courtyard in the back. In here, he could sit on the sofa and look outside while he prepared his sermons or talked to God. The room was furnished with a desk, two sofas and several chairs along with many bookshelves filled with various religious texts. He spent most of his time combing through the text here as he searched for answers. There was also a computer for their use at the desk, but he must be careful since it was a shared computer. He wasn't prepared to answer questions about his research at this moment, and his search history would bring many questions. They may even wonder if his faith was slipping, but that was far from the case.

Father O'Connell made himself comfortable on the sofa opposite of Father Trahan, "Now, my son, what is on your mind?"

"A detective came to me with questions about demons, purgatory, and possession. She is working a case where these elements have been brought up. She believes the suspect is using or practicing voodoo."

Father O'Connell stroked his beard as he contemplated what Father Trahan told him, "Well, my son, this is New Orleans. There are a lot of believers in the voodoo religion here. I do know that over the years the Catholic religion has become deeply intertwined with the voodoo religion. However, you will not find any books in our library that reference voodoo or demons."

"What about exorcisms? Have you ever witnessed or heard of one being done?"

Father O'Connell shook his head, "Not that I recall. I'm not even sure if there is an actual finding of someone being possessed. Now, you may find a voodoo priest or priestess here that will attest to performing an exorcism. The Vatican may have someone who does exorcisms, but I can't swear to it."

"Do you believe that some people are the epitome of evil?"

Father O'Connell nodded his head in agreement, "Oh my yes. We are human after all and history books are full of evil people. Now if they were born that way or made that way by society, I cannot say. I do believe they let the devil enter their soul, though, and turn away from God. That is the sole reason they do what they do."

"Thanks, Father O'Connell. I may have my work cut out for me."

"So, will you try to help this person?"

Father Trahan looked over at his confidant, "Father, I pray that I can."

As Father Trahan began his research, he suddenly felt overwhelmed. The priesthood definitely did not teach you about the paranormal or supernatural. They taught that upon death your soul went to purgatory and was not trapped here on earth.

Just when he was ready to give up, his alarm went off, reminding him he had to say Mass soon. His favorite part of the Mass was presenting his sermon. He liked to see if he had everyone's attention or if they were nodding off to sleep. He enjoyed giving his parishioners words of wisdom and emphasized that they should be thankful for what God had given them.

After Mass, he felt a renewed energy and was ready to dive into the research once again. As he reviewed today's readings, it came to Father Trahan that in the Bible the apostles were sent to address and expel the evil spirits and demons. If God asked this of them back then, he must have believed that evil spirits and demons existed.

While searching the internet, he found one site that explored demonic possession and exorcism. It spoke of how the possessor could only make someone do what they desired and nothing more. A demon coerced the victim to allow their instincts and desires rule.

As Father Trahan read the information on this site, he found himself believing what it had to say. This society of late was ripe for the picking. It would be so easy for demons to possess many souls. All they had to do was tempt man, and he would inevitably follow.

The more research Father Trahan did, the more fear crept into his soul. He found it hard to understand his being chosen for this particular mission by God. After hours of research, he finally came across some information that may be useful. It appeared as if the crucifix would come in handy as well as holy water. From what he could tell, holy water was like an acid to demons, vampires and the like.

If this was correct and holy water was this lethal, he planned to have a vast amount handy for their fight.

Chapter 31

Father Trahan had been asleep for an hour when the dreams started. He found himself wandering around the marshlands not far from the rectory. All around him, he felt eyes looking down on him. A moment of trepidation came over him as he heard his name called out.

Unable to stop himself, he moved further into the marshland as he followed the voice that called out to him. He paused in a clearing and watched as an apparition made its way to him. The souls surrounding him warned him of danger, pleading with him to go back. He found himself frozen in place and unable to back away. He gripped the crucifix in his hand tighter, needing to feel its comfort in the palm of his hand. He refused to let his faith falter.

He let out a small gasp as the apparition before him took shape; it was a woman. The evil that consumed her had turned her into a ghastly figure.

Bianca laughed when she heard him gasp in surprise, "What is wrong Father? Do you not find me pleasing to the eye? I was once a beautiful seductress and can make myself so again in the blink of an eye."

To prove her power, she turned herself back into a young seductress. "See, Father I can be very pleasing to the male eye, but why should I waste my power and energy on you?" She looked him over and sneered, "Or maybe I should try to sway you with my charms?"

Seeing the disdain in his eyes, she returned to her true self, "You see, Father Trahan, I can be whatever it is that a man desires. I can control a man by his very desires!"

"Man can only be controlled if he allows sin into his mind and body."

Bianca let out a laugh, "Father Trahan, can you be so naïve? I have ways of making a man do my very desires. Soon, this world will not belong to man, but to me and my minions. These mere mortals will merely be cattle for us; they will be bred to feed us and nothing more. For you see, Father Trahan, I am more powerful than even the one you call God."

Father Trahan shook his head in disbelief, "No, you are incorrect. No one is more powerful than God. He will see to it that evil does not win."

She snarled at him, "You are wrong! I will have you begging for mercy before I am done with the likes of you. I will show you just how insignificant you are to this God of yours."

Without warning, four creatures flanked him and pinned him to the ground. He tried to break free, but their hold was too strong. As this woman stood above him, he stared into the never-ending depths of her black sockets. For a moment, he swore that he could see the souls of those she'd claimed hiding in those depths. He peered deeper, trying to confirm what he thought he saw there.

She moved in closer and her lips peeled back in the most grotesque smile. His eyes widened in horror as a row of pointed teeth smiled back at him. Where each one of her teeth was supposed to be were instead pointed fangs that filled her mouth.

When she breathed down on him, he could smell the heady scent of death on her breath. He feared his time had come.

He watched as his soul left his body and hovered overhead. He was carried away to the city where he watched in horror as creatures fell on their prey with such savagery. All around him, the night air echoed with screams of the dying as their bodies were torn open.

Waking from the horrid dream, Father Trahan bolted upright in bed. As he looked around to confirm his surroundings, he found little comfort from his room. The dream had been a premonition. The voodoo priestess must be stopped!

That afternoon, Father Trahan felt the sudden need to go to the library downtown to do some research. As he walked into the library and saw the books, he feared this may be an overwhelming experience. The librarian looked up at him from her desk, "May I help you with something, Father?"

Clearing his throat, he asked, "I need to do some research on voodoo priestesses and vampires."

The librarian never raised an eye to his request. Before he knew it, the librarian brought him stacks of newspapers, magazines and books on both subjects. Most of this would be pointless, but he dove into the first book. Most of what he'd read so far was nothing more than the myth of vampires.

As he was reading, the librarian walked up to him, "Father, I did find an article written by a local reporter here in New Orleans."

Taking the material from the librarian, he thanked her as he perused the article. The reporter talked about the rise in missing persons' reports filed in the city during Mardi Gras and how no one in the police department seemed to be concerned about it. This particular reporter was convinced that there was more to it. This article was of little help to him, but he wondered if the investigative reporter wrote any other similar articles.

Sure enough, he found another article recently written by this journalist. In the article, he talked about how he believed evil had taken over the city. He thought that evil elicited immoral behavior from the tourists and residents of the city. He noted that once again there was an increase in missing persons' reports being filed with the New Orleans police department and bodies being discovered mutilated. He then went on to write about how he believed that the Mafia was still practicing here in New Orleans. With the death of Dominic St. Germaine, it was his belief that one of his underlings took over the family, but he also disappeared from the face of the earth. No one had seen or heard from Brian Donovan in weeks.

Father Trahan leaned back in his chair and absorbed what he read so far. It may be worth visiting this investigative reporter to see if he could shed some more light on what he believed was happening here. This particular reporter left out his true feelings in the story. Just reading it had your mind wandering into the unknown.

The reporter went on to write about how he personally believed that the voodoo priestess who helped Dominic St. Germaine may still be lurking about, and building herself a following. He went on to state that she practiced secret ceremonies in the cemetery. Father Trahan feared that the voodoo priestess was indeed visiting the cemeteries here. Maybe he should confer with the voodoo priest to find out how they could keep her away from the cemetery.

As Father Trahan was picking up to return his materials, he noticed an article he'd somehow missed. It was an occult magazine that talked about consuming the soul of one's enemy. It went on to state that collecting souls would not only extend your lifespan, but you would also assume the powers and memories that your enemy possessed.

As he sat down to read what the writer had to say, a chill swept through Father Trahan. As he continued to read the article, he found where the author referenced a soul collector that worked for the devil. This creature was basically the devil's bounty hunter and collected souls that wandered the earth instead of going to hell as expected. Could this be what was trapped in the mirror? Did the vampire figure a way to catch the creature to have it do the vampire's bidding? Father Trahan made a mental note to find out more on these soul collectors.

Chapter 32

Hutch looked around her, unsure if she was in heaven or hell. The ground chilled her feet as trepidation crept over her. She had seen this place in previous dreams. The air around her was thick and a dense fog swirled around her, making it hard to see. Uncertainty gripped at her heart. She wanted to run, but if she wanted to learn anything, she must stay. She desperately needed to find the answers.

She must wait; he would come. He always came. Her heart beat even faster as the dense fog parted enough for her to see him. She did not know his name, but she knew his face. She had seen him numerous times in her mind. She tried to block him from penetrating her thoughts.

He was more powerful than before. Just in his stance, she could see the power he emitted. She must not let her guard down. As he moved closer to her, he reached out to touch her. She stepped back, fearing his very touch. An apparition stepped in between them and whispered, "You must go. You don't belong here now."

In the blink of an eye, the vampire and apparition both vanished. She stood amid the misty darkness, left alone with ghosts and shadows.

Hutch bolted upright in bed. Her gown clung to her sweat drenched body. She gulped for air as she tried to calm her beating heart. This was the first time the vampire had tried to reach out to her. She swore she could actually touch him in her dream.

Who was the apparition that warned her? It was not the same one who called out for help before. No, this was a much older woman.

Chapter 33

Archbishop John Paul Waguespack returned Father Trahan's phone call later that afternoon. The Archbishop arranged a meeting with a Catholic priest here in New Orleans who did local exorcisms. The priest wanted to keep his anonymity so he would meet Father Trahan at the rectory in the morning.

This gave Father Trahan enough time to meet with the voodoo priest here in New Orleans who claimed to have performed over a dozen exorcisms recently. As Father Trahan walked into the voodoo shop, he began to feel guilty, and instantly chastised himself for feeling this way. If God did not want this of him, He wouldn't have sent the detectives to seek him out. No, this was what God wanted, and he must complete this mission. Maybe between this voodoo priest and the Catholic priest, they could save the trapped souls in the carnival rides.

He saw the voodoo priest, Paul Decimus, sitting behind the cash register sipping on a cup of coffee and reading the newspaper. Father Trahan was surprised by the man's appearance. He expected someone dressed in haunting garb and to have a more evil look. No, he was an ordinary everyday man dressed all in black. He wore a simple cotton t-shirt and black jeans. There was nothing menacing about him. If he'd passed him on the street, he would never think he was a highly sought after voodoo priest who performed exorcisms on a daily basis.

Paul stood up and walked over to Father Trahan. Extending his hand, he stated, "Father Trahan, please sit."

Father Trahan picked up the thick Haitian accent, "Thank you for agreeing to talk to me. It was very difficult to find any information on freeing trapped spirits and exorcisms."

"I must admit, you had me intrigued when we spoke on the phone. What makes you believe that you have trapped spirits that must be freed?"

"I had a young woman come to me explaining that she could talk to the dead or, more importantly, she could read the energy that they leave behind. She is extremely worried about some souls that she believes are trapped here on earth."

"She is certain then that these spirits are trapped?"

Father Trahan nodded his head in agreement, "Yes. Do you remember when a carnival came to New Orleans at Mardi Gras and it was discovered that several murders had occurred there?"

"Yes, I recall something to that effect. There have been whispers that the supernatural had more to do with it than what was released to the public."

Father Trahan replied, "There is much more to it than what was let on. I was privy to some of the information, but I believe there is more than what they told me. I have done my own research and from the information I ascertained, we may be facing a true battle of good versus evil."

As Paul finished his tea, he looked down at the tea leaves, "Father, I believe you may be correct in that assumption. The signs appear more frequently that there is a shift in the power between good and evil. I have heard whispers that the voodoo priestess is still here in New Orleans practicing her own special brand of magie noire. If my signs are correct, her powers are strengthening."

"The young lady that I spoke of believes that the voodoo priestess may have taken a partner. They are planning something big and very diabolical."

The voodoo priest took Father Trahan's hand in his and turned it palm side up, "You had visions yourself, have you not?"

"I had a very vivid dream is all."

Paul shook his head, "No, there is more to it than that. I believe your God is preparing you for your mission. He chose you because you are more receptive to the supernatural. Yet, your faith remains unshaken. He has chosen wisely in you."

"I pray that he has. I fear what could come to fruition if this evil is not stopped."

"You must trust your instincts and never lose faith. Your God put several people in your life in hopes that together evil can be overcome. You must remember that good, and evil, can come in all shapes and forms."

"Yes, I have found out that evil can take many shapes and forms."

"It very well can indeed. Let me start off by telling you that performing an exorcism is a very nasty business. It took me a while to become desensitized to this kind of thing. I no longer get a chill down my back when I witness a demon leaving a body. The smell of burning flesh will soon no longer turn your stomach.”

Father Trahan watched as the voodoo priest pulled out a string of prayer beads from his pocket and placed it on the table. “This set of prayer beads has sizzled the flesh of more possessed humans than I would ever want to guess. The sheer number is more than you can ever fathom and with each exorcism that I do, it seems as if two more souls become possessed by evil spirits or demons.”

Father Trahan interrupted, “So, I am correct in my understanding that the crucifixes will help when it comes to the supernatural.”

“Oh my, yes. When the prayer beads come into contact with another human that is possessed, the human skin immediately begins to sizzle. It won’t take long before the heady smell of brimstone and sulfur fills the air. No matter how desperately the possessed begs, you must not stop what you are doing. You must drive the demon out of their body. The possessed will jerk and spasm beneath you, and yet you must continue. When you see the irises of their eyes transform from a mottled black and red to their normal color, it is then safe to stop the exorcism. You must also remember that a possession is one of the most painful things a person can live through. To free a possessed soul, you must first kill that person then bring them back to life, Father Trahan.”

“Those that I must free are already dead.”

"Yes, well, I need to do a little more research before I can give you a definitive answer on how to free these souls. It is likely that someone put a spell on them."

Father Trahan finished the last of his tea and set the cup down. Paul picked it up to study the leaves, "You will have a visitor soon. He is coming to help you with your mission. Do not turn him away, despite your intuition. God has indeed sent him. You must remember your faith above all else. There will be one in sheep's clothing sent by the devil. This one cannot be trusted. All is not as it seems."

As Father Trahan listened to what the voodoo priest had to say, he prayed that God would send others to help him in this mission. When the time came, he hoped he chose wisely on those he could trust.

Father Trahan asked, "What would it take for you to consider joining the team?"

Paul gave Father Trahan a wicked smile, "Father, you don't even have to ask. This will take everything we have, but I need more information from you. You have not told me everything."

"You are correct, mon ami. Some things may be hard to believe. I must show you."

Paul walked over to the "Open" sign and turned it off while locking the front door. "We can exit through the back."

Father Trahan followed Paul out the shop, "We can take my car. It is parked on the side street not far from here."

Paul let out a laugh, "What's wrong, Father? You didn't want anyone to see a Catholic priest go into a voodoo shop?"

Laughingly, he replied, "No, that's not the case at all. There weren't any parking spots out front."

"There never is Father. This place is always busy. You were lucky to find a parking spot."

As they made their way to where the carnival rides were stored, Father Trahan called Detective Hutcherson, "Detective, this is Father Trahan. I am taking someone to the carnival rides so that he can get a feel of what is there first hand."

Detective Hutcherson replied, "How far away are you? I can meet you there."

"You don't have to do that."

"I know that, Father, but I want to. I want to help those poor souls as much as you do. It kills me to know that they are trapped in there."

Paul overheard the conversation and asked, "Did I hear you correctly? Are we going to a carnival?"

"At one time, it was a carnival, a popular carnival. Now it is merely a shell of what it was. The evil that was there still permeates the surroundings."

Instead of asking more questions, Paul contemplated what he was told and what he overheard. Soon all of his questions would be answered, but would it be answers that he wanted to hear?

* * *

As Hutch was leaving, she informed Guy and Mike where she would be. Mike asked, "Do you need me to go with you?"

"No, I will be fine. Besides, Father Trahan will be there. He is bringing someone who may be able to help us."

Guy grabbed his keys, "In that case, I think we should all go. If he is going to be a member of this team, he needs to meet us and hear what he may be dealing with first hand."

The closer that Hutch got to the impound lot, the more she could sense the trapped souls. They were reaching out to her, pleading for help. She hoped that sooner rather than later she could free them.

Father Trahan pulled up at the same time as the detectives. After making the proper introductions, Father Trahan replied, "There was no need for all of you to come. I wanted Paul here to witness first hand what we were dealing with rather than telling him."

Guy stated, "We may as well give him the good and the bad if he is considering helping us out." Looking directly at Paul, he said, "We have done some research as well. It appears that the voodoo priestess and her lover boy are up to something. A few calls came in about zombie sightings but nothing concrete as of yet. There were a few more vampire related deaths and a few unexplained deaths where someone tried to blame a vampire, but the evidence points another way."

Paul stated, "It could be that the voodoo priestess developed a taste for blood and has found a way to drain the blood from the body."

Guy nodded his head in agreement, "The DNA on one of the bodies did point to the suspect as being a woman. Why would she need to use a poison when she could just have her boyfriend subdue the target?"

Father Trahan contemplated this, "She was betrayed by a man once already. Maybe, she hasn't informed her partner of her taste for blood. Without him, she might need the poison."

Paul replied, "These deaths could also be done to distract you from what they are really doing. Maybe, they are giving you suspicious murders to keep you too busy to solve the real case."

Mike replied, "That could very well be the case. With each new killing, we have to take time away from what we were doing to solve the case in front of us. Some cases take days, even weeks, before we can devote more time to this case."

Father Trahan thought back to the dreams he'd had, "I have a feeling that the time for games is over. I expect they will make another move soon, one that will not be just to distract you."

Hutch nodded her head in agreement, "Yes, he has been quiet lately. I fear they are up to something. It has been a while since he felt the need to taunt me."

Paul, being the newcomer, looked at the others with bemusement. Hutch informed him, "What you are about to see was done by a vampire. I have yet to figure out how he did this or how to solve the problem at hand. You are about to find out why we asked you so much about exorcisms and freeing souls."

As they made their way through the impound lot, they could sense a change in the air. The evil was so heavy it became difficult just to breathe the air here.

Paul noticed the carnival rides right away and observed the thick ring of white substance on the ground. Mike saw Paul eyeing the ring. "It is salt. We weren't sure if there was a way for the creatures to escape. If they did escape, we needed to keep them confined. Salt was our best guess."

Paul nodded his head in agreement, "Salt will protect you from evil. Salt, at one time, was poured over a gravesite to keep the dead from rising."

Guy replied, "I found that same research which is why we chose to do this."

Father Trahan asked Paul, "Do you still have your prayer beads on you?"

Paul took them out of his pocket and wrapped them lovingly between his fingers, "I never go anywhere without them or my gris-gris bag."

As they stepped into the circle of salt, Paul felt a shift in the air. It was frigid within the circle of salt.

Hutch took a deep breath before speaking, "We have brought someone to try and help you. Do not be afraid. He means you no harm."

Paul looked around at the carnival rides, and a chill ran down his spine. "Were these rides made with human bones?"

Mike nodded his head in acknowledgment, "Yes, we confirmed that these were indeed human bones. The tents were made out of human and animal skin. It looked as if one of the reasons they were never discovered was they made sure not to leave behind any bodies. When the general public observed the carnival and its appearance, no one could even conceive that the bones and such were all in actuality real. Even more disturbing was when the carnival was impounded and brought back here for processing, it was discovered that the meat used for consumption was human. The vampires were excellent at what they did; they used every spare part as some part of the carnival. They would feed off of the victims and then dispose of their bodies as needed." Even now, Mike could not look at a hamburger or hot dog and not wonder what he was eating.

The carousel caught Paul's eyes. It was so unusual, so dark and haunting. A movement in the mirror caught his eye. He looked around to see if there was someone else lurking about whose image was captured in the mirror. After looking around and not seeing anyone, he heard Hutch come up to him, "They are trying to free themselves even now. Something in there keeps them trapped. I am not sure what it is, but it is evil."

No sooner than Hutch had spoken, Paul saw a creature coming at them. He pulled her back just as the glass of the mirror rattled violently. This creature was one of the devil's legion of that he was certain. "There is black magic at work here."

Hutch watched as the creature continued to ram against the glass in an attempt to free itself from its prison, "Do you see why we need your help? These souls cry out to me, pleading to be set free."

"Cher, I am sure they do, but not all these souls are good. I can sense the evil that is trapped here. We must be very careful in freeing these souls. There are some we do not want to walk this earth."

Guy replied, "That is why we have the circle of salt. I am unsure how long these mirrors will hold."

Paul could barely make out an inscription etched on the mirror. He took out his phone and took a picture of the etching. He needed to do some research on this language. He asked Father Trahan, "Did you notice this before?"

Father Trahan inspected the etchings in the glass, "No. It looks like an older version of Latin. I saw something similar when I was in the seminary, but I can't be certain. Can you please email me a copy of the picture? I know a priest who specializes in ancient languages. It is a pastime of his."

Upon the discovery of the etchings in the mirrors, they inspected the remaining rides and found similar engravings. Paul replied, "It looks like we found the incantation that keeps the souls confined to their prison. Now, we must see if we can get this translated in hopes of freeing the souls."

Hutch prayed that this may be the answer she needed to free these souls. She hoped that once they were freed the voices inside of her head would quiet down. It seemed as if the vampire opened a portal that she wanted closed. It was okay when she could channel the energy at crime scenes, but she was unaccustomed to spirits seeking her out and intruding on her thoughts at all times of the night and day. More and more lately they reached out to her. She must learn how to keep them from barraging her constantly. There had to be a happy medium.

***

Father Francis Metz was not what Father Trahan imagined. He expected an old, staunch priest, but instead, Father Metz was in his late thirties and very much interested in everything going on.

They spent several hours talking before Father Metz stood up and stated that come morning light they would go to the impound lot and free the tortured souls.

After showing Father Metz out, he went back into the study. As Father Trahan looked out the window, he took in the dark cloud that slithered across the skyline like billowed ghosts. An angry breeze whipped through the rectory, shaking the windows. Was this an ominous prediction of what was to come? Was this a signal from heaven or hell to leave the souls where they were?

Father Trahan was about to delve into the dark, metaphysical world of exorcism. He found it very comforting that Father Metz agreed to let the voodoo priest participate in the exorcism.

The next morning, by the time they arrived at the impound lot, the turbulent storm clouds were right above them. Father Metz gave each of them a St. Benedict medal and instructed them to not take it off, no matter what happened. They used ancient Bibles, holy water mixed with special oils, sacred relics and the power of the Almighty God. It took them almost all day to free the souls, but it was well worth the exhaustive efforts.

Once they were done, Father Metz pulled Father Trahan aside to inform him that he would stay on at the rectory to assist him in defeating the voodoo priestess and the vampire.

Chapter 34

Clank. Clank. Clank.

Bianca awakened to the sound of chains rattling outside of her bedroom window. "Damn!" She pulled herself out of the bed to see what was going on. More than likely one of the zombies broke free and was roaming the grounds. They needed to purchase stronger chains for the zombies to keep them more placid.

Their growing army seemed to run into problems that must be taken care of. She was also worried about Joshua. He seemed distant. Bianca was certain he planned on controlling his legion of soldiers on his own and betraying her. She forbid him from restarting his own family, but she had a strong suspicion that he had done so. He was stronger than she initially believed. She was foolish to think she could control him. She may have to take care of him sooner than she suspected. He had outgrown his usefulness, and she couldn't have him gaining control of a family once again.

She should have known he would want to rule his own kingdom. In order for him to do that, he would try to dispose of her or take over the army she had created. She must be on constant guard.

She called for her second in command, Abraham, "They are dealt with your highness."

"Thank you, Abraham. I knew I could count on you. The necessary pieces are falling into place."

"Everything is going as you planned."

Bianca asked, "Did you do the other preparations?"

"Yes, your highness. Everything will be ready."

"Good, keep me informed. It is imperative that everything goes smoothly. We are on the edge of an epic moment. It won't be long before we can take over New Orleans."

Abraham replied, "It will all go as planned."

"I have waited too long for this to fail."

With a wave of her hand, she dismissed him. She knew that Father Trahan and his group were making preparations to stop her. They were of no concern to her.

Chapter 35

As Father Trahan walked back to the rectory, a man in ragged clothes approached him. For a moment, a wave of apprehension came over him, but he quickly chastised himself. This was one of God's children who may be in need of help.

The derelict man asked, "Do you have any change you can spare?"

"I don't keep cash on me, but the church has a soup kitchen if you are looking for a meal to warm you."

Without warning, the man's arm grabbed hold of Father Trahan's arm with a vise grip. As Father Trahan looked into the man's eyes, his breath caught. This was what the voodoo priest had warned him of, mottled black eyes with hints of red. Could this be a demon who had sought him out? How did he know to come after Father Trahan specifically?

An intense headache overcame him as this demon tried to read his thoughts. Now he knew how Hutch must feel when the vampire tried to intrude her thoughts. Fearing that this demon may jump from the body he inhabited for his own, Father Trahan said a prayer as he reached for the rosary in his pocket. Without thinking, he pulled out the rosary and pushed it into the demon's chest. Immediately, the smell of sulfur filled the air as the demon's skin sizzled. The demon's screams pierced his ears.

"Back demon. In the name of God Almighty, go back to the hell you came from."

The demon hissed at him and stumbled backward. The demon's true self showed itself as it tried to flee. This creature was an unholy abomination. Its scale like skin was black as night. It almost had the appearance of a dragon with a man's head. It was a sight he would not soon forget. You could smell the scent of death that lingered on him.

The demon's forked tongue slithered out of his mouth as he stated, "Preacher man, you won't always have your trinkets to protect you. We will get you when you least expect it."

"That is where you are wrong. I always have my rosary and crucifix on me. I also have my faith; it is unfaltering."

The demon let out a hideous laugh, "Fool, how wrong you are. We can get to you in your dreams also."

"Who sent you here? Who told you where to find me?"

"My master knows all, of that you can be certain. She has a message for you."

"Well then spit it out and be on your way demon."

"Oh, I can't wait to take you down, preacher man. You will be a delicious treat. My master wants you to take heed; she will win. If you wish to spare any of your minions, you best take leave and let her be."

Father Trahan let out a laugh, "I can't do that. I will not allow evil to win. If it means my death in order to keep the likes of you from winning, then so be it. I am ready to die; my soul is free of sin, unlike yours."

The demon had the most sinister of smiles formed across his face as he spit a vile, thick black liquid from his mouth, "You have been warned. Soon we will rule this world."

Father Trahan watched as the demon disappeared into the darkness of the night. He still wondered how this demon or his master knew what Father Trahan was up to. Did they have a traitor in their midst? Who among them could be working for the voodoo priestess and vampire? Father Trahan was confident that the voodoo priestess was the demon's master.

***

Their screams haunted her as his maniacal laughter echoed through her mind. His dead eyes seemed to pierce right to her very soul. He deeply inhaled their last breath, making each victim a part of him. He relished the terror on their faces. The smell of fear gave him a rush as did their impending death. He wanted to hear them plead for their lives. She could see the moonlight as it gleamed off of his fangs.

The taste of blood on his tongue ignited his senses. The rush of power was so dominating. These mortals were weak. They were nothing more than sheep and he the wolf.

For a moment, he let them think he would set them free. He offered them a glimmer of hope; however, he had no intention of setting them free. His only desire was to take their souls and make them part of him. They would be introduced to the never ending darkness that was his.

Hutch bolted upright in bed. She'd seen more into the vampire than before, and it sent a chill down her spine. He must be stopped. He would not stop killing unless they stopped him.

As the images of the dream dissipated like puddles of rain on the sun-scorched Louisiana pavements, Hutch rolled onto her back and let out a soft moan. This dream left a throbbing pain deep inside of her head. The headache quickly escalated into a migraine. The pressure building up inside of her head felt as if it would explode at any moment. This was the first time a vision left her with such an excruciating headache. All the sounds around her were blocked out by the roar of her pulse in her ears.

Before the vision left her mind, she tried to recap what she saw. Maybe this time she could figure out where the vampire was and stop him? When it came to the killing, she could remember each action vividly, but the surroundings were always muddled. This time was no different.

Chapter 36

The fog had eyes tonight. Mesmerizing green eyes with barely a slit for pupils hovered suspended in the mist without a body. Officer Jack Boudreaux never looked out into the fog, or he would see the strange phenomenon. Instead, he slowly made his rounds of the French Quarter. Unfortunately, Officer Boudreaux would all too soon see those mesmerizing green eyes.

A light fog had settled over the entire city earlier this evening, creating halos around the lights that lined the cobblestoned streets of the Quarter. Despite the fog and weather, tourists were still out at this hour. He took in a deep breath and caught an all too familiar smell. His mouth watered and he could just taste the gumbo. If only he could buy him a big ole bowl, but as soon as he did a call would come in and he would have to leave the tantalizing concoction. You never had to worry about starving in New Orleans. The food here was the best in all of Louisiana. The restaurants around here catered to the variety of economics that came to the city. In some restaurants, a meal cost as much as his paycheck and there were some vendors on the street and smaller restaurants where a home cooked, satisfying meal could be bought for a very reasonable price. Those were the restaurants Officer Boudreaux visited. He doubted the more expensive restaurants served food any better than his favorite places to eat.

The eyes in the fog never blinked as they followed Officer Boudreaux. They hid in the mist with their translucent stare, but the gaze always remained firmly trained on the young officer.

For the last two years, Officer Boudreaux had walked this part of the French Quarter. As he walked up the levee, he looked back over the Quarter. He noticed that the fog was even thicker; it was beginning to shroud the city.

A horn from a passing ship in the river filled the night. As he looked towards the river, the gentle sway of the water could barely be seen as the fog continued to roll in. He shivered for a moment, unaware of the greedy eyes focusing on him or the strange mist that formed around him.

As the horn of the passing ship sounded once more, Officer Boudreaux gazed thoughtfully at the river and the lights of the ship that could barely be seen through the fog. What would have become of his life had he not listened to his mother and joined the Navy. He had wanted to see the world and joining the Navy would have given him that opportunity. His mother feared she would never see him again if he enlisted in the Navy. She begged and pleaded for him to stay here at home with her. He had never traveled further than Mississippi; it was time he saw more of what this world had to offer.

Behind him, the fog that encircled him began to grow. A skeletal shape appeared in the undulating mist and reached for the young police officer. The apparition was gone in a flash when a noise from the officer's radio crackled through the air.

The noise brought Officer Boudreaux out of his reverie, and he listened to what the dispatcher had to say. Since it was nothing for him to worry about, he lowered the volume of the radio. The eyes greedily hovered over the young officer. With one quick look around, Officer Boudreaux headed back to the streets of the French Quarter.

The mist wasn't far behind him; it stealthily approached him with its hungry green eyes. The hand formed once more, waiting for the opportune moment to strike.

As Officer Boudreaux continued his rounds, he caught an unpleasant scent. It was almost sulfuric in odor. He stopped to see where the smell might be coming from. The last thing this area needed was a leak of some kind.

When he stopped, he noticed a mist crawling up his legs. He watched, frozen in horror as the mist moved quickly up his body. Officer Boudreaux tried to shake it vigorously off to no avail. His pulse pounded deafeningly in his ears. A shiver of fear snaked across his body as cold beads of sweat broke out. He was paralyzed in terror and could produce no scream as the mist reached eye level. The wicked eyes stared back at him while the vaporous shape continued to wrap itself around his body in a deathly coil.

Petrified, he found his body no longer obeyed. A nightmare of visions and hallucinations gripped his mind as the mist strangled the last breath from the young officer's lungs. In sheer desperation, he gulped for another gasp of air that never had a chance to fill his lungs. As the mist encased him, his flesh rapidly dried to a leathery state. His body was wracked with excruciating pain. He felt an unknown force penetrating his mind.

Time seemed frozen, and the torment never ending as the creature engulfed his mind, senses and finally his entire body. The gurgle that escaped his throat was barely more than a rasp. The eyes seemed to mock him as it finally let go of his body and dropped it heavily to the ground like a rag doll. The leathery skin was almost falling off the body, and the sunken eyes and mouth were wide open in a grimace that was reminiscent of a horrible, silent scream.

***

Ron Grady and Bill Thompson were ready for the day to be over. They were on their last delivery. Ron hollered out to Bill, "Come on, man. Let's get this done so we can get home."

Bill rolled his eyes, "I'm waiting on you. I got a woman waiting for me at home. She already sent me a text saying she is ready for me to come home, and we both know what that means."

"Yeah, I know, but I don't need that image. I get to go home to an empty apartment."

"Not my problem. I told you I could set you up with one of Jill's friends."

A shudder went through Ron as he thought about what Jill's friends would look like, "Yeah, that's okay. I will keep trying my luck at the bars."

Bill let out a laugh, "Come on, mon ami, Jill's friends aren't all as bad as the one you met."

As the two unloaded the truck and joked around, they failed to notice the heavy fog that was beginning to encircle the area.

As Bill took out the last box, he informed Ron, "That's the last box." Ron looked over the manifest before heading into the restaurant to let the manager know the complete delivery was in the warehouse.

As he walked to the back door, the mist encircled his legs and prevented him from moving. The two men trembled as the dense fog intensified rapidly around them. It grew so thick that they were unable to see in front of them. Ron tried to feel around his legs in order to find out why he wasn't able to move. He didn't see any ropes on the ground, but his legs must be trapped in something. Ron shouted over to his friend, "Dude, my legs are caught on something. This fog is so thick I can't see anything."

Bill tried to go to help his friend, but found that he couldn't move as well, "Mon Dieu, my legs are stuck too."

Despite the wind blowing in off the river, the fog remained thick and heavy. The men shuddered as the fog moved up to encase each of them. A strong, pungent smell of sulfur filled the air, and the men began to choke. The air became more acrid as the mist continued to snake upwards. Ron desperately tried to free himself as the fog pulsated from the inside.

Their struggles were futile. Fear penetrated the men straight to their bones. The mist paralyzed their very movements. Suddenly, glowing green eyes appeared in the mist. The searing stare bore right into their minds. They felt their minds being probed as their bodies went limp. Their skin wrinkled like old leather as death came in a single flash of horror.

***

After unmercifully dropping the shriveled bodies to the ground, Bianca felt her powers grow in intensity. She managed to leave her body and transport herself through the fog to kill. She wished she could be a fly on the wall when the pesky detectives found the bodies. Terror would soon grip this city as they realized she was unstoppable.

She used her powers to make the fog denser now and spread the mist here and there; she reached out and trailed between the streets with the fog. Soon she was able to cover almost the entire street. After hovering like this for a while, the fog crept forward even more. She moved to a single spot, near the front of the rectory where Father Trahan lived.

She used her powers to find him in the rectory. Anger quickly filled the air as she realized that he was not here. As her fury intensified, the fog exploded in all directions before once again pulling itself together into a single, billowy cloud. She made her way back to her house. What good was this new power if she couldn't taunt her enemies?

***

Mike, Hutch, and Guy all meet Dr. Ortego in the morgue. Dr. Ortego stood over the bodies and looked up to acknowledge their presence. He didn't waste any time leaving the crime scene and getting back here. He was already dressed in his green scrubs, footsies, hat, and gloves. What threw Mike off was that he had a biohazard mask and face shield on along with his usual surgical mask.

Dr. Ortego pointed to the other masks he had out for them, "I suggest y'all get suited up. We don't know what we are dealing with this time."

After suiting up, they joined Dr. Ortego by the bodies. It was a surreal experience. It was hard to believe that not long ago Mike talked to Officer Boudreaux, and right now he and the others looked more like ancient mummies rather than corpses. Guy stated, "This wasn't the work of a vampire."

Dr. Ortego shook his head. "No. I will take a sample of the remains and see if the vampire gene is present in the bloodstream though. Since we know what we are looking for, it will be easier. I have searched the body carefully for puncture wounds and found none so far. However, that doesn't really mean anything. Now that we know what we are looking for, I went back and indeed found the vampire gene in several other unexplained deaths where no puncture wounds were present. They either didn't want their existence known or that they killed for food."

Guy ran his hands through his hair, "This is going to be an impossible battle if they congregate and come at us at once. We have no idea just how many are out there."

***

As Dr. Ortego made the "y" incision to begin the internal autopsy, Hutch looked away. She never liked the noise of the saw or the way a body had to be completely exposed to find the cause of death. As he reached into the cavity, he exclaimed, "This is new; the heart and possibly the other internal organs as well are completely dehydrated." As Hutch looked at the organ, she was surprised to find that it looked more like a large raisin than a heart.

***

Joshua picked up the morning paper to see what was happening before going to bed. An article caught his attention.

A young, New Orleans Police Officer's life was cut short as well as two other men working in the Quarter early this morning.

The bodies of the two delivery workers were found this morning when Chef Pierre Robicheaux arrived at work. Officer Jack Boudreaux's body was later found when the crime scene techs were surveying the area for clues. Cause of death has not been released, but one witness stated that the bodies looked as if they dried in the sun. The police were quick to cover all three bodies upon discovery and have yet to make any comments pertaining to the case.

Joshua looked over at Bianca and wondered how powerful she was. Could it be she found a way to drain the life force from an individual? He saw what happened when a soul collector squeezed a soul from a mortal, and it was similar to what was described in the article. The skin took on a black hue, almost as if it was burned, but the skin was heavily wrinkled and shriveled instead of smooth. It reminded him of a human raisin.

He needed to discuss this with Bianca without letting her know he had an idea of what she was up to. This may be a power he had to steal from her. It could be quite useful.

***

Bianca felt Joshua watching her. She wondered if he had any idea of what she'd done last night. Currently, she was too weak to hunt. As she thought of the midnight feast she'd devoured last night, she relished the way it made her feel. She felt ethereal floating on top of the land the way she did. It was truly an out of body experience. If only it didn't drain her power as fast as it did. She hoped that killing the humans the way she had would regenerate her energy, but it had not. She didn't even have enough strength to face the day.

Chapter 37

Father Trahan stretched his leg muscles, trying to relieve some of the pain that radiated to the center of his bones. When he agreed with Guy Mayon that he needed a crash course in martial arts, he had no idea what was in store for him. The training was more physically challenging than he initially thought. Father Trahan always considered himself to be physically fit; although, he was not athletic. He was out of shape. His body screamed in shock at the number of muscles he'd just worked.

As Father Trahan stretched his legs, Hutch walked over, "Don't over do it, or you won't feel like doing anything the next day."

He let out a chortle, "I always thought I was in shape. This workout proved how wrong I was in my thinking."

Hutch smiled at him, "Yeah, well Guy has a way of showing us just how inadequate our workouts are compared to his."

Guy replied to Hutch, "Hey, I can't help that you are a little soft when it comes to working out. I figured Mike here would be keeping you fit." As soon as Guy made that particular comment, he let out a groan, "I'm sorry, Father, I forget that you are a priest at times."

"No need to apologize. We have more to worry about than the premarital affair of Mike and Grace. After this battle is over with, though, I plan on finding out when these two plan on making this affair proper by getting married."

Mike pulled Hutch closer to him and kissed her firmly on the lips, "I agree with Father Trahan. Marriage is a conversation for a later date."

***

Hutch looked up at Mike and just smiled. They'd just moved in with each other, and neither had spoken about marriage or children. This was new to her, and she wanted to take it slow. She was grateful Mike didn't push marriage on her. She loved Mike, but with everything going on, she feared bringing him in too close to her. What if the vampire went after Mike to prevent her from reading his mind? No, she couldn't live through that kind of tragedy.

Father Trahan had informed the group before they dispersed, "Soon, we will begin another form of training. We need to know how to use all of our senses if we want to win. I have found someone who can teach us how to enhance our abilities. We all do it on a subconscious level, but this person will come in and make sure we know how."

***

That night as Hutch fell asleep in Mike's arms, she began to dream. She found herself in a dark, dense part of the swamp. The trees were so thick here that she was sheltered from the torrents of rain pouring down from the night sky. With each step she took deeper into the woods, she smelled the pine needles and wet soil. Suddenly, she caught the aroma of something else.

She called out, "Is anybody here?"

Up above the tree tops, the wind gusted, and an owl called out with a lonely hoot. No one answered her. She peered into the darkness of the night, hoping she could make out her surroundings. The deeper she moved into the woods, the less the moonlight could filter through the heavy canopy of trees. She heard twigs snap. She stopped and tried to peer into the night once more.

She stared frantically into the darkness. "Who's there?"

Again, no one answered. Another branch snapped, and a chill swept through her. Without warning, something grabbed at her wrists and pulled her close. She could smell the decay that surrounded the creature. She felt the hatred radiate through the night air.

A bolt of lightning streaked across the night sky. At that moment, Hutch saw what had a hold of her. It was the vampire who constantly taunted her. She saw him for what he truly was, a monster of decomposing flesh and eyes of death.

She let out an unearthly scream, but the thunder drowned it out.

"Soon, cher, it will be time for us to meet in person." His voice sent a chill down her spine. Even the trees around her seemed to tremble in fear.

She asked, "Why do you continue to taunt me?"

Another bolt of lightning streaked through the air. She could see him smiling down on her. She could feel him looking her up and down, studying her. "Ah, cher, you intrigue me. You called out to me, wanting to know about me. I want you to get to know me before I make you mine."

Hutch shuddered at the thought of being turned into a blood sucking vampire. His gaze made her feel vulnerable, searing her soul with his voice.

Unable to go back to sleep, Hutch dragged herself out of bed and stumbled to the kitchen. She put on a strong pot of coffee and headed to the shower, being careful not to wake Mike.

After showering, she wrapped herself in an oversized bathrobe and walked into the kitchen. After pouring herself a large mug of coffee, she stepped out on the balcony just as the sky shifted from the darkness of the night to the beginning of a new day. She sipped her coffee as the morning sky awakened, transforming the black of night into a majestic palette of colors. The morning light filtered through the maze of wrought iron, creating patterns along the magnificent Spanish colonial architecture that defined the New Orleans French Quarter. Along the Mississippi River, a paradox of sun dappled diamonds glittered and muddy ripples danced across the water. There was something so peaceful and relaxing about the simple beauty in front of her. She could almost forget about the trouble brewing underneath.

This was the first time since moving to New Orleans that she truly felt as if she belonged here. Now something wanted to demolish this beauty. They couldn't let Bianca's plan come to light. Good must triumph over evil, if only it were that simple though.

Chapter 38

Deep in the swamps of southern Louisiana an old woman rocked in her chair on the front porch. Her hands lay limp and dangled off the edge of the chair's arms. Her granddaughter brought her a blanket to help warm her old bones. "Grand'mere, would you like some soup?"

Antoinette LaRue feared that her grand'mere's time on this earth was close to an end. "No, child. I want to look out on the land for now."

Antoinette went back inside to clean her grand'mere's room. She fluffed the pillows and turned down the bed. Without thinking, she picked up one of her grand'mere's most cherished voodoo dolls. For as long as she could remember, her grand'mere had kept an altar beside the bed adorned with beads, candles, and brightly colored fabric in which to make her gris-gris bags.

Antoinette learned how to make the gris-gris bags and voodoo dolls as well. Antoinette wished she had the power that her grand'mere had.

She walked back towards the front porch to find her grand'mere staring at her herb garden that she tended to with loving care. Each of the herbs here served a purpose. Some were used to cure, some to banish, some for vengeance and some were used to find love. Her grand'mere knew every herb that existed. She taught her granddaughter the meaning of each and not to fear using them.

Unlike her grand'mere, her body was still vulnerable to the power of the herbs. Sometimes, the rich smell of the herbs got caught in her throat, causing her to cough. Soon, though, she would be able to use them just as her grand'mere did.

As Marie rocked herself on the porch, a warm night breeze drifted off the bayou. Antoinette walked out onto the porch and asked, "Grand'mere, are you sure that you don't want to come inside? The heat is almost intolerable even at this hour."

Marie shook her head, "Mais non, mon cher. The warmth feels good on my old skin. My time on this earth is short. Soon, I shall leave this place for the other world that awaits me."

"Grand'mere your time on this earth is not done."

***

Marie took Antoinette's hand in hers and gave it a gentle squeeze. Marie feared that she had cheated the other world of her death for too long now. Her body cramped and ached. "Marie, it is Mariam. You must listen my dear friend. I made a horrible mistake. I should have listened to you long ago. You were right about my Bianca. I didn't want to listen. I wanted the same joy you had with your own granddaughter, Antoinette. Now, my jealousy may have brought an end to this world."

Marie listened to what her old friend was saying. She was unsure if this was a dream or a visit from her dear departed friend. "Mariam is that you?"

Mariam moved in closer, "Oui, cher. I need your help. Only you can help me."

"Ah Mariam, I am afraid my body is too frail to assist you. My time has come to join you."

Mariam shook her head, "Non, cher. You must help me stop Bianca before leaving this world."

"I am too old. My powers are faltering."

Mariam caught a movement inside the old house, "What of Antoinette? Have you taught her your ways? Please Marie, it is important."

Marie could sense her granddaughter's presence nearby and lowered her voice, "My granddaughter isn't ready to take on the likes of your granddaughter. I told you that girl was evil; yet you wouldn't listen. She bore the mark, and you chose to ignore it."

"My friend, I now see the error of my ways. I was foolish to think I could change her. I fear Bianca has become too powerful for a mere mortal to stop."

Marie looked over at the door, "Come child. I know you are there."

Antoinette stepped out on the porch and knelt down by her grand'mere, "Come inside, Grand'mere, and rest."

"Child, we need to talk. My friend Mariam Honore is here with us, and she needs our help."

Antoinette looked around as she wondered what her grand'mere saw. Her friend, Mariam, died a while back.

Marie could sense her grandchild's confusion, "Hush now, my dear. I realize that Mariam has departed this world, but she is here asking for our help. I'm afraid that I am unable to help her. I am too weak, but I can channel my power through you. That may be the only way we can stop Bianca."

Mariam explained to Marie, "I talked to another voodoo priestess who is trapped here. She enlisted the help of one that speaks to the dead as you can, cher. This young woman managed to enlist the help of a Catholic priest and a few others. There is a darkness over the group. I fear one is not what they appear to be. I need your granddaughter's help to protect them. I am afraid a gris-gris bag will not be enough."

Marie listened to what Mariam told her, making sure to repeat everything in great detail to her granddaughter. Antoinette was unsure of what to believe. Her grand'mere was aging, but she believed without a doubt that her friend was speaking to her, warning her of what Bianca planned.

In the morning Antoinette must call this Father Trahan and Detective Grace Hutcherson to find out if there was any truth to this. If there was, then she must decide what to do. She prayed that this was merely the rantings of an elderly woman.

***

Father Trahan was surprised to see a young woman at the front door of his rectory this early in the morning. "Is there something I can help you with, my child?"

Antoinette informed him, "I have a few questions to ask you, Father, and I'm not even sure how to begin."

Father Trahan had never turned away a woman in need, or anyone for that matter. He showed her into the house. "Please come in. I don't normally see people here at the rectory, but we can go into the study to talk. We shouldn't be disturbed there." To emphasize the point, he closed the study door. "Now, my child, have a seat and tell me what troubles you."

Father Trahan noticed how jittery his guest was. She couldn't sit still and fidgeted in the small arm chair. While she picked at her skirt and looked down at the floor, she informed him, "I'm not sure where to even begin. What I have to say is hard to believe, and I grew up here."

"My child, you may find I understand more than you realize."

"I've been told that as well, Father. Do you believe some people are born evil?"

"It is something I am contemplating. I also believe evil has a way of finding some people easier. If you have goodness in your heart and truly don't want evil to set in, then I believe you have the power to turn that evil away. The devil can only tempt you if you are willing."

"I feel that you are correct. However, my grand'mere believes that some are born evil. She claims this one girl should never have been born. She read the cards and saw it in the stars that this girl had evil in her heart. Even the girl's mother begged for the child not to be born."

"Could it be that the poor girl was born with a mark against her? Maybe while growing up, she let her mother program her into believing she was evil from the moment of conception? If she honestly believed she was born evil, she would be susceptible to allowing the devil in and turning her soul."

Antoinette thought about what he was saying. "But her grand'mere loved her very much and she doted on her more than she did with her daughter. Bianca never went without. Her grand'mere took her under her wing and taught her everything she knew hoping she would eventually take over for her. My grand'mere said it broke her heart when Bianca moved to New York. She moved back down right before her grand'mere passed. Mariam swore that New York changed her, but I knew Bianca growing up and she crossed over to the dark side before then. I think New York just helped her heart turn black. When she met Dominic St. Germaine down here, they fed off of each other, and the blackness just consumed her."

As Father Trahan listened to her, his excitement continued to grow. They had someone who could give them some insight into the voodoo priestess. This may be just what they needed to help defeat her and stop her plans. Before he told this woman of his plans, he needed to make sure she was on board with everything. He was warned to be careful of a serpent in disguise.

"I must know what your true feelings are regarding Bianca and what she is doing. Did you come here hoping I would exorcise the demons from her or were you hoping to stop her from continuing her black magic?"

"So you do know of Bianca and her work. Her grand'mere was right, that I should seek you out."

"Bianca's grand'mere sought you out personally?"

"She did not seek me out, but she sought out my grand'mere. My grand'mere's time here on this earth is short lived. She doesn't have the strength to fight Bianca, but to be honest with you, I am not sure if my powers are strong enough to stop Bianca. Her black magic is growing. I can feel it in the air, especially deep in the swamps. What she plans is big Father Trahan. I believe it will take both of our religions to conquer this evil and, even then, I am scared it may not be enough. There is a darkness out there waiting to consume New Orleans. I just can't see her stopping once she has New Orleans under her control. She will spread her evil over the world like a virus."

As Father Trahan listened to everything that this young woman had to say, he no longer doubted her side. She truly believed in what she just said. He wasn't one hundred percent sure of just how Mariam Honore fit into this since she was deceased. "Did I hear you correctly when you said that Mariam Honore was the one who asked your grand'mere for help?"

She fidgeted with her skirt even more; her nervousness became clearly apparent. He reached out his hand to still her hands, "Relax my child. I want to piece this all together. I have come to believe that there are ghosts among us. When we are born, God sends down a guardian angel for that child to help protect it. As you grow up, you don't need the guardian angel as much; it comes into your life only when you need it."

Antoinette let out a deep sigh. "When I first saw my grand'mere talking to someone on the porch the other day, I thought for sure she was getting ready to cross over to the other side. My grand'mere claims that Mariam came back and forth more in recent days. At first, I didn't believe her, but after talking with you, I think Mariam Honore did indeed speak to my grand'mere. Father, you should know Mariam mentioned that another was helping her stop Bianca. Mariam said that this woman was a traiteur before her death, and she is very bitter. Bianca is the one who killed her. I believe she talked to someone who was helping you, a young detective."

Now that he understood how she knew him, he needed to make sure she was ready to join their team. He informed her, "I am putting together an elite group of individuals to help in the battle of good versus evil. Before I tell you who it involves, I need to make sure that you are interested in joining. You should know that we do have very special individuals on our side. Some have unique gifts, if you will."

"I fear that I am not strong enough to fight this battle. I am still learning, but my grand'mere has done this for years. If only I took it as seriously as she wanted me to. I saw it as a way to help the sick and needy. I never saw voodoo in the same light as my grand'mere. Now, I regret not studying with her the way Bianca did with hers. She is younger than me, but more powerful."

Father Trahan squeezed her hand, "My child, the Lord will provide. You must believe in yourself, and God will take over."

Antoinette sat up a little straighter, "Father, I will help you in any way I can. Please let me know what you need me to do."

"This is a dangerous mission. People, good and evil, will die. Your life will be in danger from the moment you accept this offer. I don't know if this battle will ever truly be over."

Father Trahan watched her closely as she thought everything over. He continued, "You must also realize that you cannot tell anyone about what we are doing. I understand you will want to talk things through with your grand'mere. You must explain to her that she mustn't speak to anyone else about this. There is a chance if somebody learns of our mission their life will be in grave danger. Those that join the team must keep their wits about them."

As the young woman nodded her head in understanding, he feared that she may not truly have any idea what they were up against. There was another level of inhumanity that they were dealing with, something very dark and sinister. She may understand that they were going after a dark voodoo priestess, but was she ready to go up against vampires, possibly zombies and no telling what demons would appear?

Father Trahan informed Antoinette, "You will need to attend training with the rest of us. We start at eight o'clock at night here at the Catholic School's gym."

She looked up at him, puzzled, "Training?"

"We do martial arts and a few other exercises so that our body is ready for the fight. One of the detectives has everything ready for us to practice aiming and shooting. It is imperative that we know how to shoot a gun, as well as a crossbow. Eventually, we will begin practicing with real guns and crossbows. Until we are comfortable with the toys, it doesn't pay for us to start shooting with real ammunition and arrows. We do know that the vampires are best killed with silver bullets and stakes right to the heart, but the zombies we are unsure about. Especially those that have been raised from the dead. Those that recently died will have their organs removed prior to burial. If she raised those buried long ago, there is a chance they were buried with their organs. Unfortunately, we won't know what we are fighting until we start."

Father Trahan could see the trepidation when it swept across her face as the reality of what they were up against hit her full force. He exclaimed, "I know, my child, that this is way more than you ever imagined. This is more than any of us imagined. You have to trust me on this. There is true evil out there, and it is coming. We must be prepared to fight a battle like no one ever imagined."

"I know you don't want me or grand'mere to talk to anyone about what we are doing, but you must let her talk to Mariam. She may know some ways we can stop these zombies. Zombies are in the voodoo religion. There are spells to raise them from the dead, so there must be something that we can do to counter the spell she performed."

Father Trahan looked at her surprised. That was something he had not considered. This was a black magic spell to raise the dead, so maybe there was a spell to also send them back to where they came from.

***

Father Trahan and Antoinette had talked for a little longer before she headed back home. As she left, she suddenly felt the urge to make the sign of the cross and say a Hail Mary before leaving. That could not be a good omen.

While driving home, a shiver went through Antoinette. She did not understand the seriousness of this mission until talking with Father Trahan. This wouldn't be her casting a few spells; this would be her chance to use white magic to conquer black magic.

As Antoinette thought about everything Father Trahan had to say, she was overcome with overwhelming despair. They would be fighting and killing the undead. They could be truly up against the supernatural. She never honestly considered there would be vampires and zombies out there. Could she do this? A shudder wracked through her body as she even contemplated shooting something to kill it.

***

Later that night, Father Trahan met with the other members of the team. After explaining his visit with Antoinette, Guy asked, "Do you think she can handle this?"

"I can't say for sure. She is mighty young, but then again, she's not that much older than Bianca herself. She grew up with Bianca, which may be beneficial to us."

Mike shook his head, "She knew the Bianca before New York. Since then she has become heavily involved with black magic. She is not the same person that this young woman knew."

Father Trahan replied, "She may not be the same woman, but we can use her previous knowledge of Bianca to find a weakness we can use in our favor. As much as I hate to find one's weaknesses and use that against them, this fight is against the devil taking over. For that reason alone, I don't see a problem with using certain weaknesses against an enemy. We also know that the one thing Bianca has ever loved is her grand'mere and I plan on using that to our advantage."

Mike asked, "And how do you plan on doing that?"

"That I don't know, but when the time comes, we will figure it out. I plan on invoking every spirit, saying every prayer, reciting every scripture and using holy water as well as incense if I must. Somehow we will save these souls here in New Orleans and the world from damnation."

As Hutch listened, she feared that their time to see how successful they would be was soon at hand. She'd felt uneasy these last few days. It wasn't something she could explain, but it had her worried.

Chapter 39

One by one the souls Bianca raised entered the clearing and waited for their priestess. Off in the distance, a flickering light could be seen crossing the bayou. On the small bateau was a lone female cloaked in black. The bayou was hot, humid and lush as she glided through the water. A misty haze settled over the placid, unmoving water whose calm was interrupted by the mysterious currents. Ancient trees dripping with moss were clustered around the muddy waters which had weeds and long grass sprouting everywhere.

The closer she got to the land, the thicker the mist grew giving the bayou a ghostly haze. Trees in the distance resembled inky shadows against the white wisps of fog.

Bianca knew she could have just transported herself, but she preferred the most dramatic entrance for this ritual. In the distance, she heard the muffled screams of tonight's sacrifice. As she neared the clearing, she could see that her minions had followed her directions. The man was held down by the intestines of the last victim. There were stakes made of bone placed six feet apart with straps made of human intestines flanking the magie noire symbols carved into the ground. The man struggled as his arms and legs were bound and spread eagle.

The zombies and other members of her legion circled around the sacrifice and chanted as instructed. The chant started as an ominous whisper and rose to an excited roar.

As Bianca made her way to the ritual site, the drums began. Their beating grew louder with each passing minute. The beat of the drums was repeatedly steady and hypnotizing. The swamp seemed to come alive with the beating. The night air pulsed with the vibrations of the drums. A dense fog rolled in behind Bianca.

She watched in pleasure as her followers performed the ritual. Her chosen followers wore only goatskin loincloths. Their dark bodies glistened in the light of the fire from the special oils they used. The zombies and other members of their growing army wore soft white cotton shirts and trousers, nothing more.

The sweltering night air had the men's bodies covered in a sweaty film that radiated in the glowing embers of the fire. A handmade altar was in the center of the clearing. Her relics and fetishes needed for the rituals proudly displayed.

As Bianca stepped into the circle, she disrobed. Her naked, oiled body was adorned with bracelets, a snake and her amulet. She danced to the tempo of the drums, swaying from the hips like a snake. Each movement accentuated the power in her legs as the muscles rippled in the firelight. As she began her ritual, the drums beat faster. Her dance became more energetic and vigorous. Even the flames seemed to sway to the beat of the drums as her followers continued to chant.

The moonlight sparkled off of the sweat beads on her body. The beat grew faster and more pronounced as the chant continued to match the rhythm. Her bracelets chimed loudly as she increased her frenzied, thrusting dance.

The ritualistic dance grew in intensity, increasing in passion as two of her followers stepped from the shadows. They carried her headdress for her to wear for this part of the ritual.

As she walked towards the man, he struggled against his restraints once more. Bianca dipped her finger into the bowl of blood one of her assistants carried. She made a crude symbol on the man's chest. She took the remaining blood and poured it on the fire.

The spirits being summoned came out of the ground where each symbol was crudely drawn. Soon the area was a sea of black ecstasy as the spirits rose. The beat of the drums reached a fevered pitch and drowned out the chanting. The zombies danced in the flames of the veve. As the blaze roared to life, the various loa entered the bodies of the zombies. Each body became a vessel to offer protection for each loa. They picked up the gathered stones and pelted the sacrificial man who let out terrifying screams with each connection of a stone. Soon the man was a bloody mess.

Bianca walked up to him and drew out her dagger. She plunged it deep into his chest and ripped out his heart. She lifted the heart, dripping with blood, to her mouth and sucked from it greedily. She then stuffed the heart into her mouth and savored its delicate flavor.

She then released the remaining zombies from their chains and watched as they devoured the remains of the body in a fierce frenzy. They reminded her of wild animals, lurching about with blood dripping from their mouths. Before they could venture out of the circle she'd created, she confined them to their chains once more. She only gave them a taste of blood tonight as to keep them in a frenzy when she released them onto the unsuspecting public.

With an abrupt end to the ritual, the drums fell silent, and all dancing ceased. The dust and smoke from the frenzied activity mixed with the heavy mist that surrounded the area, quickly dissipated into the fog. As if by magic, the zombies disbursed, retreating into the darkness of the night.

Chapter 40

Stacie Allen looked over the city she had always held dear to her heart and shivered at the evil that lurked in the shadows. There was a shift in the atmosphere. She had a growing business, and she feared that the life she'd built for herself could come crumbling down around her as well as others in the city. She left her newly turned escorts with strict instructions and headed out into the night.

Before making this difficult decision, she made sure that Father Trahan would be hearing confessions tonight. Stacie could not remember the last time she'd walked into a church, much less confession. She had no idea if her kind could even walk into a church. She may just burst into flames. Soon she would find out.

She entered the church with trepidation. Surprisingly, no one was standing in line waiting to say confession. As she noticed the empty church, she wondered if she mistook the time and there was no confession tonight. As she opened the confessional door and knelt down, she wondered if the priest was in there. Before speaking, she fidgeted with her clothes. She'd made it this far without bursting into flames. She would tell this priest what she suspected and get back to her life. She began, "Father, forgive me for I have sinned."

***

As Father Trahan listened to this woman speak, he didn't recognize the voice. Even though there was a dense black grill over the small window between the priest and parishioner confessing, he had come to recognize certain people's voices.

"How can I help you my child?"

Stacie cleared her throat, "Father, I have done some terrible things in the past. Some things I am not proud of. Some things I did out of necessity and some were merely business dealings."

Father Trahan informed her, "My child, before I can absolve you of your sins I must know more."

Stacie let out a sarcastic laugh, "Father, my soul is past saving."

Father Trahan shook his head in disbelief, "No my child. If you truly wish to be absolved, then your soul will be saved, God will not turn one of his children away."

"No, Father, you don't understand. My soul has already been taken from me. There is no hope for me. What has been done is final, but I fear my maker has something evil planned."

A chill snaked across Father Trahan's spine. Without thinking, he held his rosary tighter, "My child, are you from the carnival? Are you one of his children?"

Stacie sneered at that remark, "I sometimes feel as if the only thing Joshua cared about was saving himself so he could accomplish whatever he intended. He believes I escaped the raid instead of leaving earlier. I did not care for the atmosphere in the carnival, but at the time, I didn't want to risk my neck, so I let them be. Even when I saw

Joshua the other day in downtown New Orleans, I did nothing Father. I turned my back on this town once, and I cannot do that again. When I was turned, I learned that vampires existed, and that I was one of them. There were others there that taught me that being a vampire wasn't as bad as I first feared. We do have to feed to stay alive, but we don't have to kill. When I returned to New Orleans, I discovered there were others here as well. They only want to exist among the people here. They do not kill, and they do not want our kind brought to light. That was another reason I did not want to come forward about Joshua. Once it becomes known about him and his plans, vampires will be given a bad name. Not all of us are like him. I am not saying vampires are the neighbor next door; they can be nocturnal predators, but I am saying that we are not all bad. Typically, vampires are not a threat; however, Joshua and some of his followers are vicious creatures who kill simply for pleasure Father. When Joshua had the carnival, he killed for profit. He took victims at an alarming rate which is one reason he was discovered. I fear that he has resumed his killing. I believe he wants to take over the world with his children. When I was there, he talked about one day owning blood slaves. There is a chance that he does have some. Father, he must be stopped. Joshua craves blood, and he will never be satisfied. No one is safe as long as he and his children walk this earth."

Father Trahan listened to everything she had to say and felt the anticipation building. This may be a lucky break for them, "Do you know where I can find him so that he can be stopped?"

Stacie shook her head, "I am sorry Father, but I do not. I agree that he must be stopped, but I did not think to ask him where he was staying. These recent murders were what made me realize that he must be stopped. He is taunting you, but he is also letting the world know of our existence. There are already whispers among our community that they aren't happy with his ways. Several have talked among themselves about bringing Joshua down."

Father Trahan asked, "Do you believe that these members of your community will join our team?"

"Mais non, Father. They don't want anyone to know of their existence. I have talked to them, and they want their identities kept secret. You see, Father, some are very prominent citizens here in New Orleans and they do not want it known that they are vampires."

"Okay, so do you think they would consider working with us if we kept their identities a secret? I can let you know what we have planned, assuming that you prove your trust, and we can make all of our plans that way. This way each tactical team knows what the other is doing at all times, so no one gets caught in the cross hairs."

Stacie listened to what he had to say, "I have to talk to the others, but I am sure we can work out something along those lines. These vampires want everything returned to the way it was."

Father Trahan contemplated out loud, "How is it that your existence has gone unknown?"

"Being newly turned, I wondered the same thing. One of the other vampires in the carnival told me that she believed vampires operate on a different plane of existence. I'm not sure how true that is. I sometimes wonder if it has more to do with humans not wanting to believe that monsters live amongst them or that they refuse to believe that pure evil exists. It's similar to a serial killer who hides their existence from friends and family. They all swear they never suspected him of doing something like that. However, I suspect they refuse to let themselves believe it, not that they didn't want to believe it. Who wishes to envision their next door neighbor of being able to commit a heinous crime?"

Father Trahan advised her, "I hate to tell you this, my child, but you have joined our team, whether you want to or not. I believe for the time being though it is safer for you not to let anyone else know you are a vampire."

"I agree Father Trahan. Some of your members might not be keen on joining ranks with the likes of me."

"No, my child, I don't believe that is the case. We have a rather unique group that you may fit in with more comfortably than you believe. I am worried that there is a traitor among my team, and I would hate to see him tell your master that you are helping us. For now, you and I are the only ones who should know about your addition to the team. I could not bear to have your death on my hands."

Father Trahan heard her gasp, "You believe that there is already a vampire in your group?" This was one reason Stacie did not want to get involved. She witnessed first hand what Joshua could do to those who betrayed him. She had no desire to see that happen to her.

"No, I do not believe that this is a vampire. I suspect Bianca and your master have a spy in our midst."

"Who is Bianca? I have not heard her name before."

"Bianca is a voodoo priestess that we believe teamed up with the vampire who ran the carnival."

"Joshua may not be the vampire you are looking for then Father. He is peculiar about those around him. He always had to be the one in charge."

"We believe that both are leading the other on. Bianca has no plans on keeping Joshua around and vice versa."

"Father, if that is the case, then you must be very careful. Joshua can read minds very well. He is probably already aware of the fact that this Bianca plans on betraying him, so I am sure he has set up some safeguards. Joshua has many talents he keeps hidden from the world. We were only privy to a few. I am not sure what happened to the carnival rides or if the vile creatures are even still trapped in the rides, but they were there."

"So you do know about the souls trapped in the carnival rides?"

Stacie bowed her head, "It is not something I am proud of, but I do know about the souls that Joshua trapped. I tried to do research, but I have not found anything that could be of use. There is little information about these mythical

creatures and even less about freeing souls trapped by
them."

"But these souls were trapped by a creature and not a
spell?"

"There may be a spell to keep the creatures and perhaps
the souls captured in the mirrors. I do know that the
creatures were the ones who caught the souls for Joshua. I
cannot be sure, but I suspect that Joshua still has one
capturing souls for him."

If only they'd known of this one's existence earlier, but at
least the souls were freed. It was also useful knowing that
Joshua still had a soul collector in his possession.

As Stacie and Father Trahan talked about Joshua and
vampires, she started to realize she may be no better than
Joshua himself. She turned women without their
knowledge into the very thing she had become. She never
considered that they may not want this life. Should she
have given them a chance to accept their fate? As Stacie
pondered what mistakes she may have made, Father
Trahan interrupted her train of thought. "I have something
I need to ask you, but this must be kept in the strictest of
confidence. If you were given the chance to be turned back
into a mortal would you?"

That comment floored Stacie. She was dead; her soul
claimed by Joshua. That just wasn't possible, was it? If it
were possible, could she give up this life? "I don't know
Father Trahan. I have come to accept my fate. I have done
things that I am not proud of."

"My child, I understand what I am asking is frightening and very uncertain, but please think about what I am telling you. I know someone who may have isolated the vampire gene. It may merely be a virus that can be eradicated."

The revelation blew Stacie away. Could she give up this new life she had grown accustomed to?

Chapter 41

Dr. Calvin Ortego met his wife, Irene, at the doctor's office. When he received the call from Irene that Dr. Babin wanted to meet with the both of them, dread settled deep in the pit of his stomach. He could hear the fear in his beloved wife's voice. She'd complained of headaches for years, but lately the headaches were worse. When she started complaining of seeing flashes of light with the headaches, Calvin begged her to go see a neurologist. They married over twenty-five years ago, and he couldn't imagine spending a day of his life without her. She was what made his world go round.

Dr. Babin met them in the waiting room, "Calvin and Irene, thank you for coming in together. Let's go on back to my office, shall we?"

As they followed the doctor to his office, Calvin could see the news in Dr. Babin's eyes. After taking their seats, Dr. Babin looked Irene directly in her eyes, "I am sorry Irene, but you have brain cancer. It appears to be in the early stages, but we will know more after a few tests."

Calvin saw his wife swoon and wrapped his arm around her for moral support. As he listened to everything the doctor had to say, Calvin thought about the vampire DNA he had back at the office. Could he do that to his wife? Could he infect her with that strain to keep her alive for eternity? Or could he possibly make a superior strain of the Vampire DNA that would keep his wife alive forever without turning her into a blood sucking creature?

When he and Irene arrived home, he went directly into his home office and pored over the data they had retrieved so far. The answer had to be in here. He'd dabbled in genetics and blood born pathogens years ago when there was a fear of bioterrorism. He hoped that what he knew was enough to help him do what he planned.

***

As Dr. Ortego walked into his office at the morgue, Father Trahan called, "Dr. Ortego, I may have someone who can provide you with a good sample of vampire DNA. She will come see you tonight after everyone leaves."

As Dr. Ortego listened to what Father Trahan had to say, he wondered if last night's prayers were answered.

As the night progressed, Dr. Ortego feared Father Trahan's guest chose not to come. Suddenly a woman appeared out of nowhere. Stacie looked him over, "Dr. Ortego?"

"Yes, Father Trahan told me you may be able to help us with the vampire DNA."

Stacie held out her arm, "Please, whatever you do, I don't want my name associated with this. I have too much at stake for it to become known I am involved. You have no idea just how deadly Joshua can be."

Dr. Ortego looked at her with surprise in his eyes, "You are a vampire?"

"You have nothing to fear Dr. Ortego. I won't harm you."

He shook his head, "No, I'm not afraid, just surprised is all."

As Dr. Ortego took a blood sample, she could sense sorrow about him. His thoughts seemed to intrude on her without any probing. She reached out and took his hand in hers. "Dr. Ortego, I am truly sorry to hear about your wife, but please think about what you are about to do. Death would be better than a life without a soul. I was going to hell already, but if you love your wife as much as I think you do, you don't want to inflict her with this life."

Dr. Ortego felt the tears building in his eyes and looked away. There had to be an answer in this vampire DNA.

Chapter 42

For the last couple of hours, Antoinette had sat on this front porch listening as the frogs croaked in a deep chant from the bayou. As she went over everything she'd learned today, the night sky seemed to grow darker. For the first time, she felt that there were ominous shadows lurking in the dark, watching and waiting to strike.

When the area grew silent, Antoinette wondered if the frogs sensed a predator was near. The full moon illuminated the swamp of twisted cypress trees that dripped with Spanish moss. For the first time, the moss took on a sinister appearance. What she had once found peaceful looked like haunted ghouls shivering in the breeze. Somewhere in the night a whippoorwill sang out, and her grand'mere's warning that death was near resonated in her mind.

Her mind swam with wild visions of apocalyptic horror as she stared out into the darkness of the night. Suddenly, she sensed evil lurking about the swamp, moving across the murky water. It was a dark evil.

A vision appeared before her, one that made her hair stand on end. The image was so grotesque that she wanted to look away. The vision called out to her with a voice that chilled her to the bone. "Soon our time will be near." The creature's eyes pierced her with hatred. Its mouth snarled at her; its fangs gleamed in the moonlight.

She shook her head as the image disappeared. How did this creature even know about her? Father Trahan couldn't be the one on the same side of this demon? He seemed so vehement that evil must not win. If it was not him, then who could it be? Now she was positive that she must join this fight. She would not let someone try to scare her off with threats.

Once the image disappeared into the night, the sounds of nature returned once more.

***

Hutch settled into bed with her eBook reader and found that she was already dozing off. She wanted to wait for Mike to get home, but her body craved sleep. No sooner than she drifted off into slumber, the doorbell rang. As she stumbled to the door, she figured Mike forgot his house keys once again.

Without looking through the peephole, she opened the door expecting to see Mike waiting for her. Instead of Mike, a man was standing there leering at her. There was something mesmerizing about this man. Hutch could merely stand there and stare at him.

His dark eyes seemed to glitter in the moonlight. His clothes fit him like a glove, showing off his perfect, lean form. From the doorway, she could smell his intoxicating cologne. As she took in a deep breath, attempting to draw in more of that enticing smell she caught a whiff of something else and frowned. There was an undertone to the cologne that was entirely unpleasant. The smell reminded her of death and decay.

Instinctively, she knew that this man was more than he exuded. He extended a hand to Hutch, and she stepped further into the house. If this man was who she thought he was and what she learned was true, then he couldn't come in unless she asked him to. She hoped the salt and holy water she'd placed around each of the window sills and doorways helped to keep her safe inside of her house.

A chill washed over her as he smiled, "Good evening, Detective Hutcherson. I hope I didn't disturb your slumber. I wonder if I could come in and talk with you?"

Hutch noticed when he spoke, he had a hint of a Southern accent and his words sounded almost like a song. The way he talked hypnotized her. She tried to break the trance as he watched her every movement, waiting for her to invite him in.

She shook her head, "No, I don't think so. We both know that you coming into my house and talking isn't what you have in mind."

He dropped his fake smile and fury flashed across his face. It was a ghastly expression of anger that sent a chill of fear down Hutch's spine. She used the door almost as a shield as she stepped behind it. She prayed that Mike would be home soon to protect her if this creature decided to make a move on her tonight.

In an instant, the anger was replaced by another smile; one that was almost sincere looking and hypnotic. Hutch began to feel groggy, and all she wanted was to go back to bed. She found herself drawn into his eyes, as he spoke in a soft voice, "Let me in, Detective Hutcherson. I just want to talk to you."

His voice hypnotized her, made her want to let him in. Her thoughts trailed off, and she couldn't break away from his intense stare.

He leaned in closer to her, "Come on, Detective Hutcherson, you know you want to find out about me. Now is your chance. I am a very busy person, though, and I may not give you this opportunity again."

She opened her mouth to tell him something when a cold breeze blew across her. A voice whispered in her ear, "You know better than to listen to him. Shut the door and lock it."

The voice in her ear shook her out of her trance. She went to shut the door, but he put one of his feet in the doorway to prevent it from closing. Terror filled her as she saw the rage in his glittering black eyes. She felt the anger from him rippling through her body.

Needing to rid him from her place, she informed him once more, "No! Go away. Leave!"

"I will be back Detective Hutcherson. I know where you and your boyfriend live. Maybe, I should wait for him to come home. I am famished and would enjoy a late night snack."

Hutch slammed the door and leaned against the closed door as she took in deep breaths to calm her racing heart. She made sure the door was locked and swore that the vampire was out there laughing. She was too afraid to look through the peephole to find out. She must call Mike and warn him before he came home.

After talking to Mike, she sat in a recliner in the living room and waited for her pulse to return to normal. She grabbed one of the blankets on the couch and decided to wait for Mike right there.

It wasn't long before she heard the front door opening. She grabbed her gun out of instinct. Mike sensed that she was there, informing her as he opened the door, "It's just me Hutch. I didn't see your friend outside waiting for me. He must have wanted to spook you."

She ran into his open arms, "Well, he did. Thankfully, I remembered reading somewhere that you have to invite them in, and it must be true because when I refused he became furious."

Even safely wrapped in Mike's arms, Hutch found it difficult to sleep. When she finally fell asleep, her dreams were full of monsters with claw like hands and glowing eyes. This case was beginning to get to her.

***

Joshua whistled a happy little tune as he walked down the street. He considered waiting for the boyfriend to return, but then thought better of it. Detective Hutcherson was sure to have called the boyfriend as soon as she slammed the door in his face. He suspected the man was ready to strike at any moment and was prepared to kill a vampire instantly. No, when he walked up to the man to kill him, he wanted to have the upper hand, just as he had with the beautiful Detective Hutcherson tonight.

He'd learned one important fact; Detective Hutcherson could put up a wall between him and his prey. The only question was if it was her or did she have some outside interference? Could it be that there was someone helping her block him from her mind and his black magic charms?

He needed to find out if he had any hope of killing her. He could just imagine stealing her soul and drinking in her powers. It sent a shiver of anticipation through him when he thought of having her become one with him. He must take it slowly with Detective Hutcherson though; she knew too much about vampires and their behaviors. She must have found someone to inform her about vampires and their powers, but whom? He couldn't see books having knowledge of the information she knew.

Just the thought of draining Detective Hutcherson's blood and stealing her soul caused his fangs to throb. He could taste her on his tongue. He knew she would be delicious.

As he made his way down the streets of this small subdivision in New Orleans, he smelled the blood of potential prey all around him. Unfortunately, most were tucked safely in their home, which was one of the reasons he never hunted in small subdivisions. As a group of teenagers drove past him in their car, he forced himself to hold back and not tear the doors from the hinges to feed on them. Hunting too close to the good detective was dangerous. While feeding this near her, she may sense him and come after him while his guard was down.

When he made it to the French Quarter, he found what he was searching for. A man was passed out in the alley. Even in deep slumber, the man still clutched the now empty liquor bottle as if it was his most prized possession. As Joshua looked down at the filthy man, a wicked smile came across him. He could feed on this man right here, and no one would know the difference. He would be doing the town a favor by ridding the streets of the likes of him. He wouldn't be missed, and the man would satisfy the hunger he'd felt since leaving Detective Hutcherson's house.

When he nudged the man with his shoe, the man never budged or let out a moan. Once Joshua was confident there would be no noise emitting from him, he lifted him up off the ground to feed. It wasn't until the man was in the air that he half opened his eyes, "Whatcha doing man? I was sleeping. Leave me alone."

Without answering, Joshua pierced the drunk's neck with his sharp fangs. Rich, warm blood filled his mouth. The man quivered and gurgled under his grasp. Joshua gripped the drunk's neck more securely and drained every last drop of blood from the man. As Joshua savored the last drop, he could tell the man had just drunk alcohol. His blood was heavily tainted with the whiskey. Still unsatisfied with the snack, he threw the man down. He didn't care if the police found the body. Detective Hutcherson already knew Joshua was out tonight.

In search of another snack, Joshua left the alley and headed to Bourbon Street. A shadow from an alleyway called out to him, "You look like you could use a little company honey?"

He eyed her up and down, "Perhaps." She looked into his eyes and smiled. He could smell her blood as it coursed through her body. Maybe this was what he needed to satisfy his hunger. She was normally not the type he fed on. She was too skinny, and he could tell by her teeth she was addicted to meth, but her blood beckoned him.

His eyes wandered over her body once more. He shuddered at this working girl's skimpy outfit. She had easy access for her customers and to show off her wares or lack thereof.

As his eyes turned a deep shade of black, he watched the fear build up inside of her eyes. "You know, honey, that's okay. I think I misread your needs."

When his cold hand grasped her wrist to pull her close to him, she cringed in fear. "Look mister, why don't you just move on? I am sure there are other girls out there who can satisfy your needs."

"But you are right here, so warm and willing. No, you will do nicely."

As he dragged her deeper into the shadows of the alley, he laughed at her futile attempts to free herself from his grasp. He intruded into her mind, forcing her to bend to his will. He laughed at how easy these mere mortals were to control. She didn't even struggle against the invisible bonds he placed around her. As he fed on this young woman, he noticed the blood didn't satisfy his current needs. He preferred to feed on those that had an intricate, perplexing structure to their mind. He found it enticing to feed on someone while infiltrating their mind. This young woman's mind was blank and there was nothing for him to read. He suspected that the intriguing Detective Hutcherson's mind could keep him entertained long after he'd drained her body of blood.

Joshua drank ferociously at her neck as he held her dying body, all the while he envisioned the tantalizing Detective Hutcherson instead of this woman. Feeling powerful and euphoric after draining the last drop of blood from this woman, he dropped her unceremoniously in the alley and headed out into the night once more. Sated, he briskly walked back home before sunrise.

Chapter 43

Guy slammed down the shot glass on the bar as he thought about the day, or rather night, that they'd had. He had seen deaths and worked plenty of crime scenes before, but none of the others were like what he witnessed recently. The bodies were almost mummified, but they were only dead for a short time, according to witnesses who'd just seen the victims.

Vampires drained bodies of their blood, but this was as if their very being was sucked out of them. He shuddered at the thought. He couldn't imagine the pain they must have endured. He hoped that it had been a quick death. If this was their voodoo priestess testing her powers; he doubted that the death was quick or painless.

As he continued to stare at the now empty shot glass, his vision blurred. He could no longer remember how many he'd had or how long he had sat here drinking the time away. He shouldn't be drinking. They needed to keep their wits about them, but tonight he wanted to forget, if only for a short while.

He waved the approaching bartender away and headed for the door. Any more shots of whiskey and he would not be able to walk into work in a few short hours.

Usually, Guy loved to listen to the sounds of the city, but tonight the sounds were muted and eerie. Outside, he shivered in the night air. It wasn't cold outside, yet he was suddenly freezing. Since the cop in him never truly stopped working, he looked around. The street was darker than normal, even at this hour. From what he observed, the street lights in this area were out. He should call it in. This was a heavy tourist area, and the criminals were always looking to cause trouble.

As he continued walking, the night air mixed with the various odors wafting from the surrounding bars and restaurants. Out of the corner of his eye, he caught a movement and went on full alert. The hair on his arms rose as a woman stepped out of the shadows, calling out to him, "Hello, handsome."

Her sultry voice invaded his senses. She was more intoxicating than the alcohol he'd just consumed. His gut warned him to walk away, "Not interested," he muttered as he continued toward home.

She grabbed his arm and forced him to look at her. He looked into her eyes and was instantly mesmerized. Her vivid green eyes drew him in. She was dressed in a long black flowing dress that blew seductively in the wind.

Instinctively, he stepped away from her. His body still tingled from where she had pressed up against him. He found it hard to fight the temptation not to pull her close to him. When he walked into the cemetery, he realized that he had been retreating from her without even knowing it. Even though his other senses were drawn to her, something inside of him was warning him to stay away from her.

Suddenly, she was standing next to him. She placed a hand on each side of his head, but before she could press her body up to him, he slipped away from her embrace. If he had any intimate contact with her, he feared he wouldn't have the strength to walk away.

She laughed seductively, "And here I thought I found just the man I needed to satisfy all of my desires."

He drew in a ragged breath. He found himself wishing he had not walked into the bar tonight. The alcohol slowed down his thinking and lowered his inhibitions. His libido was telling him to go for it, but his gut told him to run like hell.

As the urge to sweep her away to his apartment became overwhelming, he gritted his teeth. He found the strength deep inside to walk away. He could hear her calling out to him, "We shall meet again cher."

When he turned back to tell her not in this lifetime, he found that she had disappeared into the shadows once again. As he walked back to his house, the street lights turned on, as if someone suddenly flipped a switch. How the hell did that happen?

Chapter 44

Jonas woke up to find himself lying on a freshly disturbed grave. He was in the middle of an older cemetery. The graves and tombstones around him appeared to be ancient. He couldn't understand why he was here and why there would be a fresh grave in an older cemetery.

How had he escaped the torture pit he was trapped in for eternity? He waited to see if this was a new torture the devil had come up with. He listened to the sounds of the night, waiting to hear the screams of the damned ringing in his ears. There was nothing but silence in the cemetery.

The streetlights that lined the cemetery helped to illuminate his way. The wind blowing through the ancient oak trees gave the place a more serene look. He still couldn't shake the feeling that he was being watched.

Jonas still couldn't figure out why he was here. Why was he released from the hell he'd remained trapped in for decades now? Jonas could not deny he belonged there. He killed, or more importantly was ordered to kill, hundreds of individuals. Jonas would have done this regardless of an order; he enjoyed killing. He committed evil, true evil, in his lifetime. It didn't bother him when his momma told him that pure evil claimed his soul. She even asked the local Catholic priest to perform an exorcism on her only son. He spat in the priest's face. No matter how hard they tried, they could not vanquish the evil residing inside of him. Jonas embraced the evil, welcoming it to be a part of his soul. He developed a taste for killing early on, and the rush he received from it was like none other. He started out small with the kittens he found abandoned in the neighborhood and moved up the ladder from there.

As he walked through the cemetery, he wondered how many of these bodies were here from his hands. He kept a sharp lookout for dark shadows. Once they realized he was missing, the shadows would come to drag him back to hell. He wished he knew how or why he was released from his prison.

Had he somehow done something wrong to cause him to be rejected from the devil's playground? He didn't see the devil releasing him or anyone for that matter. Sooner or later someone would come after him. Assuming something didn't drag him back to the pits of hell, he needed to find shelter and then he must make plans. As long as he was back on earth, he may as well continue his favorite hobby. There was nothing saying while he was here he couldn't wreak havoc.

A high pitched screech pierced the night sky, and Jonas froze. Panic moved through his body as the screech echoed through the air once more. He searched the shadows; he knew what made that noise. It was from one of the devil's minions, and it sounded as if it was coming directly for him. He looked for something to use as a weapon. He refused to go down without a fight. He was used to being the one that was the hunter, the one who stalked, cornered and destroyed the prey. He didn't like having the shoe on the other foot.

He heard the wings of the devil's minion drawing closer. The air chilled as it approached. Not wanting to be out in the open, he fled. As he made it to the edge of the cemetery, he found the gates were locked tight. As he faced the bars that keep him on the inside with the dead, he gripped the bars and looked upwards to heaven. The stars overhead twinkled like diamonds against a black velvet backdrop. He could hear the demon closing in on him.

Suddenly, a voice pierced the night. On the other side of the cemetery, the devil himself manifested. "Jonas, I set you free. You have a short time to prove your worth. So far, I and those who serve me are unable to infiltrate the group that means to stop my plans. I am giving you a chance to do my bidding. If you infiltrate the group and let me know what they have planned, you will be rewarded with your own legion. You will be free to walk this earth, and create your own living hell. I know how much you like to torture and kill; you will be free to do so. You must find Father Mark Trahan; he is the leader of this group. Be careful, they have a medium in the group. She can see a person's soul. If she discovers what you are, it will be the end of you. Don't let me down."

Before Jonas could reply, the night went quiet once again, and the locked gate opened. As he left the cemetery, he breathed in the night air. It was the first time he had inhaled clean, fresh air into his lungs in a very long time. It took him a while to get used to the stench of Hell. It was the most nauseating stench that could invade one's senses. It burned the back of his throat and traveled down to his gut. It was a smell he would not soon forget; one that would help him in distinguishing the devil's minions.

He knew that there was a chance this was also the devil's way of taunting him more. This respite could merely be a way to heighten the torture. The devil could be giving him a taste of freedom before he revitalized the nightmare he lived once more. The acclimatization that he'd finally managed would be wiped clean, and his body would go into shock again.

As Jonas made his way to the church, he took on a more appealing human form. When he arrived at the church, he smiled at confirmation that there were still a few lights on. The good Father must still be here, more than likely preparing for the next day's Mass. He watched the church for a moment.

Walking up to the front doors, he wondered if they were locked. He'd heard rumors that some churches were locking their doors due to vandalism. It pleased him to no end that even the church could be desecrated by robbery. The world was slowly turning into a living hell on earth. As Jonas pulled the door handles, he found that the doors opened with ease. Inside the quiet church, one small security light shined in the sacristy behind the altar. A few votive candles were lit and a few small spotlights cast shadows on the pillars that made up the interior of this century old church.

He noticed the sacristy door open and out of curiosity, he looked in. Inside the softly illuminated room were a few altar gowns hanging on a back wall and a small oak desk.

***

Father Trahan was sitting in his office preparing his sermon. He should be heading back to the rectory, but it was as if something was holding him back here. As Father Trahan finished up, he heard the door open to the church.

Father Trahan stepped out of his office as an unkempt man headed straight for his office. Something about the man appeared unusual, but nothing he could pinpoint. Jonas looked at the priest, "Are you Father Trahan?"

"Yes, I am. How can I help you my child?"

"Father, I believe it is I who can help you. I was sent here by St. Michael to help you."

Father Trahan looked at this man skeptically. He was not what you would envision an angel of God to look like, but angels could come in many forms. "Did St. Michael say what you are to help with?"

Jonas looked at the priest, unsure if he believed him. "I am one of St. Michael's chosen angels, Father. St. Michael said that you needed an army to defeat the evil that is plaguing this town. He wants to warn you Father that demons can take all shapes so trust no one. The army is growing Father; they are gathering strength. Soon they will be ready to strike. You must be prepared."

Father Trahan looked the man up and down before opening his office door. If this man were sent to kill him, he would soon find out. However, this man could be speaking the truth, and he couldn't take the chance of sending away someone who could help their war. After what he'd learned recently, he didn't doubt this man was sent by St. Michael. After all, the devil had demons walking this earth, so why shouldn't angels. Father Trahan planned on asking a few questions to ascertain if this man was truly an angel. Although, there was a chance the demons knew just as much about religion as angels.

***

Jonas settled into the room that Father Trahan offered him as his human body began to feel fatigued. He forgot what it was like to be a mortal, having been dead for such a long time. He never liked to sleep. While sleeping, the demons could come for you. His body, in desperate need of rest, slipped into sleep's warm embrace. He felt himself tumble into the depths of slumber as his limbs grew limp, his heart slowed, and he lost consciousness.

Screams echoed in his mind as he saw the images of the faces he'd killed. They reached and grabbed for him, trying to drag him back to hell. It was as if their souls sensed he was back on this earth and wanted to vanquish him from here. A figure rose from the depths of his mind. The demon drew nearer, cloaked in a dark robe. Its sleeves billowed down to the ground, forming a four foot train behind it. The demon and the cloak hovered just above the earth, never touching the ground. Draped across the demon's shoulders was the lifeless form of a man; his skin pale and flaccid. The man's face was turned away from Jonas so he could not see who it was.

When the demon pulled its hood back, instead of a face it was a myriad of creatures, circling, swirling and always changing. This particular demon never revealed its face to Jonas, but when it spoke, it was the voice of a female, "Jonas, soon you will come and follow me. Together we can rule this world."

In his sleep, he continued to listen to the ramblings of this woman. Was she the one who was doing the devil's bidding? If only he could see her face, he would know who to look for. Somehow he must find her. He watched as she slowly receded from his mind.

***

Bianca looked down at the sleeping man. Hearing a noise down the hall, she quickly left the room. She saw his true soul and knew he would be perfect to join her army. The devil believed he needed someone in Father Trahan's group to find out their plans. Even he didn't realize just how powerful she had become. He had nothing to fear, she would succeed. This would be her hell on earth. It annoyed her that the devil did not trust her and sent others to help her. She did not need him choosing others to help her take over this area. Once she took over New Orleans, she had no plans of stopping. She would rule the world; everyone would do her bidding. She'd worked too hard to get here, and it was almost time to unleash her hell on earth.

Chapter 45

Fog slithered in through the window, filling Guy's bedroom. He stirred and rolled over before falling back into a deep slumber. The seductive woman from the Quarter entered his dreams once again. She called him, beckoning him into her open arms and pleading for him to love her. She whispered his name, her voice sultry and tempting. There was something else there though. It was as if her voice was iced with a cool twinge of death.

She seemed to fill the night air, "Guy… Guy…"

This time he wouldn't resist her; he would give in to sweet temptation. He moved towards her; every step shifted from horror, desire, repulsion, and attraction. As he moved closer to her, he could smell her very seductive perfume, but another smell was there. It was one that he knew well; the air was laced with the scent of rotting flesh.

Ignoring the warning bells going off in his head, he moved even closer to her. Her exquisite body was bathed in moonlight. He caught a glimpse of her shadow and stopped for a moment. The shadow was twisted with gnarled limbs and stringy, matted hair.

She sensed his uneasiness and whispered into the night air once more, "Guy… Guy…" He pulled her into his arms, feeling her warm breath wash over him. Her arms hugged him tightly, bringing him even closer to her. There was no escape now.

Her hands ran through his hair and she peered deep into his eyes. As he stared at her emerald green eyes, he felt himself falling deep into their abyss, losing himself. They were so alluring that he found himself powerless to withstand her. When she smiled at him, he could smell death on her breath. Blood dripped from her ivory fangs, sharpened to a fine point.

As she bent his neck back, he went limp in her arms. Her mouth opened wide, bringing with it his death and damnation. He closed his eyes as she clamped down on his neck. Warm blood flowed down his neck.

With each drop of blood she took from his body, he felt his life leave him. He could smell his blood on her breath. With crimson stained lips, she told him, "You cannot fight me. I am too strong. Join me, mon cher, and I will give you eternal life."

Startled, Guy woke up from his restless slumber drenched in a cold sweat. Every pore seemed to be drowning in a sea of sweat. His hands ran over his face as he attempted to wipe away the sweat dripping in his eyes. He kicked off the damp sheets.

Sitting on the edge of his bed, he listened to the night sounds. In his mind, he heard the cries of the doomed that were held by the voodoo priestess and vampire.

He was fairly certain that this woman was the voodoo priestess. Why did she start tormenting his dreams? He had no gifts like Hutch. What did she want with him?

He walked naked to the window and stared out into the night. A sliver of a moon hung high in the air while dark shadows danced across the street outside.

Chapter 46

As Guy watched the team train, he couldn't believe that almost a month had passed since this elite group was formed. He feared that it could be any day now that they would be forced to test their effectiveness. Even without Hutch giving updates, he could feel a change in the air outside. There was a negative energy hanging over New Orleans, as if a hurricane was forming out in the gulf. At least they were somewhat prepared.

Mike walked up to Guy, "Mon ami, I don't trust this new one, Jonas."

"I thought it was just me. Something bothers me about the man, but I can't put my finger on it."

"My primary concern is that he isn't afraid of what we are up against. He has a confidence about him that is unsettling. It is as if he takes pleasure in killing."

Guy nodded his head in agreement. He hadn't been able to obtain any background information on this man. They had no clues as to his past life which could leave the team vulnerable. "I have seen it in his eyes. I don't find him trustworthy."

"I will keep an eye on him. He likes to lurk in the shadows, listening to what is being said. Maybe we can drop some misinformation to see what happens."

As Guy and Mike walked back to the group, Guy felt Jonas's eyes burn into his back. He avoided turning back and staring at him. There was no doubt that Jonas worked hard.

He had mastered every weapon and could spout off any information they needed about demons and religion, but there was still something off about him. A twinge of impending danger raced through him suddenly.

***

As Father Trahan watched the team leave to return to their homes, a wave of sadness came over him. It settled deep inside of his heart, invading every pore and every corner of his mind. They made an impressive team and were more than capable, but there was a chance that some, or maybe all of them, would not survive. He prayed once more that he was not sending them off to their deaths. He feared that he might be leading lambs to the slaughter.

As he stepped outside to walk back to the rectory, he noticed how the city seemed to have lost its civility. He didn't look at it with the same eyes. The buildings now appeared old with damaged brick facades crumbling and breaking.

He must not allow evil to win. They would defeat the evil that was growing and waiting to take over New Orleans.

Out of nowhere, and before Father Trahan could even register what was happening, a creature stepped in front of him. With a lurid expression on its face and blood on its chin, the creature smiled at Father Trahan, mocking him. Father Trahan said the St. Gertrude prayer for the poor soul this creature had just fed on. It bothered him that this vile creature desecrated this holy ground by feeding on church grounds.

With quick reflexes, Father Trahan reached into his pocket and pulled out the holy water. Without even thinking, he doused it over the vampire. Instantaneously, the creature dropped to its knees and covered its face with quivering hands. Father Trahan stepped back and recited the St. Michael prayer as the creature's flesh boiled and bubbled. A deep, guttural scream erupted from deep inside the creature, and in the next instant, the creature burst into dust. Father Trahan made the sign of the cross as the particles of dust floated away.

Instead of going back to the rectory, Father Trahan walked back inside to call Guy. "Guy, I know you are just getting home, but I just had a visit by a vampire."

He heard Guy take in a deep breath before asking, "Are you all right? Did it get away?"

"Your training came in very handy, mon ami. The holy water worked well, but we need something that works faster. It took a minute or so before the vampire died."

Guy didn't like hearing that the holy water took a little while to kill the vampire. Then it dawned on him, "Wait a second, Father, did you say that the vampire came after you while leaving the church?"

"Yes. I fear that the creature was feeding here on the grounds."

Guy swore under his breath, "Father, I don't like that they were this close to the church. It also means that they more than likely know where we are meeting."

"It means that there are no hallowed grounds for these creatures." Father Trahan left out that he already knew vampires could walk in and out of the church freely; his visit with Stacie verified that fact. He kept praying for her lost soul and that she would let him help her.

Guy exclaimed, "Father, if the vampire did just feed then there is a chance a body is near. I will call Mike and Hutch. We will be there shortly."

***

It didn't take long for the three to return. After doing a thorough search of the grounds and not finding a body, they wondered if Father Trahan was mistaken about the vampire feeding on a victim here. Hutch tried to focus in on the area again. She walked around attempting to read the energy. She finally found what she was looking for, "The body is in the bell tower."

Neither man bothered to question her. They learned that her "instincts" were usually right. As they made their way up the narrow staircase that led to the bell tower, they shooed away a couple of pigeons. Hutch wrinkled her nose as the smell of pigeon poop assaulted her nose. But the poop would smell better than what they were about to encounter.

As soon as they opened the door, she was proven correct. Inside the bell tower was Jonas, and there was a note left on his body. Hutch didn't need to read the note to know what it said. The master vampire invaded her mind with ease, "Tell your Father he may have taken my child, but I will soon take one of his children. The devil himself learned tonight that I don't need him to send one of his minions to do my work."

Before Hutch could read the master's thoughts, he was gone, "We may be in trouble y'all. Joshua is not happy that Father Trahan killed one of his children. I believe Joshua killed Jonas as a message to the Devil."

"So Joshua sent someone to kill Jonas?"

Hutch shook her head, "No, there is another body here. The dead vampire merely carried Jonas here. Jonas was killed by Joshua so he could claim the soul and Jonas's powers."

Mike let out a long whistle, "We are getting ready to have one hell of a battle on our hands. The killing of Jonas will send the devil into a rage."

The second body was found tucked in a corner of the bell tower. It may not have been one of their team, but an unfortunate individual lost his soul.

***

As Mike called the dispatcher to have crime scene techs sent out, Guy walked downstairs to tell Father Trahan the bad news. Mike looked over at Hutch after he got off of the phone and winced when he saw her face. She was pale as a ghost. He didn't like that the creature could just slip into her mind without any warning. He was becoming bolder with his attempts and now that he also has Jonas's powers they may be in a lot of trouble.

As they waited for the CSI team to arrive, Mike thought about everything Father Trahan just went through. Since the beginning, he had claimed that he would have no problem killing a vampire or even a zombie, but now that he had done it, did he still feel the same way? Father Trahan had taken a vow before God and killing was a mortal sin; although, a vampire was already dead. Being a cop, Mike knew how hard it was to kill someone. It wasn't that long ago that Guy, Hutch and he confronted the carnival of vampires. They each looked a vampire in the eyes and sent their bodies straight to hell where they belonged.

Chapter 47

Father Trahan placed his clergy case on his neatly made bed and slowly opened it. There were a variety of items he was given for this task at hand. He carefully removed the long purple chasuble and put it over his black attire. The chasuble was trimmed in white satin and had two long gold crosses on each breast. Next, he grabbed a small crucifix that was wrapped in purple cloth. Before placing it in his pocket, he kissed it. Finally, he took his bible and held it to the heavens while saying a quick novena. Once done, he kissed that as well.

Father Metz placed his hand on his shoulder, "It will be okay. The Lord is on our side."

***

The forest was blanketed in darkness. The moon hid behind the clouds, blocking out what little light there was in the dense swampland. Each member of the team wore night vision goggles so they could see what was around them. They were careful as to where they stepped, not wanting to step on a dead branch and have it snap, alerting the quarry to their presence. The forest was unnaturally silent tonight. The animals that usually roamed during the night were even leery of this area. Could they know what stalked these woods?

Mike Bailey looked over at Hutch to see how she was holding up. He was amazed at how calm she appeared as they waited for the unknown to take place. They'd prepared for this raid just as they'd prepared for the last attack with the vampires with one exception – they were more heavily armed this time. They had holy water, garlic juice soaked silver bullets, specially equipped ultraviolet tazer guns, crossbows armed with silver arrows, hand grenades, and various other weapons they may find useful. Mike even made sure he had wooden stakes in case they ran out of ammunition. They were walking blindly into the unknown here as no one had ever dealt with vampire zombies. There wasn't a website link where you could go to find out how to kill zombies much less vampires. There weren't even experts you could talk to regarding that subject. No, all they had was what Father Trahan dug up, which unfortunately wasn't much.

***

Hutch felt Mike watching her and tried not to look in his direction. She was holding on by a thread right now. There was a lot on the line tonight. She couldn't shake the feeling that this might be the last time she would see Mike. Could it be her recent vision would come true? Would the master vampire claim Mike's very soul?

As she looked around, she found it strange how in the dark of the night the swamp took on such a menacing appearance. The trees had an ominous look, as if they extended towards the sky with gnarled hands.

Each member of the SWAT team watched the dark crevasses of the forest for any signs of movement. They slowly ventured deeper into the marshland being careful with each step. They crossed one foot over the other as they took in everything. Suddenly, Hutch held up her hand.

They were not alone. The master vampire was extremely close.

They peered into the darkness. Tension charged the air. The silence around them became overwhelming. Hutch knew that at least a few of the vampires and other creatures were somewhere in this vicinity.

As they made their way deeper into the swamplands, the moon came out. Its silvery rays shined through some of the branches giving this particular area a creepy atmosphere.

As they moved forward, they were careful to scan not only nearby but into the distance as well. The night goggles were proving to be extremely effective. It was almost impossible for their eyes to miss a thing. As Hutch looked around at the group, she wondered if their nerves were strung as tight as hers.

Tonight they were fighting the unknown. They had no idea what they would be up against, if they would be outnumbered or even if they were walking into a trap. She sure hoped the voodoo priestess's spell worked. She cast a net spell that should effectively encase a ten mile area in a bubble. It should prevent any of the creatures in this particular area from escaping.

The main problem they found with the spell was it drained most of her powers, which almost rendered her useless in the fight they were about to become involved in. The other problem was that it also kept any of them from leaving the bubble; they would be trapped in here as well. When the spell was cast earlier, Mike warned everyone that they needed to be extremely cautious since animals become the most dangerous when trapped.

As they stopped once more to survey the area, Hutch sensed something up above them. She let out a gasp. Father Trahan followed her eyes and said a prayer for this poor woman. Above them in the trees, they found Stacie Allen. She yelled at them, "Do not stop to save me. Joshua is counting on it. You must keep going. I beg of you, do not stay here."

Hutch sensed that the attack was close. They were all on the defense and on edge. They were told under no circumstances should they separate from the crowd. That would mean certain death as they would be killed one by one.

Without warning, a creature moved quickly towards them. In one fluid motion, one of the SWAT team officers had his sight locked and fired. The bullet hit its mark, and the vampire exploded into dust.

Before the dust could settle, three more vampires emerged. They went down quickly. From behind several large trees emerged something resembling a human, but it was not quite human. They moved slower than the vampires. One of the SWAT team officers shot an arrow, and it hit the creature straight in the heart. Unlike the vampires, it didn't burst into dust particles and kept advancing on them.

This wasn't good. They were dealing with some kind of mutant vampire. These must be the vampire zombies they were warned about. Now, they must figure out how to kill these creatures. Another member of SWAT aimed his gun straight at the head of the zombie. The bullet hit the creature right between what should have been its eyes. As before, the creature kept advancing. Not wanting to take further chances, Mike picked up the hand grenade and threw it at the creatures. They exploded on contact. He called out to the other SWAT members, "Use the hand grenades on the zombies, save your bullets."

As if in slow motion, creatures exploded while vampires vaporized into tiny dust particles. No matter how many they killed, more came. At least the creatures weren't coming at them at once. Hutch knew that if they did then their chance of survival was next to nil. She prayed they'd brought enough grenades as more zombies approached.

Suddenly, the night went quiet, and the sky turned blood red as lightning flashed a brilliant blue in the sky. Thunder rumbled and shook the ground. The winds picked up as evil moved in. The air around them became thick and palpable with evil, making it difficult to breath. The creatures and vampires moved to the side as Bianca made her appearance.

***

Antoinette felt her strength improving and decided it was time to confront this woman. "You are playing a sick game with these souls that don't belong to you. I have come here to stop you."

Bianca let out a laugh that turned to a dangerous smile. As she spoke, her breath created a foul stench in the air. The potent, horrid odor made it difficult to stay focused. The air became frigid around them. "My magic is too strong for the likes of you."

Father Trahan once again picked up his Bible and prayed, "In the name of the Father and of the Son and of the Holy Spirit. Most glorious Prince of the heavenly armies, St. Michael the Archangel, defend us in battle and protect us against the wickedness and snares of the devil. May God rebuke him, we humbly pray. O Prince of the heavenly host by the power of God thrust into hell Satan and all the evil spirits who prowl about the world seeking the ruin of souls. Amen…."

Antoinette summoned her powers and began the chant that she had practiced. As she raised her arms to call forth the spirits, the wind picked up. Bianca sensed what Antoinette was attempting and threw a huge ball of fire at her.

Antoinette was prepared for Bianca's futile attempt to stop her and vanished from the area. Antoinette reappeared right behind Bianca and caught her off guard. She drove a bolt of lightning deep into Bianca's back, bringing the voodoo priestess to her knees.

Father Trahan and the others each continued to pray as Antoinette resumed her chant. Numerous bright balls of light filled the night sky and changed into ghostly white bodies in misty forms. The souls that Bianca captured were being freed by Antoinette. An unearthly scream pierced the night sky as those she tortured sought their own revenge; it chilled one's soul to be a witness to such a thing.

Over the next several hours, Father Trahan continued to read prayers from the gospel. Antoinette noticed a weakness in Bianca. She instructed Father Metz to sprinkle holy water on Bianca as the words of the Lord fell from his lips.

Bianca screamed out in pain as the water hit her skin. It burned like fire and smoke rose from her upon contact. Her voice elevated to a high pitched witch-like screech that made their ears bleed.

Hutch sensed Joshua's presence and picking up the crossbow, she took aim where she saw a ripple in the "net". Joshua's last sight on this earth was the smile on Hutch's face as she fired the arrow that sent him back to the fires of hell.

As Father Trahan looked around at the destruction, he said another Hail Mary. Mike broke the silence, "We need to make sure that there are no more surprises waiting for us." For the next several hours, they combed the swamps, making sure that no more vampires or zombies were lurking about, waiting to strike. It had been a long hard fight, but through it all, good triumphed over evil.

They finally found where Bianca lived deep in the swamp. You could sense her presence even though she was defeated. As Guy opened one of the doors to a makeshift shed, he hollered, "We need ambulances. Father Trahan, I believe they need your prayers."

In one of the tiny sheds, at least a dozen people were chained to the wall. One of the girls looked up with tears in her eyes, "Please, can you get us out of here before they come back?"

By the time crime scene techs and ambulances arrived, it was close to noon. They all agreed that everything needed to be wrapped up before nightfall. No one wanted to be out here in the woods after dark.

Those that survived being the vampire blood slaves were already being transported to the hospital. The crime scene techs were busy mapping out the area so that they knew where to search for bodies tomorrow. Father Trahan walked the perimeter sprinkling it with holy water and salt that he specially blessed for this very purpose. They had incense burning in the veve to send the evil spirits back to the pits of hell. Father Trahan had no doubt that the devil was unhappy with the outcome, and it wouldn't be long before he tried this once more.

Epilogue

Rayne Simoneaud was unable to find peace even though Bianca and Joshua were defeated. There was still an evil that lurked in the marshes and it had set its eyes on Grace Hutcherson. She must warn Grace before it came after her.

Rayne also must pay close attention to those vampires that Stacie Allen helped escape right before this purging. She couldn't stand to see certain brothers and sisters of hers killed because of their father's evil. She believed that there was a chance Dr. Ortego could cure them. Thankfully, there were only a handful that Stacie had rescued.

***

Dr. Ortego thought he was dreaming when he was awakened by banging on his front door that became more incessant. He called out, "I'm coming, keep your pants on."

As he opened the door, he was surprised to see several men and women standing at his door. A woman stepped forward, "Stacie sent us to you. She said that you could help us."

As Dr. Ortego looked at them, he wondered if this could be the answer to his wife's illness. He informed them, "Go home for now and meet me at the morgue tomorrow night at midnight."

Thank you!

Dear Reader,

Thank you for purchasing this book. I hope you enjoyed reading this novel as much as I enjoyed writing it.

It is important for me to hear what you think about the book. Your reviews give me inspiration in my future writings. You can leave a review on Amazon, Goodreads or Barnes and Noble.

Your thoughts and opinions mean a lot to me.

Please enjoy a sample of Haunted Visions. Detective Grace Hutcherson suddenly discovers her psychic ability is more pronounced. The dead call out to her, begging for her help. In order to stop the serial killer from taking more victims, she must learn how to use her new abilities. Her very life could depend on it.

Also, be sure to check out my website and social media sites for upcoming books and giveaways.

Sincerely,

Mary Theriot

Links

Website **www.maryreasontheriot.com**

Goodreads for reviews -
http://www.goodreads.com/MaryReasonTheriot

Facebook - http://goo.gl/Sd0VgY
Twitter - @Mktheriot
Google+ - +MaryTheriot
YouTube - http://goo.gl/ErM1M6
Pinterest - http://www.pinterest.com/mktheriot
Blog Page - www.maryreasontheriot.me

Haunted Visions

By: Mary Reason Theriot

Prologue

The full moon did little to light the area. For the last two weeks, the security lights had been out in this particular area. No one bothered to replace them. She doubted the city even cared about replacing the blown light bulbs here. Hell, they were probably hoping that if they didn't replace the light bulbs the hookers would move on.

She let out an irritated sigh and unrolled her waistband. She hiked her skirt up another inch hoping to lure someone over, but there weren't many men out looking for companionship tonight. They were probably scared by the lack of lighting and being unable to see who they were picking up.

As she walked back to her hole of an apartment, a feeling of uneasiness came over her. She couldn't explain it, but something didn't feel right. She looked around nervously, but didn't see anyone else anywhere near. There was nothing but darkness in this particular area.

He hid in the safety of the shadows. The darkness of the night was his ally, his best friend, and his confidant. He was not afraid of the dark. He thrived in the darkness. He found safety in the shadows. In the shadows, he could watch and wait.

She never had a chance to scream before the arms reached out from the alley and dragged her into the darkness. He had been waiting and watching. She was too stunned to react at first. By the time she could utter a scream, it was too late. She felt the cold edge of the blade as it cut into her tender flesh. Her last thought was that no one would find her in this alleyway.

After each kill, he placed the precious contents he carefully collected into their respective jars, filling each jar with the liquid that would forever preserve them. After meticulously completing the task, he opened the hidden panel in the wall of his private sanctuary and placed the newly acquired trophies on the shelf. It was not until after this ritual was performed that he would completely surrender to the voices that raged in his head.

Before leaving his private sanctuary, he made sure the lock was securely latched. It wasn't until he knew that his mementos were locked away that he could leave this room. Even after this recent kill, the hunger started eating away at him again; it had become almost insatiable lately. It was too soon to hunt again. He pled with the voices to stay silent for a little while before he went out once again.

They refused to be silent. He slammed his fist down on the desk and smashed the glass containing his water. He inadvertently cut himself. He stood there and just watched as the blood flowed down his hand. It was thick and slowly congealing.

The voices mocked and laughed at him more. He trembled with hatred as he begged the voices to be silent. Suddenly, he caught a glimpse of himself in the mirror across the room. It was an old mirror that was tarnished from years of neglect. Yet his image sent a flood of memories through his mind, memories that he wished he could have long ago forgotten.

The ornate mirror hanging on the wall was one of his mother's most cherished possessions. It hung in this room like a shrine to her. It was tarnished and faded, but it still remained here in the house.

He backed away from the mirror as the image of his mother moved in behind him. Even after death, she still walked these halls. For some reason, the devil himself didn't want his mother. He ran his hands through his hair as he recalled her lectures over the years. Even though the mirror had been one of her most prized possessions, she informed him it was to remind both of them of the evils of vanity.

Still, he couldn't help but marvel at his reflection. Women often commented on just how mesmerizing his eyes were and how they could lure them into doing whatever he desired.

He thought he would destroy his mother's voice forever by removing her tongue, but it did nothing to silence her. Worse, it came back from the grave to torment him. Of all the ghosts who visited him, she was the most frequent. She hounded him day and night; he was unable to walk away from her constant nagging.

Her voice was as clear today as it had been the day she died. It was as if she was right here beside him, vehemently preaching to him about how wicked girls were and how dirty little boys were. One day, she caught him touching himself, and to this very day he could still feel the switch hitting him, leaving welts upon his tender flesh whenever he thought of touching himself.

Growing up, not a single day went by that she didn't comment on her feelings of disappointment in him and his uselessness. The hate, anger and disappointment that echoed in her voice whenever she would talk to or about anyone was deeply engrained in him. It was an intrinsic part of his psyche. She was the whole reason he was this way.

Suddenly, the image staring back at him in the mirror was a monster, the monster she created. She made it impossible for him to make any friends. He grew up isolated, only having her to talk to. He didn't know how to act in front of other children. He didn't know how to talk to a girl and shied away whenever one smiled at him.

His teachers always thought he was overly shy, but he had been scared they would demean him just like his mother. His fear of being belittled in front of others forced him to sit there quietly. She raised him not to talk unless he had permission. She believed children should not be seen nor heard from unless necessary.

His father walked out on his mother before his birth. She always blamed him for his father walking out on them, but it could be that he didn't like her demeanor. Whenever he mentioned his father, he received an unmerciful beating for whatever reason. He quickly learned never to bring up his father, ever.

He had hoped that killing his mother and cutting out her tongue would finally silence her, but it did not. It was as if her death restored her eyes and her tongue. Each woman he killed reminded him of his mother, so he purposefully removed their eyes and tongue. He kept the eyes as his mementos. He made sure to keep them tucked away from his mother's view. His mother said eyes were the windows to the soul, but these women were like his mother, soulless bitches who deserved to die. Taking their eyes removed their evil spirits and preserving their eyes meant that he could keep their souls from haunting his every movement.

He was becoming much more efficient in removing the eyes. Honing his skill with each kill. If only he could silence his mother's voice in his head; then perhaps he could stop killing.

His mind drifted towards the woman he'd met the other day at church. He had never laid eyes on anyone that lovely. He instantly knew she was someone special. She didn't even resemble his mother. Just seeing the woman sent a never felt before feeling rushing through him. He couldn't help but wonder if she could be the one to silence his mother's voice. Maybe through her, he would find true love. He must make her his.

His mother must have realized he was thinking of her once again because he heard her voice raging through his mind about how wicked women were. He picked up his knife and surveyed it. He felt the sharp blade. The knife brought him some peace from his mother's incessant nagging. She may have stopped her nagging, but he could still feel her in his mind. Silence, all he needed to do was finally make her silent.

Chapter 1

The need to hunt grew strong once again. He'd already found the perfect prey. Now, it was time for him to strike.

Renee Breaux headed out to I-10. She had a long drive ahead of her, but was ready to get home. Her parents would rather she made this drive during the day, but she preferred to drive when the roads were quiet, so she chose to drive at night. She had made this drive many times in the past and knew the roads like the back of her hand.

She stopped and picked up a venti white chocolate caramel latte for a caffeine rush and turned the radio up. She was ready for a break and some of her mom's cooking. Midterms were harder this year and she needed some time to unwind before the spring semester started.

Earlier, she'd packed all the Christmas gifts and her luggage in the car. By the time her parents woke up in the morning, she would be driving up. As she made her way onto the Pontchartrain Causeway, her car started sputtering just before it died. She let out moan as she tried to start it up once again. "Great, this is all I needed." She told her dad that the car had been acting up on her and he promised to check it as soon as she got home. Now, she wished she had taken the time to get it checked before leaving. She honestly did not think it would break down on her.

It was just her luck; there wasn't another car around at this time. She hated having to call a tow truck and delay her trip to see her parents. As she picked up her cell phone to locate a tow truck company, she saw a pair of headlights heading her way. Maybe, she would get lucky, and it would be a state trooper making rounds.

As the car approached, she noticed that it was a taxi driver instead of a cop. Standing at the rear of her vehicle, she waved her hands in the air, hoping he saw her in the darkness of the night.

He couldn't believe his luck. Here he thought he had missed her, but she was right here waiting for him. It was fate. He checked his rear-view mirror before making his move. He had enough practice and could do this fast. He kept his tools sharp for this very occasion. With no one around, he could make his move.

Renee never noticed the knife in his hand. All she felt was the searing pain as he slit her throat. She was dead before she hit the ground. With expert precision, he swiftly removed her eyes and tongue and placed them carefully in the container he brought with him. Once home, he would store them.

Not wanting to spend any more time near the scene, he shoved the body under the car and left the scene. As he drove off, he still couldn't believe how quiet The Pontchartrain Causeway was tonight. This kill was meant to be...

Available on eBook and Paperback

www.ingramcontent.com/pod-product-compliance
Lightning Source LLC
Chambersburg PA
CBHW071732190726
48292CB00003B/729